Robert H. Newell, Orpheus C. Kerr

The Orpheus C. Kerr Papers

third series

Robert H. Newell, Orpheus C. Kerr

The Orpheus C. Kerr Papers
third series

ISBN/EAN: 9783348037747

Hergestellt in Europa, USA, Kanada, Australien, Japan

Cover: Foto ©Andreas Hilbeck / pixelio.de

Weitere Bücher finden Sie auf **www.hansebooks.com**

THE

ORPHEUS C. KERR PAPERS.

THIRD SERIES.

Even M. Louvois, the prime-minister, taxed Sulli with his impudence, which, he said, by no means became a man who had no other recommendation but that of making people laugh. "Why, what the d—l!" cried Sulli; "you would do as much, if you were able!" . . . . . and Sulli got the appointment.

MEMOIRS OF THE OPERA.

NEW YORK:

Carleton, Publisher, 413 Broadway.

M DCCC LXV.

Entered, according to Act of Congress, in the year 1865, by
GEO. W. CARLETON,
In the Clerk's Office of the District Court for the Southern District of New York.

Cambridge Press.
DAKIN AND METCALF.

CONTENTS.

LETTER LXXX.

PAGE

Reporting our Uncle Abe's latest little Tale — Our Correspondent's Historical Chaunt — The Boston Novel of "Mr. Smith" — And a Funeral Discourse by the devout Chaplain of the Mackerel Brigade,   **7**

LETTER LXXXI.

Showing how a Minion of Tyranny was terribly punished for interfering with the conservative Women of America — And describing the Kentucky Chap's remarkable Skirmish with his Thanksgiving Dinner, ...   **25**

LETTER LXXXII.

Noting the utter Destruction, by an inebriated Journalist, of the Venerable Gammon's benignant Speech — Introducing the new General of the Mackerel Brigade — And describing a curious Phenomenon on Duck Lake, ...   **34**

LETTER LXXXIII.

Referring to Washington City and the President's Message, and giving the Southern Confederacy's very reasonable Peace Proposition, .   **43**

LETTER LXXXIV.

Proving that Russia is indeed our Friend — Instancing the terrific Bombardment of Paris — And telling how the new General of the Mackerel Brigade delighted all with his surprising "Shape," . .   **51**

LETTER LXXXV.

Holding the Government strictly accountable for the Occurrence of a recent " Military Necessity " — Recounting the affecting Episode of the Mackerel Drummer-Boy — And depicting the new Mackerel General's first great Battle, ...   **57**

(iii)

iv CONTENTS.

LETTER LXXXVI.

Touching upon a late Ovation to a Parent of his Country — Giving the Conservative Kentucky Map of all America — And introducing a second new General of the Mackerel Organization, ... 66

LETTER LXXXVII.

In which our Correspondent has a deadly Affair of Honor with a Gentleman from Kentucky — Experiences " Contraband " Hospitality and Melody — Attends a great Meeting in Accomac — And witnesses a prodigious Naval Achievement, ... 73

LETTER LXXXVIII.

Concerning Intellectual Giants and Pins — With a few Words as to certain Dramatic Street-Scenes supposed to be of daily Occurrence — An affecting Western Poem — And a brief Glimpse of an ordinary Cavalry Dash, ... 88

LETTER LXXXIX.

Showing how the great City of Rome has been ruined by the War — Citing a notable Instance of Contempt of Court — Describing Rear Admiral Head's wonderful Improvement in Swivel Guns — And proving that all is now Ready for the Reduction of Fort Piano, . 101

LETTER XC.

Giving a deep Insight of Woman's Nature — Presenting a powerful Poem of the Heart by one of the Intellectual Females of America — And reporting the signal Discomfiture of Mr. P. Greene, . . 111

LETTER XCI.

Containing the Venerable Gammon's Report of the Manner in which the War has conducted itself up to this Time — And the most Surprising Epitaph of a Victim of Strategy, ... 119

LETTER XCII.

In which our enthusiastic Correspondent surpasses Æschylus in the way of an Invocation — And describes Rear Admiral Head's great Naval Demonstration against Fort Piano, ... 128

LETTER XCIII.

Teeming with Consummate Strategy, and relating an extraordinary Geometrical Effort of Military Genius, ... 135

CONTENTS.

LETTER XCIV.

Affording an Instance of Imperceptible Patriotism — Presenting the profound Commentary of an eminent foreign Military Critic — And Reporting the last Effusion of the General of the Mackerel Brigade,   143

LETTER XCV.

Noting the continued Anguish of the Conservative Kentucky Chap, and the Death of Nemo — And describing an immense popular Demonstration against the Outrages of Federal Oppression,   . . . 150

LETTER XCVI.

Devoted principally to Social Matters, and the benignant Bearing of V. Gammon at a Diplomatic Soirée, ... 158

LETTER XCVII.

Introducing the great Moral Exhibition of the "Effigynia," — Glancing at a fourth new Mackerel General — And showing how the President's Draft on Accomac was protested at sight, ... 164

LETTER XCVIII.

Recounting a chaste "Reconstruction" Anecdote of the Sixth Ward — And divulging Captain Villiam Brown's ingenious Alphabetical Experiment with Company Three, ... 172

LETTER XCIX.

In which our Correspondent is betrayed into Argument — But recovers in time to give us the usual Christmas Song and Story of the Renowned Brigade, ... 181

LETTER C.

Giving divers Instances of strangely-mistaken Identity — And revealing a wise Method of saving the Country from Bankruptcy,   . . . 194

LETTER CI.

Explaining the well-meant Duplicity of the Journals of the Opposition — Affording another Glimpse of the Irrepressible Conservative Sentiment — And showing how Thanksgiving-Day was kept by the Mackerels, ... 201

LETTER CII.

Showing the ingenious Financial Energy of a greatly-reduced Politician — and Describing a Combat illustrative of the Philosophical Contentment of the well-known Southern Confederacy under all Reverses,   213

1 *

vi CONTENTS.

LETTER CIII.

Being another and final Christmas Report — Including a Small Story from our Uncle Abe — A Circular from the Secretary of State — A Supernatural Carol from Sergeant O'Pake — And a tremendous Ghost-Story from an unappreciated Genius, ... 222

LETTER CIV.

Explaining, in a lucid and perfectly satisfactory Manner, the powerful Inactivity of that portion of the venerated Mackerel Brigade residing before the ancient City of Paris, and presenting certain genial Details of a recent Festive Conglomeration, ... 243

LETTER CV.

Being our Correspondent's last Effort prior to the Commencement of a new Mackerel Campaign — Introducing a metrical Picture of the most remarkable Single Combat on Record — And showing how the Romance of Woman's sensitive Soul can be crushed by the thing called Man, ... 254

LETTER CVI.

Wherein will be found certain profound Remarks upon the Variations of Gold, etc., and a wholesome little Tale illustrative of that famous Popular Abstraction, the Southern Treasury Note, ... 261

LETTER CVII.

Recording the latest Delphic Utterances of One whom we all honor without knowing why — And recounting the truly marvellous Affair of the Fort built according to Tacitus, ... 267

LETTER CVIII.

Narrating the utterly unparalleled Conquest of Paris by the venerable Mackerel Brigade, after Three Days' inconceivable Strategy — In Fact, a Battle-Report after the Manner of all our excited Morning Journals — Upon perusing which, each Reader is expected to wrap himself up in the American Flag and shake his fist at Combined Europe, ... 277

LETTER CIX.

Which endeth the Third Volume of this inexpressibly veracious History of the War — And showeth how a Great Republic finally overcame its surpassingly Mendacious Foes, and how it evinced its unspeakable Gratitude to Providence for such a Victory, ... 289

THE

ORPHEUS C. KERR PAPERS.

THIRD SERIES.

___

LETTER LXXX.

REPORTING OUR UNCLE ABE'S LATEST LITTLE TALE; OUR CORRE-
SPONDENT'S HISTORICAL CHAUNT; THE BOSTON NOVEL OF "MR.
SMITH;" AND A FUNERAL DISCOURSE BY THE DEVOUT CHAPLAIN
OF THE MACKEREL BRIGADE.

WASHINGTON, D. C., Jan. 4th, 1863.

THE more I see of our Honest Abe, my boy, — the more closely I analyze the occasional acts by which he individualizes himself as a unit distinct from the decimals of his cabinet, — the deeper grows my faith in his sterling wisdom. Standing a head and shoulders above the other men in power, he is the object at which the capricious lightnings of the storm first strike; and were he a man of wax, instead of the grand old rock he is, there would be nothing left of him but a shapeless and inert mass of pliable material by this time. There are deep traces of the storm upon his countenance, my boy; but they are the sculpture of the tempest on a natural block of granite, graduating the features of young simplicity into the sterner lineaments of the mature sublime, and shaping one of those strong and earnest faces which God sets, as indelible seals, upon the ages marked for immortality. Abused and misrepresented by his political foes, alternately cajoled and reproached by his other foes, — his political friends, — he still pursues the honest tenor of the obvious Right, and smiles at calumny. His good-nature, my boy, is a lamp that never goes out, but burns, with a steady light, in the temples of his mortality through all the dark hours of his time:

> " As some tall cliff that rears its awful form,
> Swells from the vale and midway leaves the storm;
> Though round its base the rolling clouds are spread,
> Eternal sunshine settles on its head."

They tell a story about the Honest Abe which this good pen of mine cannot refrain from writing. A high moral, political chap from the Sixth Ward, having learned that there was a pleasing clerical vacancy in the Treasury Department, sought a hasty interview with the Honest Abe, and says he:

" I am a member of our excellent National Democratic Organization, which is at this moment eligible for office, on the score of far more true loyalty to the Union of our forefathers than can be found in any other organization of the present distracting period. I will admit," says the genial chap, in a fine burst of honesty, " that our Organization has done much for the sake of the South in times past; I will admit that we have seemingly sided with the sunny South for the sake of our party. I will

THIRD SERIES.

9

admit," says this candid chap, with a slight cough, "that our excellent Democratic Organization has at times seemed to sympathize with our wayward sisters for the sake of itself *as* an Organization. But now," says the impressive chap majestically, "having heard the recent news from Sumter, the excellent Organization of which I am a part, stands ready to sacrifice everything for the sake of the Union, and demands that it shall be admitted to all the privileges of undisguised loyalty."

Here the excited chap blushed ingenuously, and says he:

"Any offices which you might have to dispose of would be acceptable to the Organization of which I am a prominent part."

The Honest Abe was wiping the blade of his jack-knife with his thumb at the time, and says he:

"What you say about the present willingness of the Organization to sacrifice everything for the sake of the Union, neighbor, reminds me of a small tale. When I was beating the prairies for clients in Illinois," says the Honest Abe, smiling at the back of the hand in which he held the jack-knife,— "when I was stalking for clients, I knew an old 'un named Job Podger, who lived at Peoria."

Here the honest Abe leaned away over the arm of his chair toward the attentive political chap, and says he —

"Podger didn't know as much as would fill a four-inch spelling-book; but he had enough money to make education quite dispensable, and his wife knew enough for all the rest of the family. This wife was a very good woman in her way," says the Honest Abe, kindly, — "she was a very good woman in her way, and made my friend Podger so happy at home that he never dared to go away from home without her permission. Her temper," says the Honest Abe, putting one of his feet upon the sill of the nearest window, — "her temper was of the useful nature to keep my friend Podger and the children sufficiently warm all the year round, and I don't think she ever called Job Podger an Old Fool except when company was present. If she had one peculiarity more than another, it was this: she was always doing something for Podger's sake."

Here the political chap was seized with a severe cough; but the Honest Abe only smiled pleasantly at his jack-knife, and went on:

"She was always doing something for Podger's sake. Did she buy a new dress, it was for Podger's sake; did she have a tea-party and a quilting-bee, it was solely for the sake of Podger; did she refuse to contribute for the fund of the heathen, it was solely on account of Mr. Podger. But her strong point in this matter," says the Honest Abe, leaning back in his chair against the wall, and scraping the sole of his left boot with his knife, "her strong point was, that she endured a great deal of suffering for Podger's sake. Did she sprain her ankle on the cellar-stairs, she would say: 'Just see what I suffer for *your* sake, Podger;' did she have a sick headache from drinking too much Young Hyson, she would tie up her face in camphor, and say: 'Only see, Podger, how much I bear for *your* sake;' did she catch cold from standing too long before a dry-goods shop window, she would go and sit in a dark room with a flannel stocking round her

THIRD SERIES. **11**

neck, murmuring: 'I was a goose ever to marry such a fool of a man as you be, — but I am willing to suffer even this for *your* sake.' In fact," says the Honest Abe, commencing to cut his nails, — " in truth, that woman was always suffering for Podger's sake, and Podger felt himself to be a guilty man.

"One day, I remember, my friend Podger and his wife were going to Chicago to buy a new set of furs for Podger's sake, and just as Podger got comfortably nested in his seat in the car, the suffering woman ate a lozenge, and says she : 'I shan't be fit to live, Podger, if you don't go out to the baggage car again, and make certain sure that they'll get all our baggage.'

" Now Podger had been out six times before to see about the same thing," says the Honest Abe, earnestly ; " he'd been out six times before, and began to feel wrathy. ' *Our* baggage !' says he, ' OUR baggage ! Mrs. Podger.' Here my friend Podger grew very red in the face, and says he: 'I rather like that, you know, — OUR baggage ! — two brass-bound trunks and covers, belonging to Mrs. Podger ; three carpet-bags and one reticule with steel lock, the property of Mrs. P. ; two bandboxes and a green silk umbrella, belonging to Mary Jane Podger ; three shawls tied up in a newspaper, and two baskets, owned by Mrs. M. J. Podger ; one clean collar and a razor, carried by Job Podger. OUR baggage !'

" Here my friend Podger attempted to laugh sardonically behind his collar, and came near going straight into apoplexy. Would you believe it," says the Honest Abe, poking the political chap in the ribs with his jack-knife, "would you believe it ? Mrs. Podger burst at once into

12 ORPHEUS C. KERR PAPERS.

bitter tears, and says she: ' Oh, o-h! a-hoo-hoo-hoo! to think I should have to suffer in this way for my husband's sake!' It wasn't long after that," says the Honest Abe, lowering his tone, " it wasn't very long after that, when Mrs. P. took a violent cold on her lungs, from standing too long on the damp ground at a camp-meeting for Podger's sake, and was soon a very sick woman.

" What particularly frightened my friend Podger was, that she didn't say that this was for his sake for two whole days, and in his horror of mind he went and brought a clergyman to see her. This clergyman," says the Honest Abe, with reverence of manner, " this clergyman was not one of those sombre, forlorn pastors, who would make you think that it is a grievous thing to be a priest unto your benignant Creator; he rather indicated by his ever-cheerful manner that the only perpetual happiness is to be found in a life of pious ministrations. When he followed my friend Podger to the bedside, he smiled encouragingly at the sick Mrs. P., and rubbed his hands, and says he: ' How do we find ourselves now, my dear madam? Are we about to die this pleasant morning?' She answered him feebly," says the Honest Abe, feelingly, "she answered him feebly, for she was very weak. She said that she feared she had not spent her life as she should, but trusted that the prayers she had breathed during her hours of pain would not be unanswered. ' Ah!' said she, ' I feel that I could suffer still more than I have suffered, for my Intercessor's sake!'

" The moment she uttered these last words," says the Honest Abe, " the moment she uttered these words, my friend Podger, who had been standing near the door, the

THIRD SERIES. 13

very picture of misery, suddenly gave a start, brightened up with a look of intense joy, beckoned the clergyman to follow him into the kitchen, and fairly danced down stairs. In fact, the good minister found him dancing about the kitchen like one possessed, and says he:

" ' Mr. Podger! Job Podger! I am shocked. What can you mean by such conduct?'

" My friend Podger caught him around the neck, and says he:

" ' She's going to get well — she's going to get well! I knew she wouldn't go and leave her poor old silly Job in that way. Oh, an't I a happy old fool, though!'

" The clergyman stepped back in alarm, and says he:

" ' Are you mad, sir? How do you know your wife will get well?'

" Poor Podger looked upon the parson with a face that fairly beamed, and says he: ' How do I *know it?* Why, didn't you hear her yourself? *She's commenced to call me names!* ' "

Here the Honest Abe smiled abstractedly out of the window, and says he:

" She did get well, too, and lived to suffer often again for Podger's sake: You see," says the Honest Abe, turning suddenly upon the political chap, as though he had not seen him before, — " you see, Mrs. Podger had been so much in the habit of suffering everything for my friend Podger's sake, that when she spoke of suffering even for the noblest cause, he naturally thought she was only calling names. And that's the way," says the Honest Abe, cheerfully, " that's the way with your Democratic Organization. It has been so long in the habit of sacrificing

14 ORPHEUS C. KERR PAPERS.

everything for the sake of the sunny South and Party, that when it talks of sacrificing both for the sake of the holy cause of Union, it seems to me as though it is only calling names!"

Immediately upon the termination of this wholesome domestic tale, the political chap sprang from his seat, smiled feebly at the ceiling for a minute, crammed his hat down over his eyes, and fled greatly demoralized.

The New Year, my boy, dawns blithely upon our distracted country as accurately predicted by the Tribune Almanac; and having given much deep thought to the matter, I am impressed with the conviction that the first of January is indeed the commencement of the year. There is something solemn in the idea; it is the period when our tailors send in their little bills, and when fresh thoughts of the negro race steal upon our minds. How many New Years have arrived only to find the unoffending American, of African descent, a hopeless bondman, toiling in hopeless servitude, and wearing coarse underclothing! Occasionally, my boy, he would wear a large seal ring, but it was always brass; and now and then he would exhibit a large breastpin, but it was always galvanized. When I see my fellow-men here wearing much jewelry, I think of the unoffending negro, and say to myself, " from the same shop, by all that's bogus!"

Twas on New-Year's Eve that I took prominent part in a great literary entertainment at the tent of Captain Villiam Brown, near the shore of Duck Lake; and responded to universal mackerel desire by sweetly singing an historical Southern

THIRD SERIES.

ROMAUNT.

I.

'Tis of a rich planter in Dixie I tell,
Who had for his daughter a pretty dam-sel;
Her name it was Linda De Pendleton Coates,
And large was her fortune in treasury notes.

CHORUS. — Concisely setting forth the exact value of those
happy treasury notes:

The treasury note of the Dixian knight
Possesses a value that ne'er comes to light, —
Except when the holder, too literal far,
May bring it to light as he lights his segar.

II.

Miss Linda's boudoir was a sight to behold:
A Northern man's breast-bone a shelf did uphold;
Of dried Yankee ribs all her boxes were full;
Her powder she kept in a Fire Zouave's skull.

CHORUS. — Beautifully explaining Southern taste for
Northern bones, and proving that an author's bones
are sacred in the sight of Southern damsels:

Your soft Southern maidens (like nations at large,
Who take the dear bones of their authors in charge)
Are so literary, they'd far rather scan
A Norther's dead bones than the best living man.

III.

She played the piano; embroidered also,
And worked worsted poodles and trees in a row;
Made knitting-work slippers that no one could wear,
And plastered pomatum all over her hair.

CHORUS — Satisfactorily revealing to the curious fair sex why
she used pomatum when Bandoline was in fashion:

Though Bandoline surely excels all pomade,
The Southern supply couldn't run the blockade;
At first it *did* bring an exorbitant sum,
And then contrabandoline straight did become.

IV.

As Linda was practising "Norma," one day,
Her father came in in his usual way;
And having first spat on the carpeted floor,
Went on to address her as never before:

CHORUS. — Showing conclusively why this tender parent had
never done so before:

On Southern plantations when money is flush
Paternal affection comes out with a gush:
But when, as in the war times, the cash is *non est*,
The Father is lost in the planter distressed.

V.

"My daughter, my Linda," he tenderly said,
"Your mother for several years has been dead;
But not until now could I muster the strength
To tell you what all must have found out at length."

CHORUS. — Casually demonstrating how it must really have
been found out at length:

The Dixian feminines, true to their sex,
To each other's precedents pay their respects;
And if there's a secret in any girl's life,
They're bound to disclose it before she's a wife.

VI.

"That you are my child, it were vain to deny;
But who was your mother? There, darling, don't cry.
The truth must be told, though it harrows me sore,
Your ma was an Octoroon slave, — nothing more."

CHORUS. — Analytical of morals in the sunny South, and touchingly illustrative of the Institution affected by the
Emancipation Proclamation:

THIRD SERIES. 17

Your slave is your property, therefore 'tis clear
The child of your slave is your chattel fore'er;
Though you the child's father may happen to be,
That child is a slave, — otherwise, prop-er-ty.

VII.

" I've bred you, my darling, as ladies are bred,
You've got more outside than inside of your head;
But now, that your pa can no longer afford
A daughter to keep, you must go by the board."

CHORUS. — Concerning the manner of going by the board generally adopted in the land of Chivalry:

The planter on finding his funds getting low,
Right straight to an auctioneer's shambles doth go;
And " Find me a ready-cash buyer," says he,
" To take his own pick out of my fam-i-ly."

VIII.

Miss Linda sprang up with a look of dismay:
" You surely don't mean, dear papa, what you say?"
Then spake the stern parent, nowise looking blue,
But smiling, in fact: " Well, I reckon I do."

CHORUS. — Calculated to account for the complacency of the tender parent on this trying occasion:

Now what, after all, is a sale to the chit?
Some gallant may buy her and love her a bit;
One half of the women in marriages sought
Are simply and plainly and formally bought.

IX.

" Dear father," said Linda, " step out for a while,
I'll think the thing over, and merit your smile;
For if what I'd bring would relieve you the least,
I'll bring it myself, though I'm sold like a beast."

CHORUS. — Tending to deprecate any imputation on the maiden s refinement that might follow her use of that last expression:

2 *

ORPHEUS C. KERR PAPERS.

The culture of woman, as known in the South,
Tends greatly to widen and quicken the mouth;
And if a fair Southerner's language is coarse,
'Tis because nothing finer her style would endorse.

x.

The parent went out, and he stayed for an hour,
Having taken some punch and a Hennessey — sour;
And when he came back, 'twas his daughter he found
Slain by her own scissors, and dead on the ground.

CHORUS. — Suggesting facts to the coroner's jury, and clearing
up all mystery as to the lamentable suicide :

Since scissors for ripping out stitches are made,
A girl in extremity finds them an aid;
She's only to open them fairly and wide,
And give them a cut at the stitch in her side.

XI.

Beside the dead body a billet displayed,
Said, " See, dearest father, the mischief you've made ;
I couldn't survive to be sold ; for you know,
I'd far rather die than a sell-ibate go."

CHORUS. — Commenting genially on the idiosyncrasy of female
character evidenced in this revelation :

All over the world it is plain to espy
That woman a husband has e'er in her eye ;
And if no fine fellow her husband can be,
She'll even take up with a *felo de se !*

XII.

The neighbors came in. " What a pity ! " said they,
" To lose such a daughter, and in such a way."
" My daughter be hanged ! " said the parent sublime, —
" *It's one thousand dollars I'm euchred this time !* "

CHORUS. — Deducing a beautiful and useful moral from this
burst of paternal agony :

THIRD SERIES. 19

My dear fellow-citizens, lay it to heart:
Who'd sell a young woman must work it up smart:
Or else, like the planter, whose story I've told,
He'll only go selling to find himself sold.

When I had finished singing, Captain Samyule Sa-mith exhibited a small manuscript, and says he:

"The noise having ceased, I will proceed to read a small moral tale, written by a young woman which lives in Boston, and is destined to become an eddycator of mankind. The fiction is called

" MR. SMITH. *

" The first of April. You know the day. A point of time, an unit of twenty-four hours, with a night on each side of it, and the sun laid on top to keep it in its place. You have undoubtedly passed the day in New England at some period of your miserable life. You have felt your coarse nature repulsed, too, when some weary and desolate little child has dreamily pinned a bit of paper to the hindermost verge of the garment men call a coat, and then called the attention of passers-by to your appearance. You have despised that little, weary, hollow-eyed child for it. Beware how you strike that child; for I tell you that the child is the germ of the thing they call man. The germ will develop; it will grow broadly and largely into the full entity of Manhood. In striking the present Child you strike the future Man. Ponder this thought well. Let it fester in your bosom.

" John Smith sat at his table, in the lowest depths of a

---

* The idea that this moral and exciting tale appeared originally in the *Atlantic Monthly*, is scornfully repelled by the Editor of this work.

dreamy coal-mine, and helped himself to some more pork and beans. I know not what there was way down in the black recesses of the man's hidden soul to make him want so much pork and beans. I look into my heart to find an answer to the question, but no answer comes. Providence does not reveal all things to us. Is it not well it should be so?

"He was a hard, iron-looking, adamantine man. His eyes were glowing furnaces for the crucibles of thought. You felt that he saw you when he looked at you. His nose was like a red gothic tower built amidst broken angles of sullied snow, and his mouth was the cellar of that tower. His hair was of the sort that resists a comb. You have seen the same sort on the heads of men of great thought. It is the tangled bush in which the goat of Thought loses itself.

"John Smith hiccupped, as he helped himself to some more pork and beans. He did not notice that the foot which he had semi-consciously placed on a pale, sickly child, was beginning to move. But it did move, and there crawled from under it the shape of a diseased dwarf of womanhood. This timid, pallid thing, uplifted itself to its bleeding feet, and nestled to the side of John Smith.

"'Y'o hae been separated by unspeaking space from dis humble leetle place for some hours longer that zis boosom could uncomplainingly indure, — y'o have.'

"The child meant to say, in its coarse, brutal, unlettered way, that the man had been absent too long.

"John Smith helped himself to some more pork and beans. He was a man, you know, and could not answer without deep thought. He took his knife and wiped it

THIRD SERIES. 21

thoughtfully upon her head, and then sawed off a sickly yellow curl. When he placed that curl on the same plate with the pork and beans, its coils seemed like those of some golden snake.

" ' Girletta,' he said, with the ring of iron in his tones, ' why is it that the beasts never want to marry? God made them as He made us; yet they never ask priests to make them slaves to each other.'

" The sickly little waif cringed closer to that inscrutable great heart which underlaid a soul of eternal questioning. She shuddered like a wounded hog, but could not answer. An inward fever was devouring her.

" The man took some more pork and beans. ' Girletta,' he said, almost fiercely, ' the beasts teach me a lesson; but I will not, dare not, SHALL not heed it. I want a home; my heart demands some one to work for me; to support me. I am weary of labor, and want some one to labor and toil and suffer for me, and do my washing. I love you. Have me.'

" The atom of womanhood contorted her diseased features into the pale twist of agony, and her bosom heaved with stormy wavings, like the side of a tortured and choking brute. Falling to the ground, she writhed, and struggled, and kicked convulsively, as though seized with some inward pang. Then she rose slowly to her shattered little feet, and drew an old cupboard to the middle of the wretched cave and beat her head against it.

" It was the child's first taste of that great mystery of perfect love which woman is doomed to share with the thing called Man.

" ' Yo' air indulging in secret cachinnation, at the expense of my sair heart.'

"The child meant that he was laughing at her.

"John Smith helped himself to some more pork and beans, and sat back in his stern, dark chair. What were his thoughts as he looked down on that miniature fragment of womanly humanity? Perhaps he thought that there might be angels way up in heaven just like her. Bright seraphs, with ruby eyes, and silver wings, and golden harps, and just such pale, haggard, gaunt, sunken, bleared little faces.

"'Girletta,' he said, 'I hereby make thee mine. Take some of these pork and beans.'

"She fell upon his bosom.

"There let us leave them. Do you think they were any less happy, because they were way down in a dreamy, rayless coal-mine, where men work their souls away to give others warmth? If you think so, you have never felt what true love is. Your degraded and starless nature has never had one true soul to lean upon. When you lean upon a soul, you see everything through that soul, which gives its own hue to everything. Man's love is a pane in his bosom, and through that pane the eyes of woman look forth to see the new world. The medium is the ultimatum. God gives us love that we may live more cheaply and happily together than if we were separate. A bread-pudding is richer where there are two hearts, than plum-pudding is to one alone. The world will learn this yet, and then the lion will lie down with the lamb, and even you will be less depraved. The First of April found John Smith unmarried, but it left him nearly wedded. Let us think of this when the spring birds sing again. It will make us more human, more charitable, and fitter to be blest."

THIRD SERIES. 23

As Samyule finished reading this excellent religious tale, my boy, I stole from the tent to meditate in silence upon the terrible revelation of human nature. Are there not dozens of Smiths in this world, — ay, even John Smiths? I should think so, my boy, — I should think so.

On Friday morning, I went to Accomac, to attend the funeral of a young chap who had finished with delirium tremens, and was deeply affected by the funeral sermon of the Mackerel Chaplain, who had kindly volunteered for the occasion.

Having shaken hands with the parents of deceased, the worthy man commenced the service.

He said that man was born to die. He had known a number of men to die, and believed that death was every man's lot. If our dear brother here could speak, he would say that it was his lot. What was death, after all, but an edict of liberty? Death was the event that set us free, and freedom was a priceless blessing. Political demagogues pretended to believe that certain men should be the slaves of other men, because their skins were a little darker than the others. What a bright argument was this! If dark skins disentitled men to freedom, he (the speaker) could point out more than one Democrat who certainly ought to be a slave. (Great laughter.) Freedom was plainly the condition Providence intended for all men, without regard to color, no matter what Tammany Hall might say to the contrary. It was because we had permitted a violation of this condition in the cases of four millions of fellow-beings, that this terrible war had come upon us. We could only conquer by declaring the slaves, now and forever, FREE! (Tumultuous and enthusiastic applause.)

2

24   ORPHEUS C. KERR PAPERS.

It was the duty of every loyal man to see that this principle was carried out, even as they were about to carry their departed brother out : though it must not be inferred that he meant it should be carried out on *beer*. (Great laughter.) When we had once settled this matter at home, we could afford to say to John Bull and Louis Napoleon: "Interfere if you dare. We are ready for you both." [Male parent of the deceased — "Why don't you go and fight yourself?"] That gentleman who spoke then, is as bad as the patient who said to the doctor who was recommending some wholesome medicine to him: "Why don't you take it yourself, if it's good?" (Great laughter and applause.) But he would detain them no longer, or the papers would say that he had talked politics.

At the conclusion of this discourse, my boy, the male parent of the deceased offered the following preamble and resolution :

WHEREAS, It has pleased an inscrutable and all-wise Providence to free our departed brother from the bonds of life ; and

WHEREAS, Freedom is the normal condition of all mankind : therefore, be it

RESOLVED, That we will vote for no man who is not in favor of Universal Liberty, without respect to color.

Passed, unanimously.

Politics, my boy, are, in themselves, a distinct system of life and death ; and when we say that a man is politically dead, we mean that even his en-graving is forgotten ; and that the brick which he carries in his hat is a species of head-stone.

Yours, post obit,

ORPHEUS C. KERR.

LETTER LXXXI.

SHOWING HOW A MINION OF TYRANNY WAS TERRIBLY PUNISHED FOR INTERFERING WITH THE CONSERVATIVE WOMEN OF AMERICA; AND DESCRIBING THE KENTUCKY CHAP'S REMARKABLE SKIRMISH WITH HIS THANKSGIVING DINNER.

WASHINGTON, D. C., Jan. 7th, 1863.

As I make it a practice to pay all my honest debts, my boy, and have never flagellated a person of African descent, I could not properly come under the head of " Chivalry " in an American dictionary, though I might possibly come under its feet in the " Union-as-it-Was ; " yet I have that in my nature which revolts at the thought of a war against women, and am sufficiently chivalrous to defend any cause whose effects are crinoline. The bell-shaped structure called Woman, my boy, was created expressly to conquer unresisting adversaries ; to win engagements without receiving a blow, and to do pretty much as she pleases, by pleasing pretty much as she does. She is a harmless creation of herself, my boy ; and to war directly against her because she may chance to influence her male friends to war against us, is about as sensible as it would be to execrate our hatter because a gust of wind blows our new beaver into the mud. If the hatter had not made the hat, the wind could not have blown it off, and if God had not made women, she could not encourage the well-known Southern Confederacy against us ; but

(25)

shall we turn enemy to the hatter, or to the woman, on this account? Not if we know ourselves, my boy, and recognize the high moral spirit of justice observable in the Constitution.

Being thus possessed of a reverence for that sex whose bonnets remind me of cake-baskets, I cannot refrain from frowning indignantly upon that horrible spirit of national tyranny which has inspired Sergeant O'Pake, of the demoralized Mackerel Brigade, to issue the following

"GENERAL ORDER.

"For the purpose of simplifying national strategy to those conservative women of America who, while engaged in the pursuit of happiness as guaranteed by the Constitution, desire to visit the Southern Confederacy, it is ordered that they shall answer the following paternal questions before passing the lines of the Mackerel Brigade:

"I. For how many years has your age been Just Twenty-two?

"II. How many novels do you consume per week?

"III. Were you ever complained of to the authorities for inordinate piano-forte playing?

"IV. Do you work slippers for the heathen?

"V. If so; for *what* He, then?

"VI. What newspaper's 'Marriages and Deaths' do you consider the best?

"VII. In selecting a church to attend, what colored prayer-book do you find most becoming to your complexion?

"VIII. How much display of neck do you consider

THIRD SERIES. 27

necessary to indicate a Modesty which shrinks from showing an ankle?

"IX. Did you ever stoop to folly? or is it Folly alone that stoops to you?

"X. Did you ever eat as much as you wanted at dinner, when members of the opposite sex were opposite?

"It is also ordered that no female visitor to the celebrated Southern Confederacy shall carry more than eight large trunks and a bonnet-box for each month in the year; and that no female shall pass the line, whose dimensions in full dress exceed the ordinary space between two pickets, as the latter will, on no account be permitted to edge away from their stations at this trying crisis in the history of our distracted country.

" O'PAKE,

" Sergeant Mackerel Brigade."

This inhuman order had scarcely been issued when there came to the Mackerel lines in front of Paris a virtuous young female, aged 23 with the figures reversed, who was disgusted with the great vulgarity of the North, and wished to visit the marriageable Southern Confederacy, having heard that the Confederacy was carefully Husbanding its resources. Being a poor girl, with "nothing to wear," she only had seven Saratoga trunks, ten bandboxes, fourteen small carpet-bags, and a lap-dog; yet the ill-bred O'Pake was suspicious enough to examine one of her trunks.

He ruthlessly opened it in her presence, my boy, and quickly met with the horrible fate which was at once im-

28 ORPHEUS C. KERR PAPERS.

mortalized by the Mackerel Chaplain in the following awful presentment:

"THE AVENGING SKELETON.

"When tyrant purpose made the martial fool
  With brief authority profoundly drunk,
Unto his minions issued forth a rule,
  To search each Southward-going woman's trunk.

" There was a Sergeant of the Mack'rel ranks
  Made one attempt to carry out the law;
But ah! — to Providence a thousand thanks! —
  He met a doom to fill the soul with awe.

" Scarce had his impious hands the task begun; —
  Scarce had he ope'd the vast and mammoth thing, —
When, from the trunk's interior Phlegethon,
  Came forth a horrid phantom, with a spring!

" It was a dreadful monster, without flesh,
  Made up of ever-less'ning, perfect hoops;
More terrible to vision than secesh,
  With all his ragged, whiskey-drinking troops.

" The wretched Sergeant started back with fear,
  And would have 'scaped the penalty incurred;
But, ah! the spectre caught him by an ear,
  And held him trembling like a prisoned bird.

" Wrought up to frenzy by mishap so dire,
  He struck the phantom in his thoughtless rage;
But 'twas like fanning to put out a fire,
  And straight his hand was tangled in a cage!

THIRD SERIES. 29

" And then his other tyrant hand he tried
　To ease the springs that pressed him ev'rywhere ;
His futile blow the Skeleton defied, —
　His other hand was taken in a snare !

" Then round his form the dread avenger coiled,
　Like snakes' backbones in unelastic curl ;
By prison-bars his wished retreat is foiled,
　And in a cage behold the trembling churl.

" Still mad with terror at his grievous plight,
　He lifts a foot, as though to kick at last ;
When, lo ! his leg goes through an op'ning slight,
　And there two wiry circles hold it fast.

" He plunges, staggers, tries to tear the bands ·
　Which make that woman's Skeleton complete ;
Then reeleth blindly unto where she stands,
　And falls in helpless bondage at her feet ! "

When the poor tool of tyranny was released from this terrific skeleton, he looked as bewildered as one who had just returned from the outskirts of civilization; but still his fiendish taste for trunk-inspection was not conquered. He returned to the edge of the wardrobe abyss, drew forth an immense white article, and says he :

" Do my spectacles relate a fiction, or is this indeed a Sibley tent for the use of the Confederacy ? "

At this moment the excellent young woman hastily snatched the article away from him, and says she :

" You nasty thing, that's my " — here she blushed.

At times, my boy, woman's blush is the imperial banner of virgin Modesty thrown out to catch the breeze that

30 ORPHEUS C. KERR PAPERS.

wafts the sound of coming rescue, and means: "*God is my defence.*" At other times, it is the eloquent protest of a fine intelligence which deprecates the test that would turn all its hidden beauties to the public eye, and means: *Humility is born of Genius.* But in this case, it was the lurid flush of anger, and meant — *a petticoat.*

Not wishing to further betray the reproachful fact that he was an unmarried Mackerel, Sergeant O'Pake closed the trunk with emphasis, and permitted the triumphant young woman of America to trip it lightly to the South.

The Mackerel Brigade at present constitutes one of three parallel lines, the other two being the celebrated City of Paris and the well known Southern Confederacy. Paris is the central one, and may be called the line of battle, over which the Orange County Howitzers are continually hurling shot and shell at the glorious sun. During the day it is much frequented by Southern Confederacies, who drink anything that will pour into a tumbler; and in the evening it is visited by our indomitable troops, who go to look at the empty bottles. You may ask, my boy, why the Confederacies are not routed, and Paris occupied? I answer, that the new General of the Mackerel Brigade will not attack an inferior force, and is waiting until there shall be something worth killing on the opposite side. Too often did the former General of the Mackerel Brigade make the mistake this high-minded conduct is intended to avoid; too often, after an interval of only a few months, did he lead the majestic Mackerels ahead of him into the field, and then hastily retire, upon finding that the Confederacies were too inferior in numbers to make their conquest worth while. But we shall have no more such

THIRD SERIES. 31

mistakes, for the new General will not move against the foe until the latter is strong enough to make carnage desirable. Besides, the man who was to build a bridge across Duck Lake, could not come last week, on account of the rain, and there are no ferryboats running.

On Thanksgiving Day, however, we had a skirmish of thrilling intensity. The conservative Kentucky chap, my boy, has got command of Company 2, Regiment 1, and having drilled them in swearing, to the sound of the Emancipation Proclamation, for a whole fortnight, he has brought them to a high state of discipline and profanity. On Thursday morning, just after one of our scouts had cleaned his spectacles, he beheld a Confederate turkey emerge from this side of Paris and proceed to insult the United States of America by hideous gobblings. The alarm was at once given, and after swearing at his men to give them confidence, the conservative Kentucky chap led them forth to capture the obscene bird. Onward pushed the spectacled veterans, with fixed bayonets, addressing their eyes with pleasant oaths, and hoping that they might meet Horace Greeley. -

The Confederate turkey was eating a worm at the moment, and only paused long enough to eye our troops with that species of disdain which comes of Southern birth. He felt, as it were, that he was protected by the Constitution of our forefathers.

The conservative Kentucky chap, being fond of turkey for dinner himself, waved his glittering sword above his head, and says he:

" The South has brought this upon herself. Make ready. — "

2

32 ORPHEUS C. KERR PAPERS.

He was about to add " Fire ! " my boy ! but he had just put on his spectacles, and a sudden change came over his Kentucky countenance. Says he :

" For Heaven's sake, don't fire♣ Vallandigham me," says he, staring right over the turkey, — " Vallandigham me, if I didn't come near telling them to shoot! And there's a nigger coming after the turkey as sure as death. Ah ! what an escape ! "

A Mackerel chap, who had noticed his staring and great agitation, approached respectfully, and says he :

" Does a obstacle to victory protrude ? "

The conservative Kentucky chap spat at a copy of the " Tribune," which he threw upon the ground for the purpose, and says he :

" Notwithstanding any Proclamations whatsoever, Kentucky is not waging this war against the institution of slavery. In the dim distance I behold a contraband apparently approaching the turkey; and there must be no bombardment until he has returned to his rightful owner."

The Mackerel chap wiped his boots with the " Tribune," and says he :

" I do not see our brother Africa at all."

Here the Confederate turkey, who had finished his worm, turned heavily from the scene, and presently disappeared on the other side of Paris.

The Kentucky chap still kept staring afar off, and says he :

" Why, I can see him, though he appears to be at a great distance."

Now it chanced, my boy, that while the conservative Kentucky chap was saying this, the Mackerel chap gazed at him fixedly, and then says he, in just astonishment :

THIRD SERIES. 33

" Methinks there is a object on one of the glasses of your spectacles, Capting."

Frantically the Kentucky chap tore off his spectacles, and discovered upon one of the glasses an object indeed. It was a small picture of a negro minstrel, my boy, cut from the show-bill of some country band, and pasted upon the spectacles . of Kentucky's rising son. It had been secretly placed there the night before by a Democratic chap from the Sixth Ward, to give a constitutional turn to the war.

The mind's eye of Conservatism, my boy, looks upon the war through spectacles so seldom cleaned, that what most offends it, is more than likely to be what exists only in its own looking-glasses.

Yours, spectacularly,

ORPHEUS C. KERR.

LETTER·LXXXII.

NOTING THE UTTER DESTRUCTION, BY AN INEBRIATED JOURNALIST, OF
THE VENERABLE GAMMON'S BENIGNANT SPEECH; INTRODUCING THE
NEW GENERAL OF THE MACKEREL BRIGADE; AND DESCRIBING A CU-
RIOUS PHENOMENON ON DUCK LAKE.

WASHINGTON, D. C., Jan. 15th, 1863.

THE venerable Gammon, has melted sadly home to Mugville since the removal of the late idolized General of the Mackerel Brigade, and a worshipping peasantry are exasperated at his unnatural wrongs.

I cannot exactly, see, my boy, how this venerable man is so deeply injured by the said removal; in fact, it does not appear to me that he can have any interest in the change whatever; but his appearance of deep affliction has called scalding tears to all beholding eyes, and the attached populace crawl in the dust at the subduing aspect of his inexpressible woe.

It was on the Tuesday evening of this revered and aged patriot's arrival in adoring Mugville, that he was tumultuously serenaded by the brass-band of the Young Men's Democratic Christian Association, which is composed exclusively of constitutional chaps. He was frantically besought to respond; and then it was that he fell a hapless and venerable victim to the great, heart-rending mistake of an inebriated reporter for a reliable morning journal. The beloved old being meant to make only a few pithy,

(34)

THIRD SERIES. **35**

telling remarks to the enthusiastic band, and this was, in fact, his veritable

SPEECH.

" Thank you for your compliment. (A voice: ' *How are you, old boots?* ' ' *We're the boys to give the Rebels comfort!* ' and cheers.) We are here to-night to stand by the Constitution. (A voice : ' *What's old Abe about?* ' ' *Locking up good Democrats in Fort Lafayette!* ' ' *Well, it's our own fault, you know.*' ' *We deserve worse treatment!* ' and hisses.) We abhor these Rebels as much as the Black Republicans (a voice: ' *We can give the Rebels what they want!* ' and applause), but we also hate home-tyranny. Why was the idolized General of the Mackerel Brigade removed? (A voice: ' *To please the Rebels!* ' ' *We have licked the Black Republicans in New York!* ' ' *We've done the Rebels!* ' ' *Good!*'') To spite us! That's so, boys! (A voice: ' *And we'll make them love us yet?* ' ' *The New York election tickles them!* ' and cheers.) Whose good was he removed for? (A voice: ' *For Jeff Davis!* ' ' *Three cheers, boys!* ' and great enthusiasm.) Let History show! (A voice: ' *We'll make him President in* 1864 !') Good night.''

Here you have the true speech of the Venerable Gammon, my boy, with all those patriotic interruptions which lend such a chaste rhetorical charm to the extemporized oratory of our distracted country; but how shall I express the pangs which tore the breasts of the fond populace, when the reliable morning journal of Mugville came

36 ORPHEUS C. KERR PAPERS.

out next morning with six pounds of heavy editorial to show that the Venerable Gammon had ruthlessly betrayed the excellent national Democratic organization! How shall I depict the public misery that ensued in Mugville when that reliable morning journal, upon the authority of its inebriated reporter, gave *this* as a correct report of the revered patriarch's

SPEECH.

The speaker said : " How are you, old boots ? (A voice : ' *Thank you for your compliment.*') We're the boys to give the Rebels comfort and cheers. (A voice : ' *We are here to-night to stand by the Constitution!*') What's old Abe about ? Locking up good Democrats in Fort Lafayette ! Well ; it's our own fault, you know ; we deserve worse treatment and hisses. (A voice : ' *We abhor these Rebels as much as the Black Republicans!*') We can give the Rebels what they want and applause. (A voice : ' *But we also hate home tyranny!*' ' *Why was the idolized General of the Mackerel Brigade removed?*') To please the Rebels we have licked the Black Republicans in New York ; we've done the Rebels good. (A voice : ' *To spite us, that's so, boys!*') And we'll make them love us yet ! The New York election tickles them, and cheers. (A voice : ' *Whose good was he removed for?*') For Jeff Davis three cheers, boys, and great enthusiasm. (A voice : ' *Let history show!*') We'll make him President in 1864 ! (A voice : *Good night!*')"

You see, my boy, this horrible twistification was the result of the reporter's getting confused about who was

THIRD SERIES. 37

the speaker — him on the hotel balcony or the talkative chaps in the street. If our excellent national Democratic Organization would have less talking during their public speeches, my boy, there need be no such inhuman mistakes as that which has calumniated and utterly prostrated the Venerable Gammon.

On Wednesday I took a trot on the war-path upon the architectural street, Pegasus, and found the veteran Mackerel Brigade back at Paris again. They had made a great march from the Blue Ridge, my boy, and when I reached the front I found a scientific chap from Cincinnati taking observations. He stuck a tall stick into the ground, and scratched a long line on the damp sod, from the foot of this stick to the extreme right of the spectacled Brigade, letting the toes of the front rank of the Mackerels just touch it. Then he attached a powerful magnifying-glass to about the centre of the upright stick, and commenced looking through it very intently all along the line he had drawn.

I observed him attentively, and says I: " What is the nature of your contract with the Government, my serious friend ? "

He rubbed the glass with his blue silk pocket-handkerchief, and says he : " I have invented this useful arrangement to ascertain whether or ·not the Army of Accomac is really advancing. I closely watch the line to which the toes of the front rank of the army are already very near, and could almost swear that the forward movement is still going on. The average speed of this army," says the scientific chap, calculatingly, " has hitherto been six miles in six weeks ; but now that the war is about to com-

38 ORPHEUS C. KERR PAPERS.

mence in earnest, I think that the troops are making better time."

And so they were, my boy, so they were; for the heel of the first rank's boots were almost on the line in less than an hour, — no Confederacies being in sight.

Noticing a circle of Mackerel Officers a short distance in my rear, I dismounted from Pegasus and walked thither for greater speed, discovering that the brilliant staff were admiring the great equestrian gambols of the new General of the Mackerel Brigade.

The new General is a dignified, middle-aged chap, my boy, with a face which expresses many whiskers, and an eye to look you through and through when your meaning is transparent. He is not quite two yards high, has a head which looks like a lustrous apple-dumpling, dropped into the middle of a window-brush, and graduates downward into his boots without seeming to be either growing out of them, or running through them.

And he is none of your military popinjays, my boy, all plastered with buttons and gold lace, but an earnest, hardworking soldier. His dress for the field is characterized by genuine republican simplicity, and consists of hardworking corduroy breeches, sternly patched; an earnest pea-jacket, resolutely out at the elbows; a pair of straightforward slippers, unflinchingly ragged around the toes, and an untrifling silk hat, determinedly mashed-in at various points. You feel as you look at him, my boy, that he means hard work, and is indifferent to good clothes as long as he can save his distracted country.

On the majestic brow of a true hero, a shocking bad hat is a far nobler, more glittering crown, than the circle

THIRD SERIES. 39

of filthy lucre which surmounts the head of Europe's bloated despot. Grander, far grander is the nightcap of a Washington, than any style of army cap I have yet seen.

The new General was mounted upon a long-tailed cob, and his horsemanship thrilled this manly bosom with rapture. Did he wish to deliver an order to his aid, he but slightly tightened the reins of his horse, and at once the noble animal arose to his hind legs and fired off a pistol held for him by an orderly. Did he wish to go the rounds, he but touched the left flank of his horse, and straightway the sagacious charger struck into a graceful waltz, leaping over five-barred gates as he went along, and dashing through hoops held aloft by the troops. Did he desire to approach one of his Generals for consultation, he had but to give a low whistle, and forthwith the intelligent animal limped about on three feet, as though lame, and drank a bottle of wine presented to him by an orderly. Did he have an inclination to review his troops, he was compelled only to gently pinch his horse's neck, and at once the graceful beast laid down upon his side and pretended to die as naturally as any human being.

In short, my boy, it is argued from the earnest new General's bad clothes, that he will speedily bring the war to a good close; and from his being such a particular horseman, that he will never become any party's footman.

But let me change my subject for a time, and relate the great triumph of our new naval artillery on Duck Lake, which majestic sheet of water has returned to earth with the late rains.

Rear Admiral Head has so improved the deadly swivelgun of the Mackerel iron-plated squadron, that it will

40 ORPHEUS C. KERR PAPERS.

send a ball some distance without kicking the gunner overboard. The secret of this improvement is known only to the Government, my boy, and will be used to advantage when our gory conflict with combined Europe comes off.

It was on Thursday morning, my boy, when an enthusiastic military mob, consisting of Captain Villiam Brown, Captain Bob Shorty, and myself, stood once more upon the familiar shore of Duck Lake. The squadron, which has been named the "Secretary Welles," having been launched upon the treacherous element by Rear Admiral Head and one Mackerel, we took out our pieces of smoked glass and prepared for the naval pageant.

We could plainly see the stern old Rear Admiral bustling about on the gallant Grandmother of the Seas, as I may term the noble craft, and hear him swearing in his iron-plated manner.

"Fracture my turret," says the old sea-dog, "if I don't think this gun will surpass the Armstrong; blockade me, if I don't."

When it became the duty of the solitary Mackerel crew to load the awful instrument of destruction, it was discovered that the ramrod had been left behind at the Navy Yard Foundry. This nautical disaster might have marred the experiments, had not the Rear Admiral chanced to have his brown gingham umbrella along with him. This was used as a rammer, and the experiment proceeded.

The first charge was twenty pounds of powder, not more than nineteen of them running out of the touchhole. The ball slightly touched the water and went

THIRD SERIES. **41**

down, the recoil of the squadron being only the width of Duck Lake.

The second shot was made with only one pound of powder, as it was feared that the rudder might be strained by too much concussion, and we saw the ball drop into the ocean wave. At this shot, the "Secretary Welles" only hopped out of the water a few inches. The third shot was made with half a pound of powder, as it was not deemed advisable to do too much damage to the surrounding country by the gunnery.

We were gazing intently at the merciless implement of death, through our smoked glass, when this shot was fired, and suddenly beheld a phenomenon which made us catch our breath.

Mixed up with the fire and smoke, there emerged from the mouth of the swivel-gun, what appeared to be an immense brown bird of some kind, spreading its huge wings as it came out, and skimming wearily to the shore!

Captain Bob Shorty commenced to quake, and says he: "It's a Confederate insect!" •

"No," says Villiam, lowering his smoked glass, and speaking in a solemn whisper, "It's the distracted bird of our country, floating spectrally on the battle-smoke. Ah!" says Villiam, abstractedly uncorking my canteen, "our distracted bird is no inseck."

Was it indeed a majestic Eagle, my boy, stooping from his clouded heights to sanctify the terrible naval scene? I guess not, my boy, — I guess not; for we presently ascertained that, when the careless Mackerel crew rammed home that last charge, he heedlessly left Rear-Admiral

4*

42 ORPHEUS C. KERR PAPERS.

Head's brown gingham umbrella sticking in the gun, and it was the flight of the umbrella we had witnessed.

An umbrella, my boy, and a horse, may be said to have some relations. We put one up when it rains, and we rein the other up when we " put."

Yours, good-naturedly,

ORPHEUS C. KERR.

LETTER LXXXIII.

REFERRING TO WASHINGTON CITY AND THE PRESIDENT'S MESSAGE,
AND GIVING THE SOUTHERN CONFEDERACY'S VERY REASONABLE PEACE
PROPOSITION.

WASHINGTON, D. C., Jan. 28th, 1863.

THE city of Washington, my boy, without her Congress, is like a maiden without her plighted young man. She surveys herself in the mirror of the Potomac, and says she : " Where's my Congress, without whom I am like a gas bracket deserted by its old flame ? " Alas! all flesh is gas, my boy, and some of our congressmen are very fleshy. Their presence it is that makes Washington a light for the world, and many of them who once rode high horses have alighted. At the present moment our distracted country is enveloped in darkest night, and the day seems so far off that many Mackerels despair of ever seeing payday, even. At such a time what a blessing is that Congress which burns to illumine us after the manner of an elaborate chandelier ! It passes away to leave everything dark ; it returns, and behold all is darkey.

I was in my room at my hotel, when Congress commenced to arrive, conversing with Captain Bob Shorty ; and, as a seedy-looking, middle-aged chap passed by on the opposite side of the street, the captain looked out of the window, and says he :

" That's one of the new legislators, my Pythias."

44   ORPHEUS C. KERR PAPERS.

"How can you tell a new Solon from an old one?" says I, curiously.

"Why," says Captain Bob Shorty, profoundly, "an old congressman never wears a tall hat. An old congressman," says Captain Bob Shorty, sagely, "always wears a soft hat, so that it wont be injured by being knocked over his eyes."

I pondered deeply over this idea, my boy, and it seemed to me that a soft hat must be the real Cap of Liberty.

Passing over the organization of Senate and House, which suggested thoughts of ancient Rome about the time she was saved by geese, I shall proceed to notice the Message which our honest Abe fired into Congress from his intellectual breastworks during the week.

You have undoubtedly read this Abe L. paper, my boy, in the reliable morning journals, making due allowance for the typographical outrages committed by printers of opposite politics; but there was one portion of it gotten up for the honest Abe by the Chaplain of the Mackerel Brigade, and this portion is so mutilated in the publishing, that I cannot refrain from giving you the true version. Speaking of the cost to the country of Emancipation with compensation, the Chaplain wrote:

"Certainly it is not so easy to pay something as it is to pay nothing; but it is easier to pay a small sum than it is to pay a large sum; and it is easier to pay any bill when we have the money, than it is to pay a smaller bill when we have no money. Compensated Emancipation requires no more money than would be necessary to the progress of Remunerated Enfranchisement, which

THIRD SERIES. 45

would not close before the end of five hundred years. At that time, we shall undoubtedly have five hundred times as many people as we have now, provided that no one dies in the mean time; and supposing the premium on gold to increase in the same ratio as it has increased since our last census was taken, the premium on the specie belonging to five hundred times our present population will be amply sufficient to pay for all persons of African descent.

"I do not state this inconsiderately. At the same ratio of increase as we now realize, American gold will soon be worth more than all Europe. We have ten millions nine hundred and sixty-three thousand miles, while Europe has three millions eight hundred thousand, and yet the average premium on specie, in some of the States, is already above that of Europe. Taking the brokers in the aggregate, I find that if one gold dollar is worth $1.30 in one year,

It will be worth $2.60 in two years,
" " " " 3.90 " 3 "
" " " " 5.20 " 4 "
" " " " 6.50 " 5 "

This shows a yearly increase. If a gold dollar is worth $6.50 in five years, it will, of course, be worth $3,250 or five hundred times as much in five hundred years. Thus, when our population is five hundred times as great as at present, supposing each man to have a single gold dollar, the premium of $3,250 on his gold dollar will enable such man to purchase thirty-two and a half persons of African descent from the loyal slaveholders of our border States at

$100 a piece, though he would be virtually expending but one dollar himself.

"This scheme of emancipation would certainly make the war shorter than it now has a prospect of being. In a word, it shows that a dollar will be much harder to pay for the war than will be a dollar for emancipation on the proposed plan."

You will observe, my boy, that this same great mathematical idea is advanced in the Message as it is printed; but our Honest Abe has chosen to vary the terms somewhat. If you have a gold dollar, my boy, salt it down for five hundred years, and some future generation of offspring will call you blessed for leaving them $3,250 in postage-stamps.

On my last journey toward Paris, finding the Mackerel Brigade still halting before that ancient city, I rode straight to the tent of Captain Villiam Brown, whom I found making himself a fall overcoat from some old newspapers, while the Chaplain sat near by, making himself a pair of shoes from a remnant of calico.

"Well, paladin," says I to Villiam, "what is it that so long detains our noble army on the path of conquest?"

Villiam sighed as he used a little more paste to fasten the sleeves of the garment he was constructing, and says he:

"It's the overcoats."

"Why," says I, epigrammatically, "don't they go far enough forward in front?"

"Ah!" says Villiam, thoughtfully, "they come far enough forward in front, but then they leave the rear exposed. On Monday," says Villiam, reflectively, "Company

THIRD SERIES.

47

Three's overcoats arrived, and I requested the warriors to attire themselves after the designs of frequent fashion-plates. But scarce had their manly forms commenced to assume the garments, when the garments tore frantically from their warlike shapes."

" Hum!" says I, questioningly, " the overcoats were Rebels in disguise."

" No," says Villiam, gloomily, " but it took two Mack-erels to hold an overcoat together while another warrior put it on, and when it was buttoned in front, the rear presented the aspeck of two separate departments. I am now making myself a stronger coat of Democratic newspapers," says Villiam, explainingly, " in order that my Constitution may be protected from harm."

I glanced at him askant, my boy, and says I, innocently, " I see a still better reason for your clothing yourself for battle in newspapers."

" Ah!" says Villiam, complacently, " you think that I adopt the intellectual garment to show that my line of battle is ten cents a line."

" No, my hero," says I, pleasantly, " I think you clothe yourself for battle in printed matter, to make sure that ' he who runs may read.'"

I would not say positively that Villiam " saw " this agreeable remark, my boy. I am not prepared to affirm that he took the hit; but as the canteen left his hand, my ears recognized a hasty whiz, and the effect upon the side of the tent, near my head, was perforating.

Turning from the spot, I next had my attention attracted by a tall whiskered chap, in a paralyzed whirlpool of gray rags, who was closely examining a stack of Mackerel mus-

3

48 ORPHEUS C. KERR PAPERS.

kets near at hand. Hearing me ask his object, he remarked casually that I was a " mudsill," and says he :

" As the unconquerable Southern Confederacy has a great contempt for the Yankee army, it has sent me here to see whether these muskets are worth taking. If they proved to be worth taking, the war was to continue ; if not, I was to offer indirect proposals for peace, as the Sunny South does not wish to protect a struggle that does not pay."

Instead of replying to him, I stepped aside to give place to the Conservative Kentucky chap, who had just been denouncing the Message to the Mackerel Chaplain in the tent, and was greatly outraged by the Chaplain's response.

It seems that he had abruptly addressed the Chaplain, and says he : " If that Message wants to make the nigger the equal of the conservative element by implication, I hereby announce that Kentucky considers herself much offended. I fight for that flag," says he, hotly, pointing to the national standard, — " I fight for the stars on that flag, to aid the cause of the white man alone ; and with the black man Kentucky will have nothing to do whatever."

The Chaplain looked dreamily at the flag, as it patched the sky above him, and says he :

" For men of your way of thinking, my friend, that banner should bear a sun, rather than the stars."

" Hem ! " says the Kentucky chap. " How so ? "

" Why," says the Chaplain, gravely, " beneath the stars alone, you cannot tell a black man from a white man. The master and slave of the broad noonday are equals under the stars ; for if the sun shines upon the one

THIRD SERIES. 49

working that the other may be idle, the gentle planets of the night make master and bondman of one hue and perfect equals in Nature's own Republic, — starry Night. The banner for you, my friend, should bear the sun, to show that it is but for a day."

The conservative Kentucky chap came away swearing, my boy; and hence, it was in no very good humor that he now saluted the Confederate raggedier.

"Hem!" says he, ungraciously, "where did all those rags come from, and what is their name?"

The Confederacy hastily put on a pair of white cotton gloves, and says he:

"Am I addressing the Democratic Organization?"

"You address the large Kentucky branch," says the Conservative chap, pulling out his ruffles.

"Then," says the Confederacy, "I am prepared to make an indirect proposition for peace. My name is Mr. Lamb, by which title the Democratic Organization has always known the injured Confederacy, and I propose the following terms: Hostilities shall at once cease, and the two armies be consolidated under the title of the Confederate States Forces. The war-debts of the North and South shall be so united that the North may be able to pay them without confusion. An election for a new President shall at once be held, everybody voting save those who have shown animosity to the sunny South. France shall be driven out of Mexico by the consolidated armies, the expense being so managed that the North may pay it without further trouble. Upon these terms, the Confederacy will become a peaceful fellow-man."

"Hem!" says the Kentucky chap, "What you ask is

50   ORPHEUS C. KERR PAPERS.

perfectly reasonable. I will consider the matter after the manner of a dispassionate Democrat, and return you my answer in a few days."

Here I hastily stepped up, and says I, " But are you not going to consult the President at all about it, my Jupiter Tonans ? " ·

" The President ? the President ? " says the Conservative Kentucky chap, with a vague look. " Hem ! " says he, " I really forgot all about the President ! "

The Democratic Organization, my boy, in its zeal to benefit its distracted country, is occasionally like that eminent fire company in the Sixth Ward, which nobly usurped with its hose the terrible business of putting out a large conflagration, and never remembered, until its beautiful machine was all in position, that another company of fellow-firemen had exclusive possession of all the waterworks.

Yours, comparingly,

ORPHEUS C. KERR.

LETTER LXXXIV.

PROVING THAT RUSSIA IS INDEED OUR FRIEND; INSTANCING THE TERRIFIC BOMBARDMENT OF PARIS; AND TELLING HOW THE NEW GENERAL OF THE MACKEREL BRIGADE DELIGHTED ALL WITH HIS SURPRISING "SHAPE."

WASHINGTON, D. C., February 2d, 1863.

THE sagacious Russian bear, my boy, is found to regard the Eagle of our distracted country with more than his ordinary liking for fancy poultry, and our shattered bird may feel proud of a friendship proffered by such an excellent beast. Truth to tell, the present aspect of our national chicken is not calculated to inspire an idolatrous passion in the breast of European zoölogy. All his tail-feathers have seceded, and are in rebellion against him ; and he has got a black eye, my boy, from strategic gambols with the playful Southern Confederacy. Hence, we should accept the bear's affection as a marvel of disinterested emotion ; for I am almost sure, my boy, I am almost sure that nothing handsomer than a bear could have much real love for such a fractured fowl.

A relative of mine, named A. Merry Kerr,* went to Russia some time ago, being secretly deputed by Government to expend the amount of his passage-money in a judicious manner. He writes to me of his friendly reception by Gorchakoff, and says he :

* Excepting Mr. Bayard Taylor, no ordinary traveler ever excited so much wild affection in the breasts of foreign kings and noblemen as this gentleman.

(51)

"Mr. Gorchakoff ordered my trunks to be put away under the throne for the time being, and then hastened me to his own private bedroom, whose windows command a full view of all you can see through them. Having brushed me off and kissed me, he ordered some fried candles for two, and then says he :

"How comes on the Union cause, whose pregnant misery on Potomac's shore has caused the heart of the Czar untold anguish? How often has his majesty said to me: 'The North *must* triumph, Prince ; and mark me when I say, that two more centuries will not roll by without witnessing the fall of Richmond.' "

"Sir," says I, —

> "'The lightning-motion of the fish,
> Beneath the sea, will just compare
> With victory's impulse to our flag, —
> That stripéd bass of upper air.' .

"The North must conquer, you see, Mr. G."

Upon hearing me speak thus, Mr. Gorchakoff laid my head upon his bosom and smoothed my hair, and says he : "Oh, how I love your country! Russia will never join any scheme of foreign intervention against your beautiful fish."

He said this in such a tone of real fondness that tears sprang to my eyes, and says I :

"Heaven bless you, my Muscovy duck ! "

With a look of the deepest tenderness, Mr. Gorchakoff now extended himself at full length upon the top of a bureau near my chair, and allowed his head to hang over in such a manner that he was enabled to press his cheek against mine.

THIRD SERIES.   53

"Wilt thou do me one favor, noble youth?" says he, with much emotion.

I placed a hand upon my heart.

"Then," says he, "just ask Mr. Seward not to write so many letters to me every week; because when my mail is so large, I don't have any time to attend to my family."

I promised to do so, and then went out to get some oysters. The candles had made me quite light-headed.

From this, my boy, you will perceive that Russia "may be counted upon in an emergency;" as the man said of the bear-skin upon which he was reckoning his small change.

On Thursday, bright and early, I mounted my gothic steed Pegasus, and started for Duck Lake.

Upon reaching the Mackerel camp, I found all the spectacled warriors under arms for a fray, the unaccommodating Confederacies on the other side of Paris having urged some rifled objections to the construction of a pontoon bridge across Duck Lake. The chap who was building the bridge had only just untied his second paper of nails, when a potato from some Confederate marksman, in the second-story of Paris, hit him violently in the stomach. Simultaneously the cover of a dinner-pot cracked his knuckles, and, as he fell back in good order, a brick-bat tapped him on the head. Believing that hostilities had commenced, the new General of the Mackerel Brigade hastily put on all his dirty clothes, and ordered the Orange County Howitzers to commit incendiarism with Paris, simultaneously directing Rear Admiral Head to moor the "Secretary Welles" abreast of the nearest Confederacy and shell him with great slaughter.

54

ORPHEUS C. KERR PAPERS.

Under command of Captain Samyule Sa-mith, the Howitzers were opened upon Paris, and commenced such a tornado of round shot and grape that the surrounding landscape was very much defaced. There was much noise, my boy, — there was much noise.

But the great sight of the hour was the manœuvring of the iron-plated Mackerel squadron on the tempestuous waters of Duck Lake. After hastily making a fire in the stove on the quarter-deck, and placing a tumbler where it could warm, the stern old Rear Admiral ordered the Mackerel crew to report how much water there was in the hold. The crew repaired to the stern-sheets and reported " One pitcherful and two lemons ; " whereupon the hardy old sea-dog swore in his iron-plated manner, and ordered the swivel-gun amidships to be trained upon the basement windows of Paris. Everything being in readiness, the word was given to fire !

Bang ! went the horrid instrument of carnage, and the hideous missile went crashing through the back basement windows, cutting a bow from the cap of a venerable Florence Nightingale, who was at that moment making a sponge-cake for some sick Confederacies, and driving the stove-pipe clear through the wall. The aged Nightingale thought that something had happened, and says she : " Well, I never did ! " .

Rear Admiral Head smiled ; but it was the horrid smile of naval bloodthirstiness. " Revolve my turret ! " says he, grimly, " I fight not against women ; but the other window must be broken."

The venerable Neptune leaned over his columbiad to make sure of this shot, unconsciously pressing his stomach

THIRD SERIES. 55

against the but-end of his gun. There was a report, my boy; the swivel-gun kicked, and the Rear Admiral fell upon the deck with a promiscuous violence.

Meanwhile, Company 3, Regiment 5, under Captain Villiam Brown, had waded across Duck Lake in as many divisions as there were Mackerels, and immediately commenced a tremendous fire of musketry at the upper windows of Paris, wounding a Confederacy who kept a shoe-store up there, and reducing two flower-pots to fragments.

Whilst I was witnessing this bombardment, my boy, and admiring the courage with which Villiam was slashing around with his sword, I noticed that the squadron had suddenly ceased firing.

It had ceased firing, because Rear Admiral Head had unexpectedly discovered that his Mackerel crew was a Black Republican; and had therefore engaged him in single combat, greatly to the detriment of the regular engagement.

Scarcely had I turned to view this new phase of war, when the firing of howitzers and musketry behind me instantly ceased, and I heard a low murmur of wonder arising from the whole brigade.

Quickly turning about again, I was hastening to where Captain Bob Shorty strode with the Conic Section, when I beheld General Wobert Wobinson, the new General of the Mackerel Brigade, cantering along the shore of Duck Lake on his trained charger, and exhibiting a form to petrify the whole world with admiration.

" Ah! *there's* shape! " was the low cry of the spectacled veterans, as they gazed breathlessly at the picture.

56   ORPHEUS C. KERR PAPERS.

Captain Bob Shorty cleaned his glasses to make sure that it was no illusion, and says he: "By all that's Federal, it appears to me that I never saw so much Shape!"

A Confederacy, who had just appeared on the roof of Paris with a horse-pistol in his hand and slaughter in his thoughts, caught sight of the equestrian vision, and instantly dropped his merciless weapon of destruction as though paralyzed.

"Oh!" says he, panting, "what Shape!"

Rear Admiral Head heard the sound in the midst of his single combat, and paused to ascertain what it was. His spectacles scanned the horizon round and round, until they finally rested upon the figure of the new General of the Mackerel Brigade.

"Fracture my armor!" says he, ecstatically, "did I ever survey so much Shape!"

The battle was over for that day.

Shape, my boy, is a great thing in a General; for when Heaven's Great Printer commenced to set human type in the "galley" of earth, He must have needed considerable General matter to fully make up His "forms;" and when a General has a form fully up to His make, we may consider him well set up.

Yours, typographically,

ORPHEUS C. KERR.

LETTER LXXXV.

HOLDING THE GOVERNMENT STRICTLY ACCOUNTABLE FOR THE OC-
CURRENCE OF A RECENT "MILITARY NECESSITY;" RECOUNTING
THE AFFECTING EPISODE OF THE MACKEREL DRUMMER-BOY; AND
DEPICTING THE NEW MACKEREL GENERAL'S FIRST GREAT BATTLE.

WASHINGTON, D. C., Feb. 9th, 1863.

I AM no longer on speaking terms, my boy, with the Government of our distracted country, and beg leave most respectfully to inform it that the imbecile cold weather of the past few days may disgust, but can never discourage me. Being of respectable though Democratic parentage, I scorn to associate with an Executive and Cabinet so lost to all sense of national comfort, that it permits the weather to become a constant outrage on our Constitutions, frequently freezing loyal Democrats for no other offence than that of protecting defenceless lampposts after nightfall. I am very cold, my boy, — I am very cold, and my hatred of the present Cabinet is intense.

But what shall I say about the agency of this same Government in producing a Military Necessity at the late great battle of Paris? Let me put on my overcoat and express my cold in a passionate cough, as I remark that its agency in this matter forcibly reminds me of a chap I once knew in the sixth ward.

He was an aged chap of much red nose, my boy, and

(57)

58   ORPHEUS C. KERR PAPERS.

lived with his youngest broadcloth son in the same house
with his Wayward Sister. The Wayward Sister being
an old maid of severe countenance, occupied such por-
tions of the residence as seemed most safe from the in-
trusion of that sex which seeks to make Woman its
broken-hearted slave; and as long as the patient old chap
answered the door-bell and didn't smoke in the house, she
got along with him after the manner of a Methodist
angel. Things went on pleasantly through the winter,
the high-minded maiden using the coal of her aged kin-
dred, and employing all his black tea without complain-
ing; but in the spring she joined a Woman's Rights
Convention, and commenced to hold indignation-meetings
of virtuously-indignant females in the best room in the
house. These meetings having decided, that,

" *Whereas*, Man is a ojus creature which is constantly
preying upon that sex which it is his mother's, and deny-
ing to it those inalienable Rights without which Woman's
sphere cannot exist. Therefore be it

" *Resolved*, That Woman is the Superior Sex.

" *Resolved*, That union with man is incompatible with
the good of a sex which it is ourselves; and that we will
immediately take that household furniture of which
Woman is the only rightful owner, and only ask to be let
alone."

The aged chap received a copy of these resolutions, my
boy, and says the Wayward Sister: "I can no longer
consent to live in the same house with an inferior being."
The chap heard her in silence, and might have let her
have her own way, under ordinary circumstances, but
when he came home next night he found that she had

THIRD SERIES. 59

packed up all the furniture in the house to carry off with her, and expected him to give her his watch and night-key. He scratched his head, and says he: "I cannot permit this sort of thing, because I really want some furniture for my own use." The Wayward Sister threw her thimble at him, and says she: "Our male parient bought this furniture only because he got married to one of the Superior Sex; and as it was Woman which solely occasioned its purchase, it clearly belongs to Woman."

But the chap could not see it in this light, my boy; and as soon as his son came home he told him all about it. The manly youth took a look up the stairs to where the maiden and four or five other spring bonnets were intrenched behind the furniture, and says he:

"It's an unnatural thing to have trouble with relations; but I'm just going up there to capture that big chair."

By this time some of the neighbors had come in, and commenced to urge the old chap to take vigorous measures. He looked at his son, and says he:

"Can you do it Tommy?"

The child of his bosom winked twice, and immediately prepared to perform the feat, only pausing long enough to look in the glass and see if his necktie sat well. Then, gaining the head of the stairs, he leaned across a bureau barring the way, and was about to grasp the big chair, when the Wayward Sister hit him over the head with a broom, and presently he found himself prostrate at the foot of the stairs, with a violent pain in his nose.

On witnessing this disaster, all the neighbors shrank with indignation from the aged father, and said it was all his doings. The poor old chap scratched his head, and says he:

60

ORPHEUS C. KERR PAPERS.

"I don't see how it's my fault."

"Why," says a neighbor of much fatness, "you're always interfering, — that's what you are. Now, you'll never get back any of your furniture."

"Interfering?" says the paternal chap, innocently. "Why, how *could* I interfere with Tommy, when I only let him do, in his own way, what he gave me to understand he was able to?"

Here all the neighbors sighed grievously, and says one:

"Miserable old man, we believe you mean well enough; but the fact is, you are a species of old idiot. It was your business to have had *another son,* who would have been this one's brother; so that if one met with a heart-rending failure on the stairs, the other could simultaneously have entered that back window by a ladder, and taken the chair by the rear. But you are always interfering. Take our advice now, and either give up drinking altogether, or arrange it so that those who drink with you may be persons not distinguishable from ourselves."

And they all departed, shaking their heads, my boy — they all departed shaking their heads; leaving the unfortunate old chap to bind up his offspring's nose, and to reflect upon the great iniquity of interfering with one son's success, by not having another.

The Government of our distracted country, my boy, is so very much like this well-meaning but imbecile old chap, that the failure of any one of its generals is entirely due to its interference in not having another general; who, in case that general did not succeed, could take his place before he failed to do so.

The Military Necessity produced by this interference

THIRD SERIES. 61

took place at Paris, very recently, and shortly after the new General of the Mackerel Brigade had so nearly won the battle by that revelation of manly Shape to which I referred in my last letter.

Finding that the terrible bombardment of Paris, my boy, had routed the straggling Confederacies from that ancient city, the whole Mackerel Brigade marched safely across Duck Lake, leaving only the Orange County Howitzers on this side. Scarcely had the spectacled host occupied the city, when there appeared upon the main street the overwhelming Shape of the new General of the Mackerel Brigade, mounted upon a steed which was almost as sagacious as a human being; and holding his hat in one hand, after the manner of Washington entering Trenton. It was as though Frank Leslie's illustrated artist had just been commanded to draw a warlike picture, my boy, representing one of those equestrian heroes who all appear in precisely the same attitude, and seem to have lifted their hats for the particular purpose of showing with what mathematical precision their hair is parted.

Instantly there arose cheers so loud that they must have been heard by the cowardly Confederacies on the hills behind Paris, and several Mackerels became so enthusiastic to be led against the enemy, that they actually started on the war-path by themselves, and only turned back when they discovered that they happened to be going in the wrong direction.

Having received all the cheers, and immediately dispatched them to the reliable morning journals around the country, the General of the Mackerel Brigade ordered the Conic Section, under Captain Bob Shorty, and Company

62 ORPHEUS C. KERR PAPERS.

3, Regiment 5, under Captain Villiam Brown, to march out of Paris, and form in line under the guns of the Southern Confederacy; at the same time directing Captain Samyule Sa-mith, to take Company 2, Regiment 1, and strike through a defile in the hills.

Samyule formed his veterans in the shape of a horse-shoe, and says he:

"Comrades, now is the time to repent of your sins, for you haven't got much time left. As for myself," says Samyule, seriously, "my sins are all those of commission, and those who gave me my commission are responsible for them. If any of you younger Mackerels have in your possession the last things your mothers gave you, now is your chance to look upon them for the last time."

As Samyule spoke thus, a small blue object, carrying a drum, toddled forth from the ranks, and saluted. It was a small Mackerel drummer, my boy, who had enlisted only ten days before, and his small eyes were wet with tears. The heroic child wiped his little nose on his sleeve, and says he:

"*My* mother gave me something."

Samyule was greatly affected, and says he:

"Was it the Family Bible, sweet cherub?"

"No-o-o," sobbed the innocent, as though his little heart would break.

Samyule wiped his tear-dimmed spectacles, and says he:

"Perhaps it was her daguerreotype?"

The infant wept afresh, and says he:

"No-o-o."

"Then," says Samyule, in a broken voice, "it must have been her blessing."

THIRD SERIES. 63

"No! no-o-o," cried the small Mackerel drummer, with quivering lips.

"Then what in thunder was it that your mother gave you?" says Samyule, greatly bewildered.

"It was a spanking!" screamed the affectionate little creature, cramming both his little fists into his little eyes, and blubbering unrestrainedly.

Samyule gazed a moment at the child, and says he:

"Well may affection bid thee weep, thou tender little one! When a sweetheart blushingly places a rose upon her lover's breast, the scene is affecting; but my own memory of childhood tells me that a far deeper feeling is excited when the tender mother selects a different flower, and places upon the back of her child the modest lady's slipper."

Immediately after this affecting little incident, my boy, Samyule led his men to their duty, and they marched into one end of the defile as soldiers, to pass out of the other as spirits.

Along the front, "Forward!" was the word, and the Conic Section swept to the assault, like a sea of bayonets dashed against a shore of adamantine rock from the hollow of an Almighty hand. Were it possible, my boy, for bullets to ascend perpendicularly until they just reached the top of mountain breastworks, and then slant down at an acute angle to where the foe lay hidden, it is possible that the frequent volleys from the Conic Section might have produced some carnage; but as the face of the hill before our troops was straight up and down, with the noisy Confederacies on the extreme summit, the Mackerel musketry simply occasioned a rise in Federal lead, without a fall in Confederate leaders.

64 ORPHEUS C. KERR PAPERS.

Some Confederacies in their lofty intrenchments just tipped over a few cannon, so that the balls might roll out upon the mackerels, and, says one of them:

" If you mudsills will stay there a little longer, we'll manage it so as to drop the shells on you from our hands, without using the guns at all."

Captain Bob Shorty heard this jeer, and as he tied his handkerchief over a wound on his forehead, a sickly smile illustrated his ghastly face, and says he:

" We might as well all die here together. The grave, after all, is a softer bed than many of these Mackerel beings have been accustomed to."

Sergeant O'Pake who always takes things literally, turned to Bob, and, says he :

" What makes it soft ? "

" Because," says Captain Bob Shorty, looking vacantly at the sergeant, " it is a bed of down. Did you never hear the old song of ' Down among the Dead Men ?' " But let me not linger over the scene, my boy.

That night, the remaining Mackerels silently recrossed Duck Lake, and the General penned the following

DESPATCH.

" I have withdrawn the Brigade across Duck Lake. The position of the Confederacies is impregnable. It was a Military Necessity to attack the enemy or retire. I have done both.

Wobert Wobinson."

Just as the spectacled veterans gained this side of Duck Lake again, my boy, the Mackerel Chaplain was accosted by a Republican chap from Boston, and says he: " This

THIRD SERIES. 65

really looks like action at last my friend. Our troops are evidently all enthuasiasm to be led once more against the foe."

The Chaplain shaded his eyes with his hand, to look at the speaker, and says he:

"They are indeed enthusiastic, my friend. So enthusiastic, in fact, that at least half of them would not come back to this side at all."

"Ah!" says the Republican chap; "the noble fellows."

"Yes," says the Chaplain, as softly as though he were speaking in a sick-room; "they remain there sleeping upon their arms. And, oh, my friend, they will never come back again."

He spoke truly, my boy: and may a kind Heaven see naught in the blood welling from their loyal hearts but the blush of a soldier's honor; the glow of a patriot fire in which all their human errors went up to God as the smoke of a glorious sacrifice. They sleep their last sleep upon the arms of their Country; and whether those arms, with which she folds them into her heart, be white with the ermine of winter, or green with the drapery of summer, the clasp shall be none the less strong with all a Mother's immortality of love.

Yours, gravely,

ORPHEUS C. KERR.

LETTER LXXXVI.

TOUCHING UPON A LATE OVATION TO A PARENT OF HIS COUNTRY; GIVING THE CONSERVATIVE KENTUCKY MAP OF ALL AMERICA; AND INTRODUCING A SECOND NEW GENERAL OF THE MACKEREL ORGANIZATION.

WASHINGTON, D. C., March 8th, 1863.

I HAVE been very ill, my boy — I have been very ill; and even now, the hand which grasps the pen trembles with weakness, like the hand of the wind upon a slender rush. I have been reminded of my latter end, and of our Excellent National Democratic Organization, by an outrage upon my Constitution and the Arbitrary Arrest of my health, — proceedings which seem to prove that the well-known Southern Confederacy is entirely right in this war, and that the North is chiefly composed of Honest Old despots. (See proceedings of Democratic Organization, Resolution 290.)

As I lay sick in Strategy Hall the other day, so desolately lonely that I almost wished to die, and without energy enough to finish reading the greenback I had commenced that morning, there came to see me an affable Democratic chap who had just recovered from a severe bilious attack brought on by the Conscription Bill, and wished to consult me as to the propriety of nominating Dr. Brandreth for President of the United States in 1865.

THIRD SERIES. 67

"Why, my future Jefferson," says I, feebly, "what are you going to do with McClellan, then?"

"Really," says he, just stepping across the ward to spit on a copy of the Tribune, which served as a window-curtain, "really, I forgot all about that manly form. Oh!" says the pleasant Democratic chap, replacing the Constitution in his hat, from which it had just fallen, — "Oh! what heroism do we find embodied in that youthful shape! The voice of a assembled universe asks: 'Shall G. B. McClellan go unrewarded?' There is no echo at the time. It asks again: 'Who, then, shall be President of the United States in 1865?' And echo triumphantly answers, General George Barnum McClellan!"

Here the affable Democratic chap took off his spectacles, my boy, and beamed undisguisedly at a small black bottle on the table.

"But," says I, softly, "his name is not George *Barnum* McClellan at all. His middle name is not Barnum."

"Hem!" says the Democratic chap, with a severe aspect, "I don't know that it is. Really," says the Democratic chap, hastily picking up his umbrella and moving away, "really, I don't know that it is."

Mistakes, my boy, will happen in the best-regulated organizations; and, if we construe them maliciously, we deserve, like a parcel of scandal-mongering old Bohea-mians, to be confined all our lives to small *coups* of Phineas T.

It was during my illness that the adoring citizens of Mugville discovered that the Venerable Gammon had been defeated ten times in the election for County Clerk in his youth, and frantically instigated an overflowing ovation therefore to that venerable man. I know not, my

68 ORPHEUS C. KERR PAPERS.

boy, what this aged and shirt-collared picture of perpetual beneficence had done to be such an idol. I cannot conceive why repeated defeats in his youth should entitle him to the adoration of a fond populace at the present exciting period ; but the leading citizens presented him with a silver butter-knife and a serenade, my boy ; and he made a benignant speech to show that he and Providence desired only the applause of their own consciences.

"My children," says the Venerable Gammon, waving benefactions in his fat and heartfelt manner, "I accept this butter-knife, — not for my own merits, but because it symbolizes the only true means of restoring that Union of which I am a part. This knife," says the Venerable Gammon, eying the costly gift with oily and benignant satisfaction, — "this knife teaches us that only fiendish Abolitionism would think of using the Sword of Radicalism to conquer the erring Confederacy which is still our sister, when the Butter-knife of Conservatism was to be had."

Then all the leading citizens of Mugville observed joyfully to each other that the country was redeemed at last, and four-and-twenty reliable morning journals published six columns each about the triumphant progress of the Venerable Gammon in the affections of the people.

Among those present at this sublime ovation was an aged chap selling apples, who immediately burst into tears when the voice of the venerable man fell upon his ears. On being asked to explain his emotions, he cast his dim eyes upward toward an American flag which was being used by a merchant near by to advertise some patent pills, and says he, brokenly :

THIRD SERIES. 69

"When I hear that woice, and see that flag, all my manhood crumbles into scalding tears."

He was an apple-seller of fine feelings, and had once served as a deserter in the Army of the Potomac.

Pathetic little incidents like these, my boy, humble though they may be, are pregnant with a deep and touching meaning, of which I have not the remotest conception.

There is a new Mackerel Hotel recently erected on the borders of Duck Lake, near Strategy Hall, for the benefit of Brigadiers who have not been accustomed to doing without a bar; and it was in one of the rooms thereof that the Conservative Kentucky Chap recently fell a victim to the most remarkable optical illusion of this distracted century. He was sitting with his back to a window, my boy, his head drooped upon his breast beneath the weight of the Emancipation Proclamation, and, with arms folded and legs screwed awry on his chair, he was contemplating the opposite wall from under his Conservative hat.

"Hum," says he, with subdued ecstasy, "How sweet it is to look upon the map of my native land, of which Kentucky is the guiding star! As I look upon that simple map," says the conservative Chap, thoughtfully, "and reflect upon the recent improvements in Kentucky, it becomes a question in my mind whether Kentucky is the United States, or the United States is Kentucky."

Following the direction of his eyes as he said this, I beheld upon the wall opposite where he was sitting:

A CONSERVATIVE KENTUCKY MAP OF ALL AMERICA.

"Look here, my absorbed Talleyrand," says I, in astonishment, "that's not a map! It's only your own shadow on the wall."

He moved as I spoke, and then, for the first time, discovered his illusion.

"Hum!" says he, "it is a map of the Union in the sense that the Union is but a shadow of its former self."

The Conservative Kentucky Chap is actually so insufferably egotistical, my boy, and so imbued with the idea that Kentucky is the whole country, that it is almost impossible for him to sit on a chair without throwing his body into almost the exact shape of the American Continent.

Having induced a small Mackerel drummer to bring me my chaste architectual steed, the Gothic Pegasus, I

THIRD SERIES. 71

mounted the roof of that walking country church, and moved off in an organ-waltz to inspect the national troops.

The Mackerel Brigade grows hoary with antiquity, and the capture of the Southern Confederacy is still delayed for the want of pontoons. And this reminds me that the Abolitionists of New England, who are entirely responsible for this war, with its taxes upon members of the Democratic Organization, have not yet sent any pontoons to the field. Whilst they would abridge the rights of white men, they even ignore white men's rights to a bridge. But let us not linger over such depravity, or we shall be delayed in our preparations for the Presidential canvass in 1865.

The last new General of the Mackerel Brigade is an officer of great age, named Cox, — known to the soldiery as the Grim Old Fighting Cox, — and I am happy to say, my boy, that he is an officer of great ability. Spurning all that vain pomp which too often makes our generals as clean in appearance as the military minions of the despotic powers of Europe, he makes it a practice to attire himself like the unostentatious dustman of a true Republic ; and when he rides abroad to inspect the regiments, it is universally admitted that he is like a father visiting his children, whose great numbers make such demands upon his means that he can't afford to dress himself respectably.

Having assumed command of the Mackerel Brigade, the Grim Old Fighting Cox immediately summoned all his officers to his presence, and, having engaged each in single combat and defeated him, he proceeded to show his great ability. He beckoned to Captain Villiam Brown, who was at that moment taking the sun's altitude with his can-

4

72

ORPHEUS C. KERR PAPERS.

teen, and, says he: "Tell me how many men are in the guard-house for beastly intoxication?"

Villiam smiled affably, and says he: "I don't remember just how many that Republican institution will hold."

"Release them ALL!" thundered the Grim Old Fighting Cox, violently rattling his sword, and firing a pistol in the air.

"Ah!" says Villiam, "here's Ability."

The next officer called was Captain Bob Shorty, and says the General to him: "How many slow-matches did my predecessor order for the Orange County Howitzers?"

Captain Bob Shorty took three steps in a break-down, and says he: "We have always ordered seventy-five."

"Make it seventy-six!" roared the Grim Old Fighting Cox, kicking over the writing-table and discharging a revolver over his shoulder.

Captain Bob Shorty gave a leap into the air, and says he:

"By all that's Federal! did 1 ever hear of so much Ability?"

As the Grim Old Fighting Cox was leaving his quarters, he came upon a Mackerel chap who was stooping down to tie his shoe, and gave him a kick that kindled conflagration in his vision. The poor chap rubbingly picked himself up, and, says he:

"It appears to me I never see so much Ability."

Ability, my boy, in its modern acceptation as applied to military men, appears to mean a peculiar capacity for surprising and startling everybody — except the enemy.

Yours, suspiciously.

ORPHEUS C. KERR.

LETTER LXXXVII.

IN WHICH OUR CORRESPONDENT HAS A DEADLY AFFAIR OF HONOR WITH A GENTLEMAN FROM KENTUCKY; EXPERIENCES "CONTRABAND" HOSPITALITY AND MELODY; ATTENDS A GREAT MEETING IN ACCOMAC; AND WITNESSES A PRODIGIOUS NAVAL ACHIEVEMENT.

WASHINGTON, D. C., March 15th, 1863.

KENTUCKY, my boy, has considered herself a general boon to mankind ever since she was discovered by Colonel Boone; but there are different kinds of boons known to mankind, and if I should chance to mention the baboon as amongst the noisiest and least respectable of the species, my remark may not be regarded as entirely destitute of a personal bearing. It was in the honeyed accents of admiring friendship that I conveyed this chaste zoölogical idea to the Conservative Kentucky chap on Monday last, as we took Richmond together at Willard's bar, and I regret to say that he made it *casus belli*. Accidentally dropping his bowie-knife on the floor, and hastily replacing his ruffles over the handle of his pocket revolver, he polished the blade of his dirk with a blood-colored silk handkerchief, and says he:

"Kentucky fought for Washington in the Revolution; she has, thus far, prosecuted the present war without fear; nor will she shrink from even shedding personal gore where the provocation is the offspring of Yankee lowness."

(73)

74 ORPHEUS C. KERR PAPERS.

He said this, with exceeding majesty, my boy, and I felt that I was indeed involved in complications with the Border States.

"I understand you, my warrior," says I, calmly; "but if this affair is to come off immediately, where are we to find our seconds?"

The Kentucky chap hastily called a small boy to him, and says he:

"Sonny, just run out into the street and ask any two gentlemen you meet to step in here for a moment." "You see," says he, turning to me, "it's better to have two brigadier-generals for seconds, as a battle might take place while we are away, and there are no private soldiers to spare at present."

"Yes," says I, thoughtfully, "that's very true."

The brigadiers were obtained, my boy, and, with murder in our hearts, we started forth to seek a spot appropriate for carnage in private. It was just the hour of midday, and we were wending our sanguinary way in silence, when, upon turning a corner of one of the public buildings, the sound of sweet music fell upon our ears, and we came suddenly upon a brass band and a party of singers, who were discoursing witching strains under one of the windows.

I listened for a moment, and then, says I: "What may be the occasion for this noonday melody?"

The Conservative Kentucky chap motioned for us to pause, and says he, feelingly: "It's a serenade to Secretary Welles of the Navy. Let us heed the voice of the singer."

Here a young vocal chap, under the window, commenced singing the following words, in a fine tenor manner:

SERENADE.

" O lady, in thy waking glance
    There lurked a wondrous spell,
To hold young Cupid in thine eye
    As in a prison cell.

" And now, the god of Slumber finds
    Thy drooping lids so fair,
He makes of them his chosen couch
    And dwells forever there."

As the last note of the singer fainted into the eternity of lost sounds, I looked at the Conservative Kentucky chap, my boy, and beheld that his eyes were suffused with the tears of an exquisite sensibility.

" Yes," says he, softly, " — ' and dwells forever there.' " Here the Kentucky chap shed another tear to wash out the stain of the last one, and says he, " Mr. Welles is indeed a lady who offers some attraction to slumber. May he rest in peace ! "

We were all too deeply affected to speak, but proceeded silently to a vacant lot across the river, where accommodations for law-breaking were ample. Everything about us here seemed fraught with the spirit of peace ; on each side, and as far as the eye could reach behind and before, were the tents of the Army of the Potomac, growing in the spots where they were planted years ago. We alone, of all the human beings within sound of our weapons, were about to be breakers of the established war — to shed human blood. It seemed like a sacrilege, and I trembled with the cold.

76 ORPHEUS C. KERR PAPERS.

At first, my boy, we had some trouble to keep the brig-adier-generals with us, as it suddenly struck them that they had not drawn their pay for two whole hours, and were frantic to return; but when I suggested, that if they should be missed from their posts, they would probably be nominated for major-generalship, they consented to remain.

When the Conservative Kentucky chap took his position, I noticed that his countenance was contorted into a horrible expression of severity, and asked him why it was?

"Hem!" says he, "this is a solemn moment, young man. We are both about to fly into the face of our Maker." Here he pointed his weapon at me; and says he: "I think you are frightened."

"No," says I, making ready.

The Kentucky chap's face then assumed the most terrific expression I ever saw, and says he:

"Are you not alarmed at your awful position?"

"No," says I.

The Conservative Kentucky chap lowered his pistol, and, motioning for the brigadiers to come from behind their trees, advanced to my side.

"Hem!" says he, frowning majestically, "I think I understood you to intimate that you were terrified."

"No," says I.

Here the Conservative Kentucky chap took me suddenly by the arm in a very confidential manner, and, having led me a few paces back, says he, in a horrible whisper: "You find yourself frightened, as it were."

"Why, no," says I.

THIRD SERIES. **77**

"Well," says the Conservative Kentucky chap, "I AM."

And we all went home together.

Since then, my boy, I have weighed and contrasted my own feelings and those of the Conservative Kentucky chap on that occasion, when I won an everlasting reputation for bravery; and I am satisfied that the bravery of a man in an affair of honor is a superior capacity for concealing terror.

It was toward the middle of the week that I went down to Accomac to attend a great Union meeting there, and it's my private opinion, my boy, my private opinion, that the human tongue is not without its province in this war. But before the meeting commenced, and whilst I was reflecting upon the fact that it was the day on which the Prince of Wales was to be married, a redeemed contraband saluted me, and says he:

" Mars'r, I hab been made a free man by Mars'r Lincoln, and hab opened a Refreshment Saloon on de European plan. If you want to dine, sar, here's my card. My name is Mister Negg."

I looked at the card as he left me, and found it to read thus: —

> ### HAMAN NEGG'S
> #### RESTAURANT.
> ICH DIEN OYSTERS IN EVERY STYLE.

There was one thing about this inscription that I did not understand, and says I to a chap near me:

78 — ORPHEUS C. KERR PAPERS.

" See here, my patriotic friend, what does this mean? What kind of things are Ich Dien Oysters?"

" Oh," says he, obligingly, " you do not understand the Hanoverian tongue. '*Ich Dien*' is the Prince of Wales' motto, and means '*I serve*.' The phrase 'Ich Dien Oysters in Every Style' means, 'I serve oysters in every style.'"

Then it was, my boy, that I saw in Mr. Negg's device the despised African's testimonial of gratitude to Great Britain for the recent reaction of anti-slavery sentiment there. A more delicate compliment, my boy, was never offered to the mother country, who has given us all at least 290 * reasons for loving her.

And speaking of redeemed contrabands, reminds me of the new African hymn, which the more pious colored Americans of South Carolina might denominate

DE GREAT HALLELUGERUM.

" My mars'r's gwine away to fight
 With Mars'r Linkum's horde,
An' now dis chile's at libaty
 To dance an' bress de Lord.
Dar's no more swearin' round de house
 When missus cut up bad;
Dar's no more kickin' niggers' shins,
 And, darfor', I is glad.

---

 * Persons who despise Europe may remember, that, " The 290," (supposed to mean, from 290 British Merchants) was the original name of the rebel pirate " Alabama."

THIRD SERIES.

"When mars'r take his horse to go,
  He kindly say to me :
' I hab such confidence in you,
  I leab you all, you see ;
Of all de niggers round de place,
  I trust to you alone.'
By golly ! dat's what mars'r say
  To eb'ry nig he own !

"' Now if dém Bobumlitionists
  Should kill me dead,' says he,
' I hab instruct your missus kind
  To set you niggers free.'
But mars'r say dat bery same
  Wheneber he get sick,
And bresséd Jesus wrastle him
  To make him holy quick.

"' Dem Yankees, dam um all,' says he,
  ' Am comin' down to steal
You niggers, and to sell you then
  For Cuba cochineal.
De Suvern chiverly,' says he,
  ' Am fightin' jist fo' you. '
Now mars'r swearum when he lie,
  And, darfor', dat wont do !

"Den mars'r trot away to war
  With 'Dolphus by his side, —
A poor cream-colored, common dark
  Dat isn't worf his hide.
He leab me and de other nigs
  To clar the place alone,
With nuffin' but to play and shake
  De fiddle and de bone.

4*

"I hab a talk with Uncle Pete,
　　De old plantation hand,
And though he am intelligums
　　Dis chile can understand.
He say de Hallelugerum
　　For cullud folks hab cum,
And dat he bresséd Lord hab heard
　　And beat his thunder-drum.

" He say dat Northern buckra man
　　Hab sent his gun an' ship
To make de rebel chiverly
　　Give up his nigger whip,
He say dat now's de darkey's time
　　To break de bonds of sin,
And take his chil'en an' his wife
　　To whar de tide comes in.

" He say dat in de Norf, up dar,
　　Whar Mars'r Greeley dwell,
De white folks make de brack folks work,
　　But treat them bery well;
He says dey pay them for de work
　　Dey's smart enuff to do,
And nebber sells them furder Souf
　　When sheriff put um screw.

"I hab a wife an chil'en dear,
　　And mars'r say to me
He nebber sell them while he live, —
　　He'd rather set them free ;
But dar's de mortgage on de house,
　　If dat should hab to fall,
Ole Uncle Pete hab told me dat
　　He'd hab to sell us all.

THIRD SERIES.

81

> " I lub de ole plantation well,
>   And missus she is kind ;
> But den dis chile's inclined to try
>   Another home to find.
> Now mars'r gwine away to war,
>   And give me such a chance,
> I'll bress de Lord for libaty.
>   And hab a Juba dance.

> " De Hallelugerum am cum
>   With glory in his eye,
> And all de niggers in de Souf
>   Am fit to mount de sky.
> My wife an' chil'en hab de spoons
>   Dat's owned by — (here a cough) —
> I hab de sugar-tongs myself,
>   And, darfor,' I is off."

Among the distinguished speakers invited to be present at the great meeting in Accomac, were: the Emperor of Russia, the Emperor of France, the Sultan of Turkey, Queen Victoria, the King of Sweden, the President of the United States, and Theodore Tilton ; but, as the walking was very bad, they did not all come. The celebrated American patriot, Mr. Phelim O'Shaughnessy, took the chair in the absence of the President, and said, that as the Emperor of France was unavoidably absent, he would beg leave to introduce Mr. Terence Mulligan, whose ancestors were once Irishmen themselves.

Mr. Mulligan was received with prolonged applause, and said, that although he bore an Irish name, he had never been ashamed to associate with Americans. His father, while yet on his way from Ireland, had been elected a Justice of the Peace in New York, and his son should be the last one to neglect the Union in its hour of need. What we wanted now, was, that the example of our Irish citizens should be imitated by the others, and that the war should be prosecuted with vigor. (Continued cheering.) Irishmen need never despair of this glorious Union, which had often been a House of Refuge for them, and could not fall without carrying Ireland with it, — so closely were the two great nations knit together. The Irish would never despair:

> "For Freedom's struggle once begun,
> Bequeathed from bleeding sire to son,
> Though baffled oft, is ever won."

When the enthusiam had subsided, the chairman expressed his regret that the Emperor of Russia had not arrived yet; but felt confident that his place could not be better supplied than by Mr. Mickey Flanigan, whose forefathers were themselves the fellow-countrymen of Daniel O'Connell. (Great applause.)

Mr. Flanigan arose amidst great cheering, and said that it was a time when every Irishman should feel as though the eyes of the whole world were upon him. He had found the natives of this country intelligent, kind, and hospitable; and though they had not taken his advice as to the management of this war, he firmly believed that no Irishman would disagree with him when he said, that Irish arms and Irish hearts would finally conquer:

> "For Freedom's battle once begun,
> Bequeathed by loyal sire to son,
> Though baffled oft is ever won."

THIRD SERIES. 83

As soon as the demonstrations of approval had sufficiently subsided, the chairman stated, that, for some unknown reason, Queen Victoria was behind time; yet he could not, for his part, feel sorry for an event which gave him an opportunity to introduce Mr. Figsey Korigan, who represented that element of the world's hidden, free spirit which had thundered in an Emmett and an O'Brien. (Great enthusiasm.)

Mr. Korigan acknowledged the glorious welcome he had received, and declared that this was a proud day for Ireland. Her sons were ever foremost in the ranks of human freedom, shedding their votes for the oppressed of all lands, and fighting all the time. He would say to that Irishman who despaired of this Union, that he was unworthy of any office, and should blush to call himself an American. The speaker's own family had always been Irish, though he himself was born in Cork, and he would be ashamed to stand on that platform if he did not believe that the free-born Irish soul would eventually triumph:

> " For Freedom's contest once begun,
>   By bleeding sire bequeathed to son,
>   Though baffled oft is ever won."

The chairman now arose, amid frantic applause, and said that the meeting was now at an end; but proposed that all the persons present should enroll themselves as members of a Union League for the Prevention of Distress among our Irish Soldiers in the Field. This was responded to with a thundering " Ay." He also proposed that each person present should contribute one dollar as a basis of a fund for the purpose. A gentleman here moved

84 ORPHEUS C. KERR PAPERS.

that the chairman's last suggestion should be amended by omitting the words " dollar " and " fund." Carried unanimously.

Then all the Accomackians went pleasantly home, my boy, except one seedy chap who had stood patiently before the platform during all the proceedings ; and there he still stood, with his arms folded, when all the rest had gone. He was a somewhat loaferish chap, with some appearance of the philosopher.

The chairman looked at him, and says he :

" What are you waiting for, my friend ? "

The chap gave an extra chew to his tobacco, and says he :

" I'm waiting for that ere Great Union meeting to come off."

" Why," says the chairman, " the meeting is all over."

" Yes, I know — *that* meeting," says the chap, explainingly ; " but I mean the Great *Union* meeting."

It is astonishing, my boy, how much ignorance there is in this world. Here was a sane human being who had attentively stood all through a meeting in aid of our sacred national cause, and yet did not know that it was a Union meeting.

Thursday was the day when I reached the head-quarters of the Mackerel Brigade, at the ancient city of Paris, arriving just in time to witness one of those strategic naval exploits which will yet cause the American name to be respected wherever there is nothing particular against it.

It appears, that after his last successful experiment with his patent swivel gun, that stanch old sea-dog, Rear Admiral Head, devoted much of his time on Duck Lake fish-

THIRD SERIES. 85

ing for bass, believing that noble expanse of waters to be free from all obstructions and open to the commerce of the world. The commerce did not come, my boy; but several insidious Confederacies did; and as our glorious old son of Neptune always sat with his back to their side of the lake when fishing, they constructed a pier which extended from the shore to the main deck of the iron-plated Mackerel Squadron, the " Secretary Welles," and had planted seven villanous horse-pistols to command the Admiral's fish-basket and umbrella before our hoary old salt discovered that the war was still going on.

" Riddle my turret ! " says the grim old Triton, in his iron-plated manner, " I believe a blockade is established ; dent my plates if I don't."

Heartily did that pride of our Navy call up the culpably inattentive Mackerel crew, who were eating clams in the stern-sheets, and quickly was the gallant " Secretary Welles " withdrawn out of the range of the Confederacies' murderous fire ; her swivel gun raking the atmosphere fore and aft, whilst the fearless old sea-dog sat down upon a reversed pail amidships, and addressed a letter breathing future vengeance to the unseemly Copperheads of the North. " Sink my Monitor ! " says he hotly ; " let them beware of the time when the Navy returns to its peaceful home ! "

But it was on Thursday, my boy, that the Rear Admiral was to run the blockade of the Confederacies' pier, and Captain Villiam Brown, Captain Bob Shorty, and myself, stood upon the edge of Duck Lake, with our pieces of smoked glass in our hands, to behold this triumph of consummate naval strategy.

86 ORPHEUS C. KERR PAPERS.

At the hour appointed, we beheld Rear Admiral Head and his Mackerel crew slipping over the stern of the Mackerel squadron into the water, and immediately the " Secretary Welles " commenced to float past the Confederacies' batteries with the tide. Onward she went, despite the plunging fire from the horse-pistols, and, presently, we could see her go safely ashore. Never shall I forget the beautiful glow of triumph that overspread the noble countenance of Rear Admiral Head, as he and his crew waded through the water to the place where we stood.

" Unrivet my armor! " says he, in his stern, iron-plated manner ; " I call that running a blockade in good style."

" Yes," says I, sceptically ; " but how are you going to get the squadron back again ? "

" Eh ? " says he, " what was that question, young man ? "

" Why," says I, anxiously, " now that the squadron has run the blockade, how are you going to get her back again ? "

" By all that's iron-clad," says the grim old sea-dog, violently, " I forgot all about that."

" Ah ! " says Captain Villiam Brown, pleasantly, " can't you dig a canal ? "

At this moment there was a tremendous explosion ; something was seen flying through the air, and then the swivel gun of the " Secretary Welles," with the Admiral's fish-basket and umbrella attached, fell beside us on the sand. In their haste to take possession of our squadron, the Confederacies had dropped some sparks from their pipes into the powder-magazine, blowing our entire armament back to us !

THIRD SERIES. 87

Providence, my boy, is evidently on our side in this war; which accounts for the fact that human naval genius has not yet entirely ruined us.

Yours, devoutly,

ORPHEUS C. KERR.

LETTER LXXXVIII.

CONCERNING INTELLECTUAL GIANTS AND PINS; WITH A FEW WORDS
AS TO CERTAIN DRAMATIC STREET-SCENES SUPPOSED TO BE OF DAILY
OCCURRENCE; AN AFFECTING WESTERN POEM; AND A BRIEF
GLIMPSE OF AN ORDINARY CAVALRY DASH.

WASHINGTON,'D. C., March 22d, 1863.

GREATNESS of mind, my boy, like greatness of body, consists no less in a capacity for making good use of small things than in an ability to master vast ones; and the intellect sublime enough to grasp the whole system of the universe, may not disdain to draw a useful lesson in human nature even from so minute an object as the Secretary of the Interior. The elephant, in the full amplitude of his physical greatness, has been briefly and comprehensively characterized as an animal able to knock down a giant and pick up a pin; and how shall the glorious human mind boast its superiority over matter, if it be not also endowed with the power of stooping as well as soaring? I believe, my boy, in the mind that picks up pins intellectual; especially in these days, when there are so few intellectual giants to knock down. Indeed, so important to the general system of intellect is the system of taking no less note of small things than of great ones, that a multitude of writers who deal only in the smallest kind of matters all their lives may themselves be denominated intellectual pins. I hold Mr. Tupper to be an

THIRD SERIES. 89

intellectual pin, and Mr. Willis has also become somewhat of a pin in these his later years.

To the youthful soul, still steeped in those romantic dreams, of which a supper of pig's feet is the best artificial provocative I know, this war is a vast phantasmagoria of almighty giants struggling together in the clouds. There was a time when I, too, was able to see it to that extent; but time, and some experience in Virginia, have reduced my giants in the clouds to brigadiers in the mud; and from seeing our national banner in the character of a rainbow dipped in stars, I have come to regard it as an ambitious attempt to represent sunrise in muslin, the un-expected scantiness of the material compelling the in-genious artist to use a section of midnight to fill up.

Down in Accomac, the other day, I overheard a sen-timental Mackerel chap, to whom I had imparted this flagging idea, inflicting it upon another Mackerel as original; but he was anxious to improve upon the com-parison, and says he:

" Our National Standard is so much like a beautiful sunrise, that I could almost wish the full idea of an eter-nal morning could be further expressed in it by something to represent the dew."

The inferior Mackerel scratched his head, and says he:

" Why, my pay has been due for some time, and I myself am eternally mourning for it."

If we cast pearls before swine, my boy, we must not be surprised to find them taken for the seeds of cabbage-heads. I once told a Wall-street broker that I considered the break of day one of Nature's most glorious sights;

90
ORPHEUS C. KERR PAPERS.

and he said that he didn't mind it himself, if he didn't happen to have any of Day's notes on hand at the time.

But, to return to the giants and the pins; the absence of all giants in the way of events for the past week has induced me to take note of the pins; and close observation of a few of the latter induces me to believe that a strong Union feeling is beginning to be developed amongst the loyal masses of the North. For instance: one of the passengers in one of the street-cars of Paris, the other day, was a venerable man of ninety-three years and seven months, who sat quietly between two lady-passengers, eating roast chestnuts, and permitting the shells to fall upon their laps. Upon his hoary locks rested a white hat, well worn and mashed-in with time; his once light overcoat buttoned close to his throat, represented a drawn battle between grease spots and torn places; his venerable lower members were encased in blue overalls, somewhat shaded about the knees; and the large feet, resting easily upon the cushions of the opposite seat of the car, wore one slipper and one disabled boot. With the exception of a scarcely heard hiccup between every two chestnuts that he ate, not a sound was emitted by this venerable and striking figure as he sat there thus unobtrusively in a public car, like any ordinary passenger.

Presently, a young and boisterous lieutenant, vain of his new regimentals, and full of the airs of a new Jack-in-office, entered the car, and egotistically attempted to make his way to a seat. A faint hiccup saluted his ear, and, looking down, he found his way barred by the aged legs of the venerable stranger, whose feet were upon the opposite cushions.

THIRD SERIES. 91

"Let me pass, old man?" says the vain youngster, with the smart air of one who wishes to get to his seat.

The venerable stranger hardly raised his stern old eyes at the flippant remark, but ate another chestnut, as though no one had spoken.

"Come, my friend," says the conceited stripling, with fresh arrogance, "Be kind enough to move for a moment. I am Colonel P——."

In an instant, the aged frame sprang to his feet, opened all the windows, turned the conductor out of the car, locked the doors, mashed his hat down over his eyes, and frantically tearing open his dilapidated overcoat, displayed *the star of a major-general!*

In an instant, the newly-fledged colonel lost all his knowing braggadocio, and cowered before the glorious old veteran, like a cowed cur (female of a bull-dog).

"Wr-r-r-etch!" exclaimed the hoary commander, in tones of thunder, relieved with the vivid lightning of a hiccup, "Do you know *me!*"

The abashed young boaster could only bow his head in shame, and took the first opportunity to dash himself from the vehicle wherein he had been taught such a lesson. And this should teach us all, my boy, that bad clothes are not always a sure sign of the wearer being only a reporter for the *Tribune;* nor do the ordinary symptoms of intoxication always indicate that the possessor lacks high rank in our national army.

Some hours later, on this same car, there transpired a somewhat different scene, but one equally calculated to prove that there is indeed a North. Twenty-three

92 ORPHEUS C. KERR PAPERS.

wealthy secessionists were in the swift vehicle, the only other passenger being a handsome lad of about sixteen, in the uniform of a brigadier. Rendered confident by their numbers, the enemies of our beneficent form of government entered into a venomous discussion of the siege of Vicksburg, assserting that the Yazoo Expedition had not yet captured forty-two steamboats of Confederacies, and that the announcement of the capture of the Mississippi River was premature.

The young soldier of the Republic went on with some candy he was eating, an apparently indifferent spectator of this symposium of treason ; but the close spectator could not have failed to observe that his whole form was invisibly convulsed with a patriotic indignation. Presently, however, when one of the more hideous conspirators heartlessly remarked that we had not heard much of our army in Virginia lately, endurance ceased to be a virtue, and the young hero could no longer restrain himself.

In a moment his whole aspect changed ; his eyes burst into a devouring blaze, and his cheeks were in flames before aught could be done to check the conflagration. Animated by the strength of a giant, in a cause which he believed to be a noble one, he shot the traitors one by one with his revolver, and buried them in an obscure swamp near the track ; he paid the driver and conductor their wages, and induced them to enlist for three years ; then, after selling both the horses at auction, he broke the car into kindling-wood for the use of the poor.

And this mere boy, who could make himself equal to an emergency, — what of him ? I can fancy him a fond mother's pride, a venerable father's hope, — ay, even a

THIRD SERIES. 93

tender sister's favorite snub. When this record of his glory reaches them, will they remember, in the midst of their proud exultation, the poor scribe whose humble pen relates to them the glories of their house? Will they drop one burning tear to the memory of him who at this moment does not know what on earth to write about next, and heartily wishes that he had been content to earn a respectable living as a reputable wood-sawyer, instead of turning writer? Will they sometimes give one idle thought to the unpretending *litérateur* who has found the glorious reward of literary merit to be an assumption by one-horse country newspapers of the right to talk about him by his family name without troubling themselves to put in the civilized courtesy of " Mr." ? Will they mention in their less urgent prayer, occasionally, the modest child of the quill, who would exceed all the horrors of the Inquisition with the foes of his country, by actually forcing them to write a column for a newspaper when they felt mentally incapable of penning a single coherent paragraph? Will they?

Ah! this is no country to appreciate genius; as they wrote upon the tomb of my early friend, the sweet-singing Arkansaw Nightingale, whose last sad manuscript to me described

" A BIG DOG FIT.

" Lige Simmons is as cute a chap
As ever you did see,
And when the feller says a thing,
It's sure as it can be.

ORPHEUS C. KERR PAPERS.

" He owns a dog — and sich a brute
    For smellin' round a chap,
I never see in all my life,
    You'd better bet your cap.

" Now Lige is proud of this here dog,
    And says the critter'll whip
As many wild-cats in an hour
    As go to load a ship.

" ' But, law,' says Lige, ' that animile
    Is awful in a row,
And other pups 'longside of him
    An't no account, nohow.'

" In fact, one day, I saw the same
    Contemporaneous pup
Pitch into a Newfounlander
    And chaw him slightly up.

" He's such a plaguy little cuss,
    You'd laugh to see him come;
But when there's chawin' up to do,
    I tell you, boss, he's some!

" One day, a pedler came to town
    With ginger-beer and things,
And patent clocks, and pious books,
    And fancy finger-rings.

" And underneath his cart was tied
    A bull-dog of the kind
That tears your musn't-mention-'ems,
    In angry frame of mind.

" Now, Lige's dog was smellin' round,
    And when he see this here,
He cocked his eye in agony,
    And acted awful queer.

THIRD SERIES. 95

"The bull-dog gin a rousin' shout,
　　As Lige's dog went by,
And gev him such a sassy nip
　　That fur began to fly.

" Then Lige's dog unfurled his tail
　　And gev the wound a lick,
And then pitched into that ere dog
　　A way that *wasn't* sick.

" The critters had it nip and tuck,
　　And made such awful noise,
That Lige himself came up to see,
　　With all the other boys.

" The pedler see him, and says he,
　　Like one to fits inured:
'I'm sorry, strannger; but I hope
　　Your yaller dog's insured.'

" I tell you, boys, 'twas fun to see
　　The grin that Lige put on,
As in his cheek he put a chaw
　　And winked his eye at one.

" ' Oh, let the varmints fit,' says Lige,
　　'My pup is awful thin,
And this here row will make him look
　　Jist like himself ag'in.'

" And all this while the fit went on,
　　With such a mess of dust
We couldn't tell the upper dog,
　　If all our eyes should bust.

" 'Twas yell and yowl, and shout and growl,
　　And stompin' awful hard,
And sometimes they'd a tail stick out
　　From where the dust was bar'd.

" Byme-by the noise began to die,
 And as it fainter grew,
The dust began to settle down,
 And you could just see through.

" At last it cleared away entire,
 But all that we could see
Was Lige's dog a squattin' down
 Beneath the axletree.

"' Law !' says the pedler, lookin' blue,
 ' What's happened to *my* pup ? '
Says Lige : ' It's my opinion, boss,
 My pup has eat him up.'

"' But where's the chain I tied him with ? '
 The pedler loud did call.
And would you b'lieve me — Lige's dog
 Had swallowed chain and all !

" One end was hangin' from his mouth
 And gev him such a cough,
We had to fetch a chisel out
 And cut some inches off.

" Then that ere brute, to show the joy
 That's nat'ral to dum brutes,
Insulted that sad pedler there,
 By smellin' round his boots.

" The pedler dropped a tear, and then
 Says he to Lige, says he :
' I'd like to buy that yaller pup
 And take him home with me."

" But ' no,' says Lige, with proud disdain
 And sot down on a log,
' That pup is plural now, you know —
 A dog within a dog.'

THIRD SERIES.

> "' He's twice as strong to fit,' says Lige;
> ' For if he's killed outside,
> I'll turn the critter inside out,
> And let *your* critter slide.'
>
> "'Well,' says the pedler, with a sigh,
> ' The pup's a trump, I think;
> But let us change the subject now;
> Say, strannger ! — do you drink ? ' "

But let me not indulge in sentiment, my boy, while it is still before me to describe the recent successful reconnoissance of the Anatomical Cavalry, whose horses remind me of the celebrated war-horse described by Job, inasmuch as it is believed that the far-famed patience of that scriptural patriarch would have stood a very poor chance with them.

The Grim Old Fighting Cox, the new General of the Mackerel Brigade, having learned from the New York daily papers, of the week previous, that a few hundred thousand freshly-drafted Confederacies were massing themselves on his right, resolved to order a triumphant reconnoissance by the Anatomical Cavalry and the Orange County Howitzers, for the purpose of discovering whether the war was actually going on yet. As the steeds of the cavalry were widely dispersed through the various gravel meadows around the Mackerel camp, my boy, and had grown somewhat wild from long disuse, I was somewhat puzzled to know how they could all be caught quickly enough, and says I to Captain Villiam Brown, who was to command the combined expedition :

" Tell me, my Pylades, how will you manage to organ-

98 ORPHEUS C. KERR PAPERS.

ize the equestrian bone-works without losing too many hours ? "

" Ah ! " says Villiam, briskly replacing the cork in his canteen, and startling his geometrical steed, Euclid, from a soft doze, " we must make use of our knowledge of natural history, which is the animal kingdom. Observe the device used in such cases by the scientific United States of America."

I looked, my boy, and beheld a select company of joyous Mackerels hoisting a huge board to the top of a lofty pole, which must have been visible for a mile distant. The board simply bore, in large letters, the simple words :

" THE OATS HAVE COME."

and scarcely had it reached the top of the pole, when the anatomical steeds came pouring into the camp with frantic speed, and from every direction.

" Ah ! " says Villiam, thoughtfully, " how powerful is instink, even in a dumb animal. I once had a dog," says Villiam, reflectively, " whose instink was so powerful, that to stop his vocal barking it was only necessary to show him a good-sized piece of bark. He felt," says Villiam, explainingly, " that it was a larger bark than his, and it made him silent."

Truly, my boy, there is often a marvellous similarity between instinct and reason, the former serving as the foundation of the latter, and not unfrequently being entirely destitute of a superstructure in military men.

The Cavalry and Howitzers having been arranged in such order that each supported the other, and a prospect of some carnage supported them both, the word was given

THIRD SERIES. 99

to advance, and the warlike pageant swept onward very much as we read in the reliable morning journals. I was proceeding at the head of the cavalcade, with Villiam, pleasantly discussing with him the propriety of digging a canal to Richmond, and using the Cavalry on the tow-path, when there rode forth from the cover of a wood near at hand a horseman, whose stately bearing and dishevelled hat announced Captain Munchausen, of the celebrated Southern Confederacy. He waved his sword courteously to Villiam, and says he:

"You bring your hordes to measure sabres with us, I presume?"

Villiam rattled his good sword Escalibar * in its scabbard, and says he, grimly, "We are met together for that purpose."

Captain Munchausen smiled superciliously, and says he, "Is this intended by your vandals to be what you call a brilliant cavalry dash?"

Villiam waved his hand majestically, and says he:

"That is the exciting phrase."

"Then," says Munchausen, with unseemly levity of tone, "I can tell you, before you go any farther, that you are out of ammunition."

Here Captain Samyule Sa-mith, of the Howitzers, who had come up while the talking was going on, suddenly slapped his knee, and says he:

"That's so. I knew I had forgotten something in this here expedition, and it's the ammunition."

---

* It is hardly necessary to state that this sword, "Escalibar," is probably identical with the invincible blade, of the same name, presented to King Arthur by the Lady of the Lake.

ORPHEUS C. KERR PAPERS.

So we all went back to camp, Captain Munchausen being too much demoralized by the bad example to pursue us.

Our latest cavalry dashes, my boy, being reduced to their simplest meaning, signify devised charges of cavalry, which are based upon charges of artillery, which have forgotten to bring any charges with them.

Yours, retreatingly,

ORPHEUS C. KERR.

LETTER LXXXIX.

SHOWING HOW THE GREAT CITY OF ROME HAS BEEN RUINED BY THE WAR; CITING A NOTABLE INSTANCE OF CONTEMPT OF COURT; DESCRIBING REAR ADMIRAL HEAD'S WONDERFUL IMPROVEMENT IN SWIVEL GUNS; AND PROVING THAT ALL IS NOW READY FOR THE REDUCTION OF FORT PIANO.

WASHINGTON, D. C., March 29th, 1863.

AFTER due consideration of the different points of the Compass, and a fair estimate of the claims of each to superiority, I am inclined to give the preference to the Great North-west. It is to the Great North-west that we are indebted for our best facilities of sunset; some of the greatest hogs of the day come from Cincinnati; the principal smells of the age belong to Chicago, and the whiskey of Louisville has almost entirely superseded the pump of our forefathers. Hence, my boy, it was with a feeling akin to reverence that I witnessed the arrival in Accomac of a delegation of high moral Democratic chaps from the Great North-west, the other day; their mission being, to protest against all further continuation of a war which was degenerated into a mere bloodshed for the sake of New England; and to suggest that a convention of all the States be at once held in Kentucky, to arrange a peace that shall be acceptable to the Great North-west. I was asking the thoughtful chairman of the delegation what were his particular grievances, and says he:

(101)

102   ORPHEUS C. KERR PAPERS.

" This war is ruining much valuable Real Estate in the Great North-west, of which I and my fellow-beings are proprietors ; and cannot continue without proving the entire destruction of some of our largest cities. Just before this war broke out," says the thoughtful chap, impressively, " I gave a three-years' note of seven hundred and sixteen dollars and fifteen cents for the city of Rome, situated on the future line of the Atlantic and Pacific Canal, and divided into four hundred water-lots of five fathoms each. As soon as the Atlantic and Pacific Canal was built, the water would have been drawn off by means of eighteen large hydraulic pumps supported by Eastern capital, leaving the lots all ready for building purposes. The main street would then have been graded, and paved with the new patent Connecticut sub-drainage pavement, and would have extended two miles in a perfectly straight line, with a horse-railroad through the centre. The various intersecting streets I should have named numerically, commencing with ' First Street,' which faces upon the Atlantic and Pacific Canal, and so going on to ' One Hundred and Seventy-sixth street,' and so on. These streets would have been occupied exclusively by brown-stone-front residences, with a flag-staff bearing our national banner on the roof of each one, and rented to small private families without children. The full lots on the main street would have been used for the City Hall, the Lunatic Asylum, the Custom House, the Home for Deranged Persons, the Merchants' Exchange, the Corn Exchange, the Refuge for the Insane, the Grain Elevator, the Institution for Friendless Maniacs, the Principal Pork-Packing Establishment, the Hall of Records, the Office of the Superintendent of

THIRD SERIES.

Central Parks, the Madman's Snug Harbor, and the Municipal Bar-Room. The sixty-eight principal banks would have discounted bills of exchange at sight, for the benefit of the numerous foreign vessels constantly arriving at the principal pier by way of the Atlantic and Pacific Canal, and the Fire Department would have been limited to twenty-three hundred hose-carriages and engines, with an educated Chief Engineer." Here the thoughtful Democratic chap gnashed his teeth, and says he:

"But the City of Rome has been entirely retarded by this here Black Republican New England war upon the sunny South, with which the great North-west has no earthly quarrel whatsoever."

I was pondering a reply to this very reasonable speech, my boy, when word was suddenly brought that one of the Mackerel pickets had just assassinated a young Confederacy, who had only fired twice upon his inhuman murderer. No sooner did the thoughtful Proprietor of the City of Rome hear this sickening news than he at once formed the other Democratic chaps into a coroner's jury, and hastily proceeded to hold a high moral inquest upon the body of the lamented deceased.

There being no witnesses to examine, and nothing in the pocket-book found upon the body, the proprietor of Rome removed two tears with his red silk handkerchief, and briefly summoned up the case. Kneeling desolately beside the cold remains, and taking one of the lifeless hands within his own, he sniffed feelingly, and says he:

"The young man which is here before us is another of them noble souls that have fallen gory sacrifices to the Mulock of War."

5*

104 ORPHEUS C. KERR PAPERS.

" You mean ' Moloch of War,' " says a juryman.

Whereupon he was commited to custody for contempt of court.

" This young man," continued the Proprietor of Rome, " may have had good cause to hate and despise the radical abolition offsprings of New England ; but he had no quarrel with the glorious Democratic party of the Great North-west, which is now blindly fighting for his wooden-nutmeg foes. I will venture to say," says the thoughtful Roman, with great emotion, " that he even loved the Great North-west in his heart. Behold how freely he permits me to clasp his left hand to my friendly buzzom, even though he is dead."

Just then there was a sudden silence, my boy, for the right hand of the deceased young Confederacy was observed to be slowly rising in the air ! Overcome with awe, the jury gazed upon the strange spectacle, like men under a wizard's spell. Slowly, slowly, the hand arose, until nearly above the face of the slain Confederacy ; then it descended until it reached the half-averted countenance of the dead, and convulsively seized the nose between the thumb and fore-finger.

The Proprietor of the City of Rome changed color, and says he : " Well — ahem ! — it can't be that —" Here he looked more closely at the body, and says he :

" I am at a loss to explain this remarkable phenomena."

A venerable juryman, of much shirt-collar, coughed to attract attention, and says he : " I should take the present attitude of our departed Confederate brother to be that of a man who smells something obnoxious."

THIRD SERIES. 105

Here the Proprietor of Rome suddenly dropped the left hand of the deceased Confederacy, and says he:

"Why, he must mean to insult the Great North-west."

"Yes," says the venerable juryman, "there can be but one construction of the present offensive attitude of this dead young being."

The thoughtful Proprietor of the City of Rome deliberately took off his spectacles, blew his nose, buttoned his coat up to his chin, and says he: "I have always advocated a vigorous prosecution of the war, and believe that full nine-tenths of our gallant troops are Democrats. What's the werdict?"

The shirt-collared juryman waved his hand impressively, and says he: "We find the deceased guilty of contempt of court in the Last Degree."

Then the Democratic chaps from the Great North-west held an enthusiastic mass meeting on the spot, and unanimously resolved that neither Kentucky nor Indiana would resist the Conscription Bill, should it be found unsafe to do so.

Believe me, my boy, when I say that the great Democratic party is stanchly loyal at heart, however strangely its head may seem to err at times; and never will it take a side with the enemies of the country, even whilst those enemies make offers to it not only aside but affront.

Upon going down to Paris on Friday, I found the well-disciplined and spectacled Mackerel Brigade greatly excited and demoralized by the insidious report that their famous new General, the Grim Old Fighting Cox, had actually washed himself. This injurious rumor, my boy, suggested such humiliating national recollections of those

106   ORPHEUS C. KERR PAPERS.

days of consummate strategy, when a certain egotistical commander indulged in the vanities of soap and hair-oil, that the Brigade were naturally terrified. Finally, however, the absurd story received a decisive quietus, when the Grim Old Fighting Cox was seen riding slowly on his unostentatious steed, the " Pride of the Canal," dressed in the unassuming republican habiliments of a stern and inflexible coal-heaver. It is needless to say that he had not washed himself. This war is at length beginning in earnest.

It is beautiful to see how the Grim Old Fighting Cox is improving the morals of the venerable Mackerels, and winning their affection, confidence, and respect. Coming, unexpectedly, upon a Mackerel, who had just laid aside his umbrella, and removed his spectacles, in order that he might weep the more freely, he fired a pistol over his head, and says he :

" What is the matter, my dear sir ? "

" Oh ! " says the poor Mackerel, sobbing, " I am in sore need of the pay which is due me for two years' faithful strategy to the Union, and know not where to get it."

The Grim Old Fighting Cox was much affected, and says he, softly : " You must humbly kneel, and beseech Providence for it."

The afflicted chap toyed with his spectacles, and says he : " But suppose Providence should refuse ? "

" Then come to ME ! " thundered the Grim Old Fighting Cox, with the air of a stern national parent.

I could relate hundreds of such significant anecdotes as this, my boy ; though when the Grim Old Fighting Cox tells them himself to all the reporters of the reliable morning journals, he invariably desires that they shall go

THIRD SERIES. 107

no further; but other great events demand my immediate attention.

It was very shortly after the victorious but disastrous blowing up of the Mackerel iron-plated squadron, the " Secretary Welles," on Duck Lake, by the infatuated Confederacies of Pier No. 1, — it was shortly after this event, which I duly recounted at the time, that our unconquerable old sea-dog, Rear Admiral Head, invented an entirely new iron-clad after the model of a Quaker hat, the turret being of solid iron all through, and so arranged that it could be used to cover the gangway amidships. In fact, my boy, the turret was a movable block of iron, with the swivel-gun mounted on top; so that if the turret happened to be hit, the artillery would not be disabled, and if the artillery was disabled, the turret would still be as good as ever. (Patent applied for.) There was some discussion as to what name should be given to this formidable monster, nearly the whole six-barrelled Indian language having been almost exhausted by our national navy; but finally it was resolved to call her the " Shockingbadhat," — an old Choctaw title of much simplicity, signifying originally " The Head what errs," but now understood as meaning " The Head waters."

There has also been a great improvement in the swivelgun, my boy, which has been so reconstructed as to remedy the evil of immediate bursting so common to our heavier ordnance. A select committee of Mackerels having been appointed to examine our national ordnance system, and discover the cause of its inefficiency, stated in their able report that the causes of the frequent bursting of our larger guns are, —

First. The powder used in propelling the appropriate missile against the enemy.

Second. The addition of an incendiary spark to said powder.

It was further stated in the report, that, although the barrel of a gun was frequently fractured when it exploded, there was no record of the touch-hole ever having burst; and the committee believed that this curious fact should serve as a valuable suggestion to the manufacturers of future heavy ordnance.

Acting upon this truly valuable suggestion, our stern old Son of Neptune caused his swivel-gun to be reconstructed upon a novel principle; the touch-hole was extended to the usual size of a barrel, and the barrel was reduced to the usual size of a touch-hole; so that, although the terrible weapon looked precisely the same as ever, it was, in reality, *completely reversed!*

But while the "Shockingbadhat" was being built, and receiving her terrific new armament, the shameless Confederacies on their Pier in Duck Lake had been industriously building Fort Piano and mounting it with their villanous horse-pistols; so that when the new Mackerel iron-plated squadron was ready for carnage and fishing, there was a hostile projection in the way.

"Chip my turret!" says Rear Admiral Head, in his iron-plated manner, "I think I shall have to blow a few more Rebels into eternity — smash my casemate! if I don't."

I stood upon the shore of Duck Lake, with a bit of smoked glass to my eye as usual, when our new monster of the deep came abreast of Fort Piano, and Rear Ad-

THIRD SERIES. 109

miral Head commenced to reconnoitre through his pocket-microscope. The venerable commander gazed steadfastly through it for a moment, and then, says he:

"Crack my plates! if I don't perceive an insect on the wall of the hostile work."

There was indeed a solitary Confederacy seated upon the front wall of Fort Piano, dining sumptuously upon some fresh hoe-cake, and says he:

"You can't pass here without a New Jersey ferry-ticket."

(New Jersey, my boy, is now a Southern Confederacy, or a Peace of one.)

I could hear the glorious old naval hero say, in a suppressed voice, to the intelligent Mackerel crew on top of the turret:

"Depress your weapon four points to windward, grease the ball, and fire at his stomach."

In another instant, the whole landscape shook with a tremendous explosion, jarring the Admiral so greatly that his spectacles fell off, and causing his blue cotton umbrella to tremble like a leaf. The ball ascended to the zenith in a parabolical curve, and was lost amongst the other planets. I do not think, my boy, that the Confederacy would have been offended at this, had not the sudden noise caused him to jump in such a manner that he dropped his hoe-cake into the dirt. Upon this occurrence, however, he sprang to his legs on the wall, drew up a long pole from behind him, disrespectfully cracked our glorious old Rear Admiral over the head with it, and then commenced shoving at the turret of the " Shockingbadhat."

Perceiving the great danger of the squadron, and unmindful of his own wound, the venerable sea-dog hastily grasped at the pole, and says he : " Ah, now, what do you want to do that for, Mr. Davis ?   What's the use of pushing my turret overboard ? "

He said this so mildly that the Confederacy burst into a prodigious horse-laugh, and drew in his pole again.

" As no possible good could be attained by taking Fort Piano, the indomitable old Rear Admiral at once returned with the squadron to his original anchorage ; having gained all that was required, and proved his iron-clad monster to be fully qualified for actual service.   Everything is now ready for the anticipated conquest of Duck Lake."

I give you the above in quotation marks, my boy, because it is the official report as it appears in all the reliable morning journals, and clearly and satisfactorily explains everything.   The first of April is close at hand.

Yours, fortuitously,

ORPHEUS C. KERR.

LETTER XC.

GIVING A DEEP INSIGHT OF WOMAN'S NATURE; PRESENTING A POWER-FUL POEM OF THE HEART BY ONE OF THE INTELLECTUAL FEMALES OF AMERICA; AND REPORTING THE SIGNAL DISCOMFITURE OF MR. P. GREENE.

WASHINGTON, D. C., April 5th, 1863.

WOMAN's heart, my boy, in its days of youthful imma-turity and vegetable development, may be felicitously likened unto a delicate cabbage, with an invisible worm feeding upon its sensitive petals. To the eye of the ordi-nary and unfeeling observer, the cabbage is in perfect health, and its intense greenness is thoughtlessly accepted as a sure indication of an unravaged system. Man, proud man, with all his boasted human wisdom, would smile in-credulously, if told that the tender vegetable — the mag-nified and nervous white rose, as it were —had beneath all its seeming verdancy, an insatiable and remorseless worm gnawing at its hidden core. Man, I say, would thus wallow in his miserable ignorance, and persist in his disgusting blind-ness. But mark that dainty little figure coming up the gar den-walk, my boy. It does not walk erect, like boastful Man, does not spit tobacco-juice like haughty Man; and as it approaches nearer, we perceive that it is a hot-house Pig. Ay, my lord: I say to you, in all your glory of human understanding and trifling degree of snobbishness, it is a Pig. Yes, madam: I remark to you, in your jewels, and

(111)

laces, and absurd new bonnet, — it is only a Pig. *Only* a Pig! O-O-ONLY a Pig! And why should we say " only " a Pig ; as though a Pig were so *very* inferior to proud Man ? We all accord to the awful and unfathomable German Mind a preternatural gift of philosophy, so far above the contemptibly-limited thing we call human understanding that no man can ever understand a word of it ; and how does that German Mind express itself when it desires to describe the Vast, the Extensive, and the Somewhat Large ? Why, it simply observes " Das is von ' PIG ' thing." And is not this unaffected remark sufficient, my boy, to raise the wrongfully despised Pig to the dignity of an adjective, at least ? But look once more at the hot-house Pig in question, as he stoops thoughtfully to the cabbage which derisive Man has esteemed perfectly sound. He pushes it once with his nose ; he raises his eyes, blinking in the glorious sunshine ; his tail vibrates a moment ; a solemn wink, — a grunt of deep reflection, — and he *turns to another cabbage!*

Yes! this despised little roasting-pig, this unconsidered Flower, as it were, has surpassed all the vaunted wisdom of stuck-up Man, and discovered the worm at the core of the sensitive cabbage !

Woman's heart, my boy, in its days of youthful immaturity and vegetable development, is a metaphorical Cabbage with a figurative worm at its palpitating core. That worm is a passionate yearning for TRUE SYMPATHY. Heartless but wealthy Man comes along, and says : " This Cabbage is in perfect health, and I will Husband it." He *does* Husband it my boy, and what is the consequence ? Not knowing anything about the existence of the worm,

THIRD SERIES. **113**

he cannot, of course, furnish that TRUE SYMPATHY which is necessary to end its horrible gnawings ; and so the worm keeps feeding until the Cabbage Heart becomes a mere shell, when the least zephyr will break it. How different the result had that Heart been — or, that is to say, how changed would the case have been had she — or, in other words, what an opposite spectacle might we — or, rather she — if he — if she — ·

.   .   .   .

Really, my boy, I am all in a cold perspiration ; for I find that I must have made some dreadful mistake in my argument. Hem! There really *must* be some strange mistake in it, my boy ; for I cannot follow it out without making it scandalously appear, that a man, to really understand a Woman's Heart, must be something of a Pig. This conclusion would be very insulting to the women of America, and there certainly must be some mistake about it.

What led me into this philosophical vein of analytical thought was a touching poem of the home affections, which was sent to me for perusal on Monday by one of the intellectual Young Women of America. It is one of those revelations of Woman's inner-self which move us to tearful compassion for a sex doomed to be the victim of man's selfishness and its own too-great sensibilities. The terrible picture of woe is called

" WOMAN'S HEART.*

"BY SAIRA NEVERMAIR.

" We went to the world-loved Ball last night, —
    Claude and I, in our robes of gold ;

* The measure of this striking poem is Owenmeredithyrambic.

He in a coat as black as jet,
And I in the jewels I wore of old.

" Diamonds covered my head in pounds,
Seventy large ones lit my neck, —
Over my skirts they burned in quarts,
Counting in all a goodly peck.

" Hopped the canary 'neath the wires, —
Spoke the canary not a word;
When to my heart the chill has struck,
How can I sing ?— can ary bird?

" We were together, Claude and I,
Bonded together as man and wife;
Little I thought, as I uttered my vows,
What was the real Ideal of life.

" He is my Husband to love and obey, —
Those were the words of the priest, I think, —
He is to purchase the clothes I wear,
Order my victuals and order my drink !

" Well, it is well if it must be so:
Woman the slave and man the lord;
She the scissors to cut the threads
After the darning, and he the sword.

" Was it for this I played my cards,
Tuned the piano's tender din,
Cherished a delicate health, and ate
Pickles and pencils to make me thin ?

" Better it were to be born a serf,
Holding a soul by a master's lease ;
Better than learning Society's law,
Gaining a Husband and forfeiting peace.

" Mortimer sighs as he sees me dance,
Percy is sad as he passes by,

THIRD SERIES. 115

Herbert turns pallid beneath my glance ;
　　All of them married — and so am I.

" Well, if the world must have it so,
　　Woman can only stand and endure ;
Ever the grossness of all that is gross
　　Rises the tyrant of all that is pure.

" Marriage, they say, is a sacred thing ;
　　So is the fetter that yields a smart.
Give *one* crumb to the starving wretch,
　　And give *one* Object to Woman's Heart.

" Claude, they tell me, should own my love ;
　　Well, I have loved him nearly a week ;
Looking at one man longer than that
　　Grows to be tiresome — so to speak.

" What if he calls me Angel wife ;
　　Angels are not for the One to win ;
Yet is my passionate love like theirs, —
　　Theirs is a love taking all men in.

" Hops the canary 'neath the wires,
　. Speaks the canary not a word ;
When to my heart the chill has struck,
　　How can I sing ? — can ary bird ? "

Let us mingle our tears, my boy, in a gruel of compassion, as we conjointly reflect upon this affecting revelation of Woman's Heart.

On Thursday last, my architectural steed, the gothic Pegasus, conveyed me once more, by easy stages, to the outskirts of Paris, where I found the aged and respectable Mackerel Brigade cleaning their spectacles and writing

116   ORPHEUS C. KERR PAPERS.

their epitaphs preparatory to that celebrated advance upon the well-known Southern Confederacy which is frequently mentioned in ancient history. The Grim Old Fighting Cox, my boy, has rashly determined, that the unfavorable weather shall not detain our national troops another single year, and there is at last a prospect that our grandchildren may read a full and authentic report of the capture of Richmond in the reliable morning journals of their time. And here let me say to the grandchild Orpheus: "Be sure, my boy, that you do not permit your pardonable exultation at the triumph of your country's arms, to make you too severe upon the conquered foes of the Republic." I put in this little piece of advice to posterity, my boy, because I desire to have posterity magnanimous.

I was conversing affably with a few official Mackerels about several mutual friends of ours, who had been born, were married, and had expired of decrepitude during the celebrated national sieges of Vicksburg and Charleston, when a civilian chap named Mr. P. Greene came into camp from New York, with the intention of proceeding immediately to the ruins of Richmond. He was a chap of much spreading dignity, my boy, with a carpet-bag, an umbrella, and a walking-cane.

"Having read," says he, "in all the excellent morning journals, that Richmond is being hastily evacuated by the starving Confederacy, I have determined to precede the military in that direction. Possibly," says he, impressively, "I may be able to find a suitable place in the deserted city for the residence of my family during the summer."

3 *

THIRD SERIES. 117

Captain Villiam Brown listened attentively, and says he :

"Is your intelligence official, or founded on fact?"

The civilian chap drew himself up with much dignity, and says he :

"I find it in all the morning journals."

Certainly this was conclusive, my boy; and yet our supine military men were willing to let this unadorned civilian chap be the first to enter the evacuated capital of the stricken Confederacy. Facing toward that ill-fated place, he moved off, his carpet-bag in his left hand, his umbrella in his right, and his cane under one arm, a perfect impersonation of the spirit of American Progress. By slow and dignified degrees he grew smaller in the distance, until finally he was out of sight.

It was some six hours after this, my boy, that we were conversing as before, when there suddenly appeared, coming toward us from the direction of the capital of the Confederacy, the figure of a man running. Rapidly it drew nearer, when I discovered it to be Mr. P. Greene, in a horrible condition of dishevelment, his umbrella, cane, and carpet-bag gone, his hair standing on end, his coat-tails projective in the breeze, and his lower limbs making the best time on record. Onward he came, like the wind, and before we could stop him, he had gone by us, dashed frantically through the camp, and was tearing along like mad toward Washington.

"Ah!" says Villiam, philosophically, "he derived his information from the daily prints of the United States of America, and has seen the elephant. The moral," says

Villiam, placidly, "is very obvious, — put not your trust in print, sirs."

If it be indeed true, that there is "more pleasure in anticipation than in reality," the war-news we find in our excellent morning journals should give us more pleasure than one poor pen can express.

Yours, credulously,

ORPHEUS C. KERR.

LETTER XCI.

CONTAINING THE VENERABLE GAMMON'S REPORT OF THE MANNER IN WHICH THE WAR HAS CONDUCTED ITSELF UP TO THIS TIME; AND THE MOST SURPRISING EPITAPH OF A VICTIM OF STRATEGY.

WASHINGTON, D. C., April 12th, 1863.

DEPRESSED, my boy, by that low-spirited sense of reverence for shirt-collared Old Age, which is a part of my credulous nature, I proceed to record that the Venerable Gammon has once more torn himself from idolatrous Mugville to beam venerably upon all the capital the nation has left; and as I mark how fatly he waves continual benediction to the attached populace, I am impressed anew with the conviction of the serious mental magnitude of large-sized Old Age. It was on Monday that a delegation of anxious civilian chaps grovelled around this aged idol of a mournful nation; and as soon as the awe-stricken spokesman of the party had crawled within speaking distance of the Venerable Gammon, he sniffed deferentially, and says he:

"Sire, we desire to know how soon we may expect an honorable peace to end the present war, which it is perpetual bloodshed."

The Venerable Gammon placidly placed his beneficent right hand between his patriarchal ruffles, and says he:

"My friends, this war is like a great struggle between

120 ORPHEUS C. KERR PAPERS.

two hostile armies ; it will continue until it has ceased, and it will cease when it is no longer continued. Peace," says the Venerable Gammon, — waving indulgent permission for the sun to go on shining, — " peace is the end of the War, as war is the end of Peace ; therefore, if we had no war, peace would be without end, and if we had no peace, war would be endless."

Then all the fond civilian chaps grovelled ecstatically at the time-honored feet of the benignant parent of his country, and four-and-twenty reliable morning journals immediately published a report that Richmond had been taken — for another year.

But what has particularly endeared the Venerable Gammon to the hearts of his distracted fellow-countrymen is, his able report of the manner in which the war has conducted itself since the First of April, 1862. I cannot exactly understand my boy, how this benignant benefactor of his species comes to know anything at all about military matters ; nor am I prepared to state that he had any call whatever to report upon national strategy ; but he has issued a startling statement, and I give the whole

REPORT.

" On the first of April, 1862, on the day immediately succeeding the 31st of May in the same year, a solitary horseman might have been seen approaching the camp of the Mackerel Brigade from Washington. He was a youth in the prime of life, and carried a carpet-bag containing the daily morning journals of that date. Upon reaching the tent of the General of the Mackerel Brigade, he sought an immediate interview with the latter, and at

THIRD SERIES. **121**

once revealed to him that it was reported in all the morning journals, that the celebrated Southern Confederacy had evacuated Manassas just two weeks previously, thereby rendering an advance upon that stronghold by our national troops a subject demanding immediate attention.

" Upon discovering that this news was indeed contained in the morning journals, the General of the Mackerel Brigade at once ordered a report of our national victory to be conveyed to the Mackerels who had gained it; and having made several promotions for bravery, and telegraphed to the excellent Democratic Organization in New York that he had rather capture Manassas than be President of the United States in 1865, he ordered an immediate advance upon Manassas. The advance took place without confusion or dismay, and on the following morning Captain Villiam Brown electrified the whole nation with the magical words :

" ' We have met the enemy, and they are hours — ahead of us.'

" The backbone of the Rebellion being thus broken, the General of the Mackerel Brigade wrote to the Honest Abe at Washington, as follows :

" ' DEAR SIR, — I have at length successfully surprised the stronghold of Manassas, and consider myself strong enough to continue the war, if you can send me a few more troops. If you can spare 60,000 under Sergeant O'Pake, and 50,000 under Colonel Wobert Wobinson, from the defence of Washington, I can wait for the other hundred thousand until I push forward again.

" ' THE GENERAL OF THE MACKEREL BRIGADE.'

122

ORPHEUS C. KERR PAPERS.

"This was on the fourth of April. Owing to the continual storms, and the difficulty encountered in procuring umbrellas for the troops, the Mackerel Brigade was enabled to advance but thirty-three and a half feet during the ensuing four months, during which time several State elections took place. On the Fourth of July, the Honest Abe addressed the following note to the General of the Mackerel Brigade :

"'General, — By your plan of drawing troops away from Washington, the capital would be left with fewer soldiers than it now possesses; and if the capital is weakened, it follows very clearly, that it will not be strengthened. My plan is directly the reverse of your plan, so that your plan is immediately opposite to my plan. Allow me to ask you the following questions :

"'I. If your plan is different from my plan, how can my plan be the same as your plan ?

"'II. If my plan does not agree with your plan, wherein does your plan assimilate with my plan?

"'III. If your plan and my plan are not the same plan, how can my plan and your plan be one plan ?

"'IV. If my plan, by opposing your plan, shows that my plan is not at all like your plan, how can your plan, by differing from my plan, save Washington according to my plan, which is not your plan ?   H. Abe.'

"Both plans were adopted, and in the course of the succeeding two months the Mackerel Brigade shot a couple of Confederacies. Shortly after this, it was decided that an advance should be made upon the city of Paris by

THIRD SERIES.

123

way of Duck Lake, the iron-plated squadron of Rear Admirable Head being detailed from the blockade to take the Mackerels across, as soon as a heavy rain should make the lake too deep for navigation by personal wading. The troops were at the landing at the appointed time, and were about to embark in good order, when it was discovered by the negro servant of one of the officers, that they had forgotten to bring any ammunition with them, and that the iron-plated squadron had not arrived. This unfortunate discovery made it necessary for the Mackerel Brigade to fall back thirty-three and a half feet, and the General thus wrote to the Honest Abe at Washington :

" ' DEAR SIR, — The safety of this Army depends entirely upon its immediate reënforcement by all the troops at Washington, as my plan is entirely different from your plan, and your plan differs somewhat from my plan. The importance of saving Washington by your plan, is as nothing when compared with the opposite tenor of my plan ; which might, after all, be the saving of Washington by my plan, though my plan does not agree with your plan. I will stay with this army, and die with it, if need be, by my plan.

"' THE GENERAL OF THE MACKEREL BRIGADE.'

" Both plans were put in force, and during the period elapsing between this date and the middle of November, the troops were busily occupied in fortifying themselves — against the inclemency of the weather. Arrangements being made and completed for the decent interment of such troops as should die of old age before the next great

124 ORPHEUS C. KERR PAPERS.

movement took place, the General of the Mackerel Brigade had just opened a correspondence with his family on the subject of the Presidency of the United States in 1865, when he received the appended note:

"'GENERAL,—You will feel immediately relieved upon receiving this, and will report immediately to your wife at Hoboken. Colonel Wobert Wobinson is hereby ordered to take command of the Mackerel Brigade.

"'ADJUTANT.'

"Upon the assumption of command by General Wobinson, it was immediately observed that he possessed a great deal of Shape. He crossed Duck Lake on his Shape, and in pursuance of the plan of his predecessor, opened an instant attack upon Paris. Shortly after the attack, the whole Brigade was back across Duck Lake again, and the new General sent his resignation to Washington. It was refused, as unnecessary; and the General then devised a plan for startling the whole country, by organizing the Anatomical Cavalry upon an equestrian basis, and making a raid upon some Confederate oats known to be somewhere in the daily journals. The secret of this movement was confided to but three parties, —the Honest Abe, the Southern Confederacy, and the public; but before the move could take place it was divulged and frustrated. The General then sent in his resignation, which was refused as unnecessary. It was subsequent to this that a third great movement was arranged, when a shower came up suddenly, and it had to be abandoned. It was upon this occasion that the General sent in his resignation, when it was refused as un-

THIRD SERIES. 125

necessary. Simultaneously, as it were, the officer popularly known as the Grim Old Fighting Cox, was appointed to the command, and here our exciting tale ends for the present.

"If the above record of a year of the war presents some discouraging features, it also offers many seeds of hope for the future, inasmuch as it would appear utterly impossible for the future to be less fruitful of national triumphs than the past has been. The greatness of our nation is sufficiently evidenced by the fact that we are spending two millions of dollars per day ; and as soon as the present rebellion shall have been crushed, the final defeat of the celebrated Southern Confederacy will become a mere question of time, and we shall be prepared to commit immediate assault upon combined Europe.

"V. GAMMON."

Alas ! my boy, what can we say to such a revelation of national strategy ? I was thinking over its developments as I wandered listlessly amongst the deserted Mackerel fortifications this side of Manassas on Thursday, —I was thinking about it, I say, when my attention was attracted by a soldier's grave located in the very midst of the dismantled earthworks. It bore a rude monument of pine-board, on which the companions of the strategic deceased had written the following inscription with chalk.

As I read this simple inscription, I could not help thinking how many Mackerels, like this poor fifer, had rushed from their homes to the war, panting for victory or honorable death, only to be slowly consumed by national

126 ORPHEUS C. KERR PAPERS.

strategy, and die of inglorious fortification and indigestion.

MUGGY JIM,

A MACKEREL FIFER,

LATE OF THE NEW YORK FIRE DEPARTMENT;
TAKEN SICK
OF INDIGESTION,
HE COMMENCED TO
THROW UP FORTIFICATIONS,
AND DIED OF STRATEGY.

....

Hic Jacet.
1..5−4.
0 .... 4 .... 1 .... 2 8,
0 .... 4 .... 1 .... 2 .... 0;
0 .... 2 ... 80 8,
0 .... 2 ... 45 .... 4.

It needs no Champollion's hieroglyphical skill to read the beautiful little verse of the fifer's epitaph, though that verse had to be inscribed figuratively, in order to get it all upon the narrow monument. In all its praise of that quiet sleep in which there are no anticipations to be disappointed, no gluttony to make sick, and no Confederacies to guard against, — the verse will be plain to all as reading:

"HERE LIES

ONE FIFER:

Nought for one to wait,
Nought for one to sigh-for;
Nought too weighty ate,
Nought to fortify-for."

The Mackerel poet who wrote those lines, my boy,

THIRD SERIES. **127**

may have been no rhetorician ; but his theme was an inspiration giving him more than ordinary mastery of the
figures of speech.

Yours, gravely,

ORPHEUS C. KERR.

XCII.

IN WHICH OUR ENTHUSIASTIC CORRESPONDENT SURPASSES ÆSCHYLUS IN THE WAY OF AN INVOCATION: AND DESCRIBES REAR ADMIRAL HEAD'S GREAT NAVAL DEMONSTRATION AGAINST FORT PIANO.

WASHINGTON, D. C., April 20th, 1863.

STAND aside, my boy, and realize your own civilian insignificance, while I invoke all the gods of Old Olympus to aid me with their inspiration, in the tale of naval grandeur it is my duty to unfold.

Fired with the soul to hail my country great, and write her honors endless to the world, full to the sun I wave the eager pen, invoking all the lightning of the gods. Descend on me, Olympian dews, descend! that this tired brain, where oft the new-born thought hath died unblossomed in the fainting soil, may catch fresh vigor from the grateful balm, and teem thrice glorious in a nobler youth. By all the fire that glows in Homer's song, to make all ages flame anew with Troy; by all the music stirred in Virgil's lay, to make Æneas ever march the world; by all the heav'nly fury of the theme, Æschylus-taken, picturing gods to men; by all the Art o'er nature raised sublime, and unto Xenophon revealed by night, to make Ten Thousand nobler in Retreat than thrice ten thousand by a Cæsar led; by All that unto All hath been their All, I charge thee, oh, thou impulse of the gods! grand as the storm and chainless as the wind, descend on me! as

(128)

THIRD SERIES. 129

lightning from the cloud descends to beacon what the storm makes dark. That I may write, in words of thunder born, such deeds as strengthen while they shake the world; that I may write, in lines to trumpets tuned, such acts as make men brothers to the gods; that I may write, in notes to mock the lute, such feats of cunning as lull Fate to sleep; that I may dip th' immortalizing pen in bright Pactolus' ever golden stream, and write, in language sweeter to the ear than Hymet's honey to soft Dion's lips, glories of arms to first make Nature crouch — then leap to something higher than herself!

(If any man objects to that sort of thing, my boy, may he be whipped to death by the aged maidens of the Confederacy, and utterly perish *per flagellationem extremam*.)

And now I feel the Homeric inspiration in all my veins as I dip the impatient quill into the Black Republican ink, and hasten to record the deathless honors recently reaped by the Mackerel Iron-plated Squadron in a deathless attack upon Fort Piano.

You may remember, my boy, that the construction of a pier on Duck Lake by some shameless Confederacies, and the erection on the end thereof of Fort Piano, was first made known to our noble old sea-dog, Rear Admiral Head, whilst he sat on the quarter deck of his original iron-plated squadron fishing for bass, by the accidental knocking of the squadron against the end of the pier. His back being turned at the time, he had not noticed the building of the terrible fortification; and when the horrible jar of the collision caused him to look that way, he found six villanous horse-pistols so planted by the disrespectful Confederacies as to exactly command his fish-

130   ORPHEUS C. KERR PAPERS.

basket and box of bait.   You may also remember my boy,
how our glorious old Neptune subsequently caused the
stanch "Secretary Welles" to run the blockade of the
fort, to thoroughly test the invulnerability of the iron-clad
principle; and how the result of that test satisfactorily
proved the iron-clad principle to be entirely testaceous.

Since then, you have heard about the building of the
new Mackerel iron-plated squadron, the "Shockingbadhat," with Rear Admiral Head's newly improved turret
and reversed swivel-gun; but you have not yet heard, my
boy, anything at all about the unique manufacture of six
additional iron-plated squadrons, to participate with the
"Shockingbadhat" in the recent severe attack on Fort
Piano.   You have not heard of these six new monsters
before, my boy, and respect for the really decent families
of the inventors forbids that I should tell you anything
descriptive about them now, save their names.

It was intended that the name of the first should be
something full of significance to perfidious England, and,
at the same time, something never used in England.
Hence, she was christened the "Aitch."

The second was to bear a name signifying the power of
bending without breaking; and so she was called after
that elastic tree, the "Yew."

In the name of the third, the Government wished to
pay a complimentary tribute to Rear Admiral Head; and,
in honor of his daughter, Emma, the squadron was named
the "Em."

The fourth iron-plated invulnerable Mackerel monster
it was deemed proper to decorate with a name expressive
of industry coupled with a power to sting; and so she was
called the "Bee."

THIRD SERIES. 131

There was some discusssion about the proper title for the fifth patent iron-clad, each member of the generous Mackerel Naval Committee saying to the other: " Why can't she be named after you?" So, it was at length decided to happily compromise the matter by calling her the " You."

By common consent the sixth invincible iron monster was adjudged to be known by the first of General George B. McClellan's initials, and was entitled the " Gee."

Add these new national champions of the deep, my boy, to the " Shockingbadhat," and you will have some idea of the glorious naval pageant prepared to administer wholesome correction to the irreverent Confederacies of Fort Piano, and teach the world that worn-out cooking-stoves can be sold to the sagacious Government of the United States of America for something better than old iron.

The " Shockingbadhat " was the flag-ship ; and, on the morning of the attack, the hoary Rear Admiral Head repaired to the top of her turret with his umbrella, fishing-rod, and pocket-microscope, taking with him the Mackerel crew to work the improved swivel-gun, which was also up there ; and giving orders to another unconquerable Mackerel to locate himself amidships with a quart measure, for the purpose of measuring the number of bushels of shots striking the turret during the first two seconds of the approaching sea-fight.

Ranged along the right shore of Duck Lake, my boy, to witness the battle and lend lustre to the landscape, was a land-force of virtuous Mackerels, under command of the venerable grandmother of Rear Admiral Head ; and she was the one whose appearance gave rise to that rumor amongst the Confederacies in the Fort, that Secretary Welles was reviewing the troops in person.

On the opposite shore of the Lake was a delegation of European chaps, come to behold the engagement; including Fatti O'Murphy, candidate for the vacant throne of Greece; the Hon. Mr. New Troloppe, of England; and le Marquis Non Puebla, French Minister to Mexico.

At the head of the Lake, my boy, I stood myself, with my bit of smoked glass in my hand; and around me were the reporters of all the reliable and excellent morning journals, spitting on their hands, preparatory to writing their exciting descriptions of personal danger.

Precisely at noon the Mackerels of the land force raised their umbrellas, the Mackerel crews got aboard their respective squadrons, and exercises were commenced by the singing of —

"My country, 'tis of thee."

As the last strain died away, we could hear that grim old sea-dog, Rear Admiral Head, swearing in his iron-plated manner, and then the whole naval pageant swept magnificently to the front of Fort Piano; the "Shocking-badhat" leading, closely followed by the "Aitch," the "Yew," the "Em," the "Bee," the "You," and the "Gee." It was a glorious sight, my boy, — a glorious sight, and moved me like the First of May.

For the purpose of testing the range and drawing the fire of the unseemly Confederacies' Artillery, Rear Admiral Head carefully let down his old white hat into the waves, and suffered it to drift slowly past the north-east face of Fort Piano. We held our breath as we saw the

THIRD SERIES. 133

artful decoy whirl for a moment in an eddy caused by a land-crab, and then drift against the pier, where it stuck. Immediately a hand was seen reaching down after it, the hat was drawn up, and a prodigious horse-laugh arose from the uncomely Confederacies in the Fort. They supposed the hat to be Mr. Greely's.

"Sink my Keokuk!" roared Rear Admiral Head, in his iron-plated manner, — "I really believe the treasonable insects have been and stolen my beaver, — obstruct my Ironsides, if I don't!"

Scarcely had the words passed his lips, my boy, when a Confederacy *en barbette* discharged a double-barrelled fowling-piece at the "Aitch" knocking off two of her front covers, breaking several bars of her grates, and piercing her oven in numerous places. Instantly the cry arose of "One of the cooking-stoves is sinking!" which so bewildered Rear-Admiral Head that he discharged his swivel-gun one point too far to the windward, and immediately found his flagship entangled on several strings with which the Confederacies had obstructed the passage.

"Disable my Patapsco!" exclaimed the indomitable old Neptune, in his iron-plated manner, "the insects have tied us fast, — bend my turrets if they haven't."

At this time, my boy, the concentrated fire of the Fort was terrific, six horse-pistols being in full play at once, and the Mackerel with the quart measure amidships reporting that the turret of the "Shockingbadhat" had been hit three quarts of times in thirty seconds.

Such being the case, and the European delegation having gone home with a view to shaking off their inclination to fall asleep, the stern old commander ordered a wet blan-

134 ORPHEUS C. KERR PAPERS.

ket to be thrown over his swivel-gun, and such of the iron-plated squadron as had not sunk were immediately run ashore. The affair had been merely a reconnoissance.

Shortly after the conclusion of this terrible artillery duel, and a few minutes subsequent to a touching exchange of congratulations between the unconquerable Rear-Admiral and his venerable grandmother, there hastily arrived from Paris an obese middle-aged chap, in black cotton gloves and a scratch wig, and says he to the Admiral:

"Allow me to bless you, Sir, — My name is Hunter, Sir, — for your excellent iron-clad conduct. We should all be grateful, sir, that you have passed safely through ' a concentric fire that has never heretofore had a parallel in the history of warfare.' "

Never heretofore had a parallel! What could he have meant, my boy? How could a *concentric* fire have a *parallel* at any time?

Yours, questioningly,

ORPHEUS C. KERR.

LETTER XCIII.

TEEMING WITH CONSUMMATE STRATEGY, AND RELATING AN EXTRAORDI-
NARY GEOMETRICAL EFFORT OF MILITARY GENIUS.

WASHINGTON, D. C., May 10th, 1863.

As it was feared on Sunday last, my boy, that the venerable Mackerel Brigade was about to commit a breach of the peace by strategically assaulting the Confederacies established in the mud between the Mackerel camp and the ancient City of Paris, I mounted my architectural steed, the Gothic Pegasus, at an early hour in the morning, and perceptibly moved toward the scene of approaching tautology. The emaciated aspect of my architectural steed of the desert was so inviting to the fowls of the air, my boy, that divers disreputable crows circled suddenly around my hat, as my animal progressed with me by miscellaneously scattering his legs around beneath himself, and at each particular " caw " of the winged ministers of famine, a perceptible shudder passed through the entire framework of the deeply agitated Pegasus. Abstractedly waving my umbrella, to inspire the sable birds for loftier flights, I pondered deeply upon the lesson taught me by the evident emotions of my aged architectural servant; to ride upon whose fluted back may be likened to sitting astride the peaked roof of a small country chapel in the midst of a hard earthquake, and holding

(135)

136 ORPHEUS C. KERR PAPERS.

on by the steeple. If this Gothic creation, which is but a horse, thought I, is so agonized by the mere breakfast notes of a few demoralized crows in the atmosphere, how much more terrible must be the anguish of the fellow-beings known as Southern Confederacies, who must ever have a dreadful presentiment of being summarily expunged from the human race by any one of our brass-buttoned generals, who happens to board in their neighborhood for a few years. If I pity this architectural servant of mine, thought I, for his anguish at the proximity of crows in the abstract, how much more tender should be my feeling for Southern fellow-beings, who are continually endangered by the much louder crows emanating from adjacent hostile Major-General roosters. As I pondered thus, my boy, a crow of much plumage and large-sized mien, suddenly alighted upon the pommel of my saddle, as though impatient to breakfast upon some pounds of horseflesh. For an instant Pegasus trembled throughout his works; he paused suddenly in his peregrination, laid back his ears as though in deep thought, twisted his head suddenly about, and bit off the tail of the crow in the abstract!

Simple as was the act, it at once relieved me, in my own mind, of all obligations to have a more tender feeling for my Southern fellow-beings than is consistent with a proper emotion of hatred against the enemies of my country. After all, we can learn much more from brutes than from men; and as Balaam's ass saw the angel before his master did, so the Angel of Victory is likely to be distinctly obvious to any poor ass in the country, before he becomes visible to the sight of our strategic great men.

THIRD. SERIES. 137

(I turn a pretty sharp corner in that last sentence, my boy; but that is only safe strategy when you find your argument getting ahead of you.)

It was high noon when I reached the Mackerel camp, and I found the spectacled veterans hastily preparing to cross Duck Lake after the manner of aquatic warriors. By some strange fatality, all the pontoons were at hand in time, greatly to the distress of our more venerable troops, who seemed to fear that such unheard-of punctuality must be an evil omen. As there were a great many pontoons, and it was not deemed best to waste any of them, two bridges were built instead of one, — it being considered that, inasmuch as it was purposed to surprise the unseemly Confederacies on the other side, two bridges would be just twice as surprising to them as one would be. There was logic in this idea, my boy — much logic and consummate strategy.

Gazing across the expanse of waters, I beheld a couple of regiments of Confederacies playing poker on the bank, and says I to Villiam Brown, who was at that moment returning a small black bottle to his holster:

"Tell me, my fearless blue-back, how this can possibly be a surprise, when yonder gray-backs are looking on all the time?"

"Ah!" says Villiam, with much loftiness of demeanor; "you are but an ignorant civilian inseck, and know nothing about war. The movement," says Villiam, placidly, "is intended as a surprise to the enemy, upon the principle that any movement whatever of this Army must surprise everybody."

I was reflecting seriously upon this unanswerable ex-

138   ORPHEUS C. KERR PAPERS.

planation of profound strategy, my boy, when Captain
Bob Shorty came rattling up with a paper in his hand,
and says he: " Attention, Company! while I read a
document calculated to restrain the licentiousness of a
corrupt and vicious press:

" GENERAL ORDER.

" For the purpose of preventing the transmission of all
news not previously published in the morning journals of
the so-called Southern Confederacy, it has been determined
by the General Commanding to require all correspondents
of the press to affix their full names, ages, and addresses
to whatever matter they transmit for publication, thus giving to the journals of our time the double character of
newspaper and business-directory. Reporters having vulgar names, like Jones, Smith, or Stiggins, will be at liberty to assume the names borne by the most popular char-
acters in the exciting tales furnished by our weekly journals of romance, — such as Lord Mortimer, Claude de
Percy, Lester Heartsease.

" Correspondents who do not comply with this require-
ment will not ·be permitted to assist in surprising the
so-called Southern Confederacy.

" THE GENERAL OF THE MACKEREL BRIGADE."
(Blue Seal.)

After we had all duly digested this useful and sagacious
General Order, my boy, Captain Samyule Sa-mith was
ordered to make a detour of Duck Lake with the Anatomical Cavalry, and dig a canal in the rear of the well-
known Confederacy; and the Mackerel Brigade, under

THIRD SERIES.

139

the personal supervision of the Grim Old Fighting Cox, commenced to cross the pontoon-bridges in two divisions. The bridge that I was upon, my boy, was at once attacked at the other end by a surprised Confederacy with a large pair of scissors, who malignantly cut that end loose. There was an aged civilian chap, from Albany, of much stomach and a broad-brimmed hat, standing near me ; and when he found the bridge beginning to move, he smote his breast, and says he :

" Where are we drifting to ? "

" Be not alarmed, Mr. Weed," says I, pleasantly ; " we shall soon repair the damage."

" Hem ! " says he, " I wish I'd gone over on the other platform at first."

He was quite an old man, my boy, slowly sinking into the rising waves of his own fat ; and for that reason appeared to have a chronic fear of some unexpected submersion.

The Mackerel Brigade, in two parts, having reached the opposite shore of Duck Lake in safety, the Grim Old Fighting Cox ordered Captain Villiam Brown and Captain Bob Shorty to take each a regiment of spectacled veterans and cautiously feel the Confederacies' lines, while he led the remainder of the national troops to a small village at hand, which had particularly requested to be immediately destroyed. It was his great strategical plan, my boy, to form his lines in the shape of a triangle, thus inclosing the unmannerly Confederacies between three fires, and winning a great geometrical victory. The Confederacies being duly surrounded, and the village being set on fire at the apex of the triangle, the Grim Old

140   ORPHEUS C. KERR PAPERS.

Fighting Cox withdrew to a tent, spread a map of the world upon a camp-stool before him, and proceeded to take topographical observations. Drawing from his saddle-bags an instrument of opaque glass, of tubular character, quite large in circumference about half-way up, and then tapering into a neck, or smaller tube, of nearly the same length, he raised it in a semi-horizontal position to a point about one and a half inches above the lower circumference of his chin, until he could look through it at an angle bisecting its greater circumference upon the map below. The light, striking through the body of this instrument, cast a wavy, fluctuating sort of yellowish glare upon that part of the map representing the well-known Southern Confederacy, accompanied by a species of soft, trickling sound. After an interval of some ten minutes, the operator saw, by this contrivance, just double the number of Confederacies he had to contend with. It only remained, then, for him to divide the number thus ascertained by two, and he knew exactly the number of his foes!

You will observe, my boy, that this singularly ingenious device at once revealed to the new General of the Mackerel Brigade the true strength of his greatest enemy, and inspired him with a strong spirit.

It was immediately after this, that the Grim Old Fighting Cox issued the following

"GENERAL ORDER.

" The manner in which the crossing of Duck Lake has been accomplished proves that this is the finest Army ever seen on the plan-it, and is likely to prove equally

fine on the do-it.   I have now got the well-known Southern Confederacy where I wished to have her, and she
must either ignominiously retreat, or come out of her
works, and be annihilated by me on my own ground,
which is ground-arms!

" (Blue Seal.)

"The General of the Mackerel Brigade."

Having let fly this General Order, my boy, the Grim
Old Fighting Cox proceeded to complete his surprise of
the enemy by leading a bayonet charge from his side of
the triangle, and immediately telegraphed to the base
of the triangle that the enemies of human freedom were
retreating before him.   This was truly the case; for the
unseemly Confederacies not only retreated before him, but
retreated with such impetus of flight upon Captain Villiam
Brown at the base of the triangle, that they actually drove
him clear out of his place, and proceeded to occupy the
base themselves.   Thus matters stood at the conclusion of
the first day.

Early on the second day, the Grim Old Fighting Cox
charged again upon some fresh regiments of Confederacies,
who retreated with such violence that they completely
pressed Captain Bob Shorty from the right line of the triangle, and remained in that line themselves.   This was
the second day's battle.

On the following morning, it was discovered that fresh
Confederacies had come up from Paris.   These were attacked irresistibly by the whole Mackerel Brigade, and
only succeeded in making a stand when they formed, as
it were, the left line of the triangle.

142   ORPHEUS C. KERR PAPERS.

You will perceive, my boy, that a great piece of geometrical strategy had been thus achieved; but it now turned out that the General of the Mackerel Brigade had made a mistake, and a most serious one. While taking his observations with his ingenious glass instrument, he had seen just double the number of triangles (2) that might be formed by certain great strategical evolutions, as he had seen just double the number of the Confederacies; but, in his haste, he had neglected to divide the ascertained number of triangles by two, as he should have done; and now he discovered that only one triangle was formed, and that by the unseemly and chuckling Confederacies. Such a nice thing is strategy, and so easily is it deranged!

Owing to this error, of course nothing more could be done, and on Tuesday evening the Mackerel Brigade returned, full of enthusiasm, to their original side of Duck Lake. The affair had been merely a reconnoissance.

Last evening, at dusk, I was talking to the Mackerel Chaplain about this singular strategical affair, and says he:

"God help us! The skeleton regiments we have left standing are scarcely more than the skeleton regiments we have left sleeping; and only the sleeping ones can look upward."

Let gentle charity, my boy, silence our tongues to the dread mistake that is past; for he who made it lost by it the glorious immortality his meanest soldier slain has won.

Yours, gently,

ORPHEUS C. KERR.

LETTER XCIV.

AFFORDING AN INSTANCE OF IMPERCEPTIBLE PATRIOTISM; PRESENT-
ING THE PROFOUND COMMENTARY OF AN EMINENT FOREIGN MILI-
TARY CRITIC; AND REPORTING THE LAST EFFUSION OF THE GEN-
ERAL OF THE MACKEREL BRIGADE.

WASHINGTON, D. C., May 17th, 1863.

WHEN great interests are at stake, my boy, and strong
passions are excited, and when it becomes necessary that
a whole nation shall be unanimous for its own preserva-
tion from destruction, we occasionally meet with chaps of
severe countenance and much shirt-ruffles, whose patriotism is purely that of descent, and not at all of assent.
Since this great strategic war commenced, I have encountered divers iron-faced and brass-mounted conservative fellow-beings, whose sentiments in action have seemed
to establish as an inevitable postulate in logic, that a man
sired by a hero of '76, must naturally be damn'd by the
heroes of '63 ; and that a man with Revolutionary blood
in his veins is entirely exempted from all legitimacy to
a propensity for spilling the least drop of that sacred liquid
in behalf of a cause not Revolutionary. It was on Tuesday, my boy, that I met the Honorable Fernando Fuel,
the member-elect from the Sixth Ward, who had come
hither for the express purpose of getting up for himself an
entirely new coat of arms, according to New York Her-
aldry, and of procuring from some scholar a recondite

144 ORPHEUS C. KERR PAPERS.

couplet that should at once serve, in motto form, to denote his Revolutionary descent, and express his high moral patriotism as apart from any partisan desire to see injuries inflicted upon the Wayward Sisters of his distracted country. He came to me, and says he:

"Learning, sir, that you are qualified to cull from your extensive poetical readings some unique couplet appropriate for my approaching coat-of-arms, I desire you to furnish me with the same, and present your bill to our Excellent Democratic Organization, of which I am Chief Indian near — In short, a Sachem local. My patriotism," says he, shading a slight cough with a black cotton-glove, — " My patriotism is doubted by none but those imbecile despots who defeated our Excellent Democratic Organization in the last Presidential election, and are now waging a bloody and unnatural war for the sake of the Demon of Africa. But my patriotism hurls back the epithet of 'traitor,' and is clearly established by the fact that I had an ancestor in the Revolution. It is my wish," says this plausibly-spoken chap, nodding to a Faro-banker as he happened to pass at that moment, — " it is my wish that the couplet should express, neatly and figuratively as it were, the exact degree of my present patriotism, and its derivation from my Revolutionary ancestor. Let it represent me clothed in patriotism, as it were."

I thought upon his words for a while, my boy, and then says I :

"For such unspeakable patriotism as yours, good Fuel, there can be no finer couplet than this :

> "'A painted vest Prince Vortiger had on,
> That from a naked Pict his grandsire won.' "

THIRD SERIES. 145

The Honorable Fuel turned very crimson in the face with intense gratification, and says he: "Ha! ha!—ahem! Yes, that's not bad. Ha! ha! very good—you infernal Black Republican you!"

He left me, as a cloud might leave the sun with which it had vainly attempted to cut up shines, and I felt for a moment, like one lost in the Wood. With the best intentions in the world, I had only succeeded in adding Fuel to the flames of treason.

It pleases me to say that Herr Suvchork, one of those eminent foreign strategists of war who have visited our distracted country for the truly benignant purpose of teaching us how we may win battles only recently lost, has honored me with a great metaphysical criticism upon the recent reconnoissance and triangular proceeding of the New General of the Mackerel Brigade against the well-known Southern Confederacies on the other side of Duck Lake. We may all learn a valuable lesson, my boy, from this able *critique*, which reads thus:

"SOMEDINGS ABOUT ODDERDINGS.

"I have notice in der bapers that der Genral Fighting Cok cross Dook Lake in two parts, the odder day, when he assaulted the Rebel Army von Lee, which was strongly post in entrenchment built especial for dees purpose. Das was vare wrong, and oppose to all the princeeples von der Great Napoleon. Das vas der great troubles with Fritz Magnus von Prussia, at Kunersdorf, where he had dirty dousand pick troops, and lost seventeen dousand, in sooch way. Genral Fighting Cok was adopting der princeeple of der Duke von Cumberland at Fonte-

146 ORPHEUS C. KERR PAPERS.

noy, when he should adopt sooch plan as that of Mare-
chal Saxe, und keep his troops all togedder, und not cross
Dook Lake in two parts. To attack sooch Rebel Army
in entrenchment built especial for dees purpose, it was
necessaire as he should do everydings togedder; keep
his troops altogedder, und fight them altogedder.

" I have not known Genral Fighting Cok in Germany,
and I knows not as he is as good Genral as Sigel; so I
cannot say as he is sooch goot Genral as Sigel und me.
But *merk auf! — es ist ein hohes wort* — he has not so
large militaire mind as A. P. SUVCHORK."

While you will join with me, my boy, in acknowl-
edging the soundness of this criticism from our able German critic, I am sure that we must both perceive something like cruelty to animals in the very common practice
of giving the exact directions for gaining a victory so soon
after the battle has terminated in defeat. It is like telling
a patient who has just taken a dose of salts, how he might
have cured himself by a course of *patés de foie gras*.

And now let me direct your most intense attention to
the Mackerel Camp on this side of Duck Lake, where the
spectacled veterans are all repairing their umbrellas for
another reconnoissance toward the first point of the compass that seems most vulnerable. They are all full of
enthusiasm, my boy, over the loss of some of their
comrades and arms in the recent triangular geometrical
proceedings against the unseemly Confederacy, and unanimously demand to be led against the enemies of human
freedom that presume to show the freedom of human enemies.

THIRD SERIES.

147

You may remember that, just previous to the recent crossing of Duck Lake, Captain Samyule Sa-mith was despatched with the Anatomical Cavalry to dig a canal in the immediate rear of the Southern Confederacy, in order that the legions of the enemies of human freedom about to be captured by surprise, might be at once set to hard labor on the tow-path. It was not more than four days after all the fighting was over that Samyule came back with his equestrian warriors, and says the General to him:

"Well, boy, is the canal finished?"

Samyule scratched his head, and says he: "Not quite, sire; but we have torn up a Confederate railroad."

It was this circumstance, my boy, that gave rise to the recent reports of the capture of Richmond, as considerable of the Rebel capital is known to be invested in railroad iron.

Shortly after Samyule's return, the Grim Old Fighting Cox took off his coat, rolled up his sleeves, ordered a couple of spies to be executed, and discharged the following

"CONGRATULATORY ORDER.

"Head Quarters Mackerel Brigade.

"The General commanding tenders to the aged Mackerels his congratulations on their achievements of the last seven days, which were week.

"If they have not accomplished all that was expected, the reason is, that more was expected than has been accomplished.

"It is sufficient to say that they were of a character not to be foreseen without foresight, nor prevented without human sagacity and attainable resources.

148   ORPHEUS C. KERR PAPERS.

"In withdrawing from the other side of Duck Lake without delivering a general battle to our adversaries, the Mackerels have proved their renewed diffidence in themselves, and their fidelity to a high standard of retiring modesty.

"In fighting at a disadvantage, instead of at the enemy, we would have been recreant to our trust in our pontoons.

"Profoundly loyal, and conscious of its strength, the Mackerel Brigade will give or decline battle whenever it considers the weather sufficiently pleasant and the newspapers sufficiently snubbed.

"It will also be the dictator of its own history and the vindicator of its own legs.

"By our celerity and secrecy of movement, both in crossing and re-crossing Duck Lake, we neither pursued, nor were pursued by, a Rebel.

"The events of the last week may swell with pride the feet of every officer and soldier in this Brigade.

"We have made long marches and countermarches, crossed and re-crossed lakes, surprised the enemy by our advance, brought back seven pieces of our artillery, and given heavier blows than the wind.

"We have nothing to regret, save the loss of our brave companions, and in this we may be consoled by the conviction that they fell in the holiest cause ever left so exclusively to the care of Providence, that very little human intelligence was deemed necessary to direct its arbitrament in battle.

"(Blue Seal.)

"THE GENERAL OF THE MACKEREL BRIGADE."

THIRD SERIES. **149**

As we consider the vast world of animated nature, my boy, and mark what apparent simplicity there is in the structure of beast, bird, and reptile, does it not seem exceedingly strange, that all of man's vaunted ingenuity has thus far succeeded in making imitative approximation only to the insect kingdom, — the apparently least difficult of all, — and to *that* only by such a spurious kind of a bug as Humbug ?

Yours, wonderingly,

ORPHEUS C. KERR.

LETTER XCV.

NOTING THE CONTINUED ANGUISH OF THE CONSERVATIVE KENTUCKY
CHAP, AND THE DEATH OF NEMO; AND DESCRIBING AN IMMENSE
POPULAR DEMONSTRATION AGAINST THE OUTRAGES OF FEDERAL
OPPRESSION.

WASHINGTON, D. C., May 24th, 1864.

THE beautiful Spring, my boy, is out in the sunshine
once more, — bowing her pretty face over her lap, as
though to breathe the odor of the fresh violets lying scattered upon her coquettish green apron, but really to hide
the blush mantling the cheeks on which the hot breath of
enamored young Summer is tempting the roses to premature birth. What a fine old world this is, after all, if we
have plenty of money in our pockets, plenty of health in
our systems, and no poor relations! As you stand on the
Arlington side of the Potomac, on any one of these fair
May days, and look around you in any direction, there is
a beauty even about the tracks of war which enables you
to comprehend why so many of our brass-buttoned generals are fond of staying in one spot so long. Behind you
rise Arlington Heights, which are disliked by our excellent National Democratic Organization, only because they
wear a covering of Lincoln green in summer; before you,
and across the Potomac is the Capitol of our distracted
country, looking like an ambitious marble-yard on its way
out of town; and close beside you is one of our national

(150)

THIRD SERIES. 151

troops extracting certain wonders of the insect kingdom from a Government biscuit. On Tuesday, I was standing with the Conservative Kentucky chap near Long Bridge, surveying this scene, and says I, —

"Behold, my Nestor, how the scars left upon Nature's face by the chariot wheels of War are turning into dimples, and all the twinkling curves of a placid smile."

"Yes," says he, hastily picking up the Jack of Diamonds which he had accidentally drawn from his pocket with his handkerchief, — "the scene is somewhat pleasant; but not equal to Kentucky, where there is more rye."

Here the Kentucky chap became so deeply affected that he was compelled to smell a cork which he took from his vest pocket, and says he, —

"Kentucky raised a great deal of rye before the breaking out of this here fatal war with the Southern Confederacy, with whom Kentucky is connected by marriage; she raised it by the bottle; in which form it becomes, as it were, the crowning glory of agriculture. Ah!" says the Conservative Kentucky chap, stirring an invisible beverage with an imaginary spoon, "how softly on my senses steals Kentucky's national anthem, —

"'If a body meet a body,
Comin' through the rye.'

And the Old Rye of Kentucky is famous for its body." The Kentucky chap hiccupped at the bare recollection of the thing, and says he: "But we can no longer say that the bloom is on the rye; for this unnatural war has killed the agriculture of Kentucky and broken many of her bottles. O Kentucky! Kentucky! how thirsty I am!"

After this speech, I could no longer profane the glory

152   ORPHEUS C. KERR PAPERS.

of God's beautiful picture by talking about it to a chap who could see nothing in a landscape but rye fields. And yet it is but natural for any Conservative chap to talk thus, after all; for I have found it to be a peculiarity of nearly all our fellow-beings, that Old Rye is forever running in their heads.

On Wednesday, while I was on my usual weekly visit to the Mackerel camp near Duck Lake, I was called to look upon the body of a poor soldier who had been shot during the night by a prowling Confederacy. He was a very young chap, my boy, with light, wavy hair, and might have been taken for a mere lad, had there not been more years in the deep lines on his brow than on his beardless chin. There he lay upon his gun, with one hand clenched in the sand, and the other upon the damp red spot on his breast. He looked like a child who had fallen asleep after unkind words from his mother. The Chaplain and a private Mackerel in rags were bending over him, and says I, —

" Who was he ? "

" He went by the name of Nemo," says the Chaplain, sadly ; " but no one knows what his real name was. He enlisted only two days ago, and kept himself apart from the other men. I think he was a gentleman."

Here the private Mackerel in rags broke in, and says he : " Yes, he *was* a gentleman. I an't no gentleman, but I know *he* was, and I can lick any man that says he wasn't ! I spoke to him last night when he was relieving guard, and asked him what fire-company he belonged to ; and he said, none. I see he looked sick, and wasn't fit to do duty, and I offered to go out on picket in his place.

THIRD SERIES. 153

It wasn't much to offer; but he squeezed my hand very hard, and said that my life was worth more than his; and that he would go. I asked him what he wanted to come to the war and get killed for; and he said he'd tried to do his best in the world, but everybody was against him, and he'd been disgraced for trying to do an honorable thing, and couldn't stay and face people any more, because all turned away from him. I told him I would lick the man who hurt his feelings, and he only said: 'They all do that,' and went away." Here the poor Mackerel in rags shed tears, and says he: " I know he WAS a gentleman."

" I see how it is," says the Chaplain, shaking his head; " he was one of those unfortunates whose sensitive natures are a legacy of unhappiness, or madness, to be cancelled only by death. And yet his kindness of heart with this rude soldier proved how much goodness there was in him that the world had not turned to bitterness."

Alas! my boy, what a pity it is that these finer natures are forever coming under the heels of everybody, and getting themselves crushed! They are like fine Sèvres vases among stout earthen pipkins, equally ready to split with the cold, or be pulverized by a tilt from their next door neighbors. It is a misfortune for such fragile natures as these to be in this common-place world at all, my boy, and they cannot do the more useful portion of humanity a greater service than by getting themselves out of it as soon as possible. I have known human porcelain vases of this kind so fragile, that they were half-cracked before anything touched them.

On Thursday, my boy, the report that a friend of the well-known Southern Confederacy had been arrested and

154 ORPHEUS C. KERR PAPERS.

court-martialled, in Ohio, for simply advising the intelligent masses to set fire to a few Union hospitals and go hunting after American eagles by the light thereof, — this report, I say, excited amongst the loyal but seditious patriots of storied Accomac an indignation that was anything but speechless. Shades of our Revolutionary sires ! was it possible that a citizen of the Republic could no longer speak pieces without being arrested for speaking peace ! Ashes of the great ! could it be, indeed, true that, even where there were no police, a man's personal liberty was no longer safe ! The people of Accomac, my boy, were alarmed for their own liberties, and at once held a public meeting, at which I happened to be present.

As all the citizens who were worth $300 each sent notes to say that they had imperative engagements to prepare for the approaching Conscription, and could not come, the meeting was composed entirely of the other citizens, many of whom engaged in single combat on their way thither, for the purpose of making the distance seem shorter. Punctually at seven o'clock, P. M., a gentleman of much muscle touched off a small field-piece with such admirable precision as to break all the windows for two blocks around, and then dexterously discharged a two-pound sky-rocket into the third-story bedroom of a venerable maiden lady living across the road. The demonstration was received with joyous acclamations by the populace, nearly twelve of whom had already arrived ; and a victim of Federal oppression, with a very large stomach, mounted the platform erected for the speakers, and said that he would commence proceedings on this occasion, by reading a short portion of Washington's Fare-

THIRD SERIES. 155

well Address from the volume of Bancroft which he held in his hand. (Great applause.) The honorable gentleman then proceeded to read something; but was interrupted by a reporter, who remarked that the speaker must be mistaken about that being Washington's Address, as he had certainly read it in the Bible. The honorable gentleman then turned his book over so that he could read the title, and said that he had, indeed, made a slight mistake about the volume. He would defer reading the Address for the present, and begged leave to introduce Mr. John Smith, the Hon. Ferdinand De Percy having failed to be present.

Mr. Smith said that it was the proudest moment of his life, and he felt it an honor to be there. They had met together to denounce and spit upon an astounding Administration, under whose tyrannical sway no man was allowed to say one word against it. A fellow-citizen had been arrested in Ohio upon the miserable charge of advocating peace, when he was really disturbing the peace all he could. How long were such outrages to be endured? He advised his hearers to strictly honor the laws; but he would also have them go home, organize into regiments, purchase artillery, procure iron-clads, and destroy every man who dared to speak in favor of an Administration under which the boldest man dared not express his sentiments. He would have them do all this peaceably; but he would have them do it. (Great enthusiasm, and cries of "Keep off my corns, durn ye!")

As Chesterfield Mortimer, the celebrated Accomac patriot, was not able to be present on this occasion,

156 ORPHEUS C. KERR PAPERS.

Mr. Jones was introduced, and made a few sensible remarks. He said that he had always been a law-abiding man, and would always advocate the strictest observance of the laws. The peaceful people, he trusted, would all procure reliable muskets and . . . . . .

At this moment, my boy, the speaker suddenly stopped short; stared at a white object which had just appeared fluttering down the street; and then, dashing wildly from the platform, tore furiously in the direction of said object, which appeared to be moving, followed spontaneously and with frantic speed by his fellow-speakers and the entire meeting. I was astounded; I was overwhelmed; for such a sudden breaking-up and precipitate flight of a great indignation meeting was never witnessed before. Quickly mounting the vacant rostrum, I drew my field-glass from my pocket, and proceeded to scan the wonderful white object which had produced such an electrical effect. It was moving on, as I fixed my glass upon it, and I found it to be a new banner, born by a fat young man in a white apron, and bearing the inscription:

> ### BROOKSES
> ### NEW BAR·ROOM,
> *JUST OPEN.*
> Free Lunch now Ready.

This it was, my boy, which had broken up one of the most significant meetings of the age, by artfully working upon the idea of its supposed inn-significance.

Upon reaching Washington, on my return, I heard

THIRD SERIES.   157

that a serious-minded chap, of Republican officiousness, had just waited upon the Honest Abe to ask if he did not intend to cause the arrest of Smith and Jones for their treason.

Our Uncle Abe smiled feebly, and scratched his head, and says he:

" What Smith and Jones, neighbor?"

" Why," says the serious-minded chap, earnestly, " the Smith and Jones of Accomac."

" Well, really," says the Honest Abe, pleasantly, " it's curious, now; but I never heard of them before."

Drawing an inference from this little circumstance of Executive conversation, my boy, it strikes me that it would add considerably to the importance of some of our large-sized local revolutionists, if they could overturn the present ignorant Administration, and establish in its place a — Directory.

Yours, double-entendrely,

ORPHEUS C. KERR.

LETTER XCVI.

DEVOTED PRINCIPALLY TO SOCIAL MATTERS, AND THE BENIGNANT BEARING OF V. GAMMON AT A DIPLOMATIC SOIREE.

WASHINGTON, D. C., July 3d, 1863.

SOCIAL life at our National Capital, my boy, as far as the native element is concerned, has not been refined by the war; and even at the White House it is scarcely possible to collect an assemblage of persons sufficiently genteel by education to speak familiarly of European noblemen of their acquaintance. At the last dinner given by the Secretary of State, there were actually three Western persons of much cheek-bones, who dissented from the very proper idea that Earl Russel's Carlton-house sherry is superior to anything we have in this country; and my disgust intensified to hopeless scorn, when an Eastern chap in a nankeen vest was brazen enough to confess that he could not tell how many pieces the Emperor of the French had in the wash on the last week of Lent. At other social gatherings in Washington I have noticed the same evidences of growing vulgarity; and I greatly fear, my boy, — I greatly fear that a knowledge of Europe will yet be more prevalent amongst Europeans than Americans. O my country, my native land! has it indeed come to this at last? In thy loftiest social circles shall we no more behold that beautiful flesh-colored being in lavender gloves and dress-coat whose etherealized individ-

(158)

THIRD SERIES.

uality broke rapturously forth in the thrilling words,
" When I was in Paris last summer " ?   Are we no more
to palpitate with ecstasy at the tones of that voice which
was wont to trill forth in liquid music from a curl-crested
fountain of white shoulders, saying : " Don't you remember, Mr. Thompsion, how the Guke of Leeds larfed that
day, at the Reception, when I told him that we American
ladies thought it was vulgar to say ' garters ' out loud ? "
Alas! my boy, our aristocracy is fading away like an
abused exotic, and it is not oftener than once in a season
that the frequenter of our Republican Court witnesses
one incident to make him recognize the polished people he
once knew.   About two months ago, at an evening party
given by Mrs. Senator ——, I did witness a social incident, showing that there is still hope for the Republic.
An interesting young mother, of not more than sixty-two
summers, attired in a babywaist and graduated flounces,
was standing near one of the doors of the music-room
conversing with me upon the moral character of her dearest female friend, when her gushing daughter, a nymph
not more than six pianos old, came pressing to her side,
and whispered behind her fan, —

" Mamma *cheri*, may I donse with young Waddle ? "

The maternal girl smiled grimly at the fragile suppliant,
and asked :

" How much is his celery, *ma petite ?* "

" Nine hundred, mamma, in the Third Auditor's."

" Then tell him, *mon ange*, that you are engaged for
the next set, and wait until the thousand-dollar clerks
come in.   You know, *ma petite*, what the Count Pistachio
said to you at Avignon about giving encouragement to
anything less than four figures."

I could not avoid overhearing this conversation, my boy, for it was not held in whispers, and I thought to myself, as I eyed the fashionable pair, " The Republic still lives."

It is, however, with the foreign embassies at Washington, that the genuine aristocratic spirit still holds its normal own ; and when I lately received an invitation from a certain convivial diplomatist of the Set to be one of a select party of distinguished gentlemen at his residence on a certain evening, I felt that there was still an available balm in Gilead. Arriving in the rooms shortly before ten o'clock, I found seven middle-aged gentlemen in cambric ruffles and scratch-wigs assembled around the wine-table, all pledging the health of the Venerable Gammon, who had come up from Mugville expressly to be present. There was the French Marquis Non Puebla, on a visit to this country to search for traces of one of the lost gravies of Apicius ; Milord Gurgle, who had been deputed to convey to New York a pair of Southdown sheep, presented by the Zoölogical Gardens to Central Park ; the Honorable Peter Pidger, who had once been to Europe to negotiate the sale of some railroad stock ; the Ambassador in person ; and three other respectable persons with no names, whose sole duty it was to indorse the Ambassador whenever he said anything about " dat signeeficant commencement of dees war at Bool Run." But the greatest of them all, my boy, was the Venerable Gammon, who smiled fatly as they drank his health, and emptied his own crystal with a soft benignity which seemed to consecrate that brand of liquor forever.

" My friends," says the Venerable Gammon, waving an

THIRD SERIES. 161

unctuous hand around the board in a manner to confer
blessings on the very nutcrackers, — " my friends, I accept
the honor for my country, and not for myself. Your
countries bask in the sunshine of a powerful peace, while
mine grows weak in despotic war. But do not spit upon
us, my friends ; do not crush us. We will do whatever
you want us to do. War," says the Venerable Gammon,
beaming thoughtfully at the nearest wine-cooler, — " war
may be called the temporary weakness of a young country
like ours ; and if we learn not to value peace more than
war as we grow older, it will only be because we do not
learn to value war less than peace as we advance to riper
years."

Then all the respectable middle-aged gentlemen nudged
each other to notice *that ;* and the Honorable Peter Pidger
observed, in an undertone, to Milord Gurgle, that if the
Government was only guided by such wisdom as that, the
country might yet hope for favor from Europe.

" Ah ! " says the Ambassador, reflectively, " I cannot
help to recollect dat signeeficant commencement of dees
war at Bool Run."

Whereupon the three middle-aged gentlemen with no
names nodded meaningly to each other, and murmured,
in pitying chorus :

" Ah, yes indeed."

As I rode home to my hotel that night, my boy, and
reflected upon the polished observations I had listened to,
it seemed to me that Europe must indeed be superior to a
weak young country like ours, and that Secretary Seward
was but showing a proper respect for the dignity of mon-
archies in yielding gracefully to them whatever they

162 ORPHEUS C. KERR PAPERS.

asked, and establishing in American history its first creation of knighthood, under the title of Sir Render. The Sword of '76 would have refused the accolade ; but that of '63 is of a milder temper.

On Wednesday, as I strolled lazily along the shore of Awlkyet River, listlessly tossing pebbles into the placid stream, and paying no attention to any visible object save the severed branches of trees and broken fragments of artillery-wheels which occasionally barred my progress, a Mackerel picket suddenly touched me on the shoulder, and says he, in a whisper, —

" You mustn't be chucking stones into that air water, or you'll wake up the Captain which is asleep."

I glanced askance at him from under my vizor, and says I, " What Captain, my trooper ? "

" Why," says he, " the Captain of the Blockade, over yonder."

I looked in the direction indicated by his finger, my boy, and beheld the sloop-of-war Morpheus at anchor near a small inlet leading to the river from the up-country.

" Why, my Union champion," says I, wonderingly, "I should like to know at what time the Captain makes it a practice to retire ? "

" Ah ! " says the Mackerel picket, leaning upon his musket, and looking dreamily over the water, " he's all the time retiring — he's been put upon the ' Retired ' list."

Here was a man, my boy, an American, like you or me, brought up in a country where education is free to all, and yet he had no clearer idea of the functions of our

THIRD SERIES. 163

Naval Retiring Board than such as happened to be suggested to his instinct by what he could see of the national blockade service !

Yours, amazedly,

ORPHEUS C. KERR.

LETTER XCVII.

INTRODUCING THE GREAT MORAL EXHIBITION OF THE "EFFIGYNIA," GLANCING AT A FOURTH NEW MACKEREL GENERAL, AND SHOWING HOW THE PRESIDENT'S DRAFT ON ACCOMAC WAS PROTESTED AT SIGHT.

WASHINGTON, D. C., July 10th, 1863.

As I wax numerous in exciting years, my boy, and observe more and more of the long-headed and strategic manner in which our wealthy but distracted country prosecutes the Restoration of the Union, the stronger grows my belief that, inasmuch as the way of the transgressor is hard, the way of the well-doer is inexpressibly " soft." Each day of the present national crisis brings fresh evidence of the exceedingly soft character of the policy by which our upright government would turn to nought the wrathful devices of its enemies, and further demonstrates the vast difference existing between everything upright and anything downright. We discomfit the well-known Southern Confederacy, at every turn, my boy, — we discomfit it at every turn ; but, the trouble is, we keep turning all the time, like a Thomas Cat after his tail, constantly believing that we are approaching the end, but never quite reaching it.

Fearing lest I should become metaphysical if I pursued this train of thought any farther, — thereby encroaching upon the bottomless province of the Awful and Unfathom-

THIRD SERIES. **165**

able German mind, which rejoices gloomily in the solemn investigation of all that verges upon muddled abstraction ; — fearing lest I should become thus erudite, profound, and snuffily unintelligible, my boy, I repress my morbid inclination to take a funereal canter into abstruse speculation on the elephants of thought, and digress from theory to fact.

This city, which is destined to become in time another Waterloo in the sense of offering everything drinkable in lieu of water, presents but very little except bar-rooms in the way of entertainment just now. Hence, my boy, we can properly appreciate the " Effigynia," as it is classically called, which a thoughtful yellow-vested chap of much breastpin, from Pequog, has just opened on Pennsylvania Avenue. According to advertisement, " this chaste and plastic exhibition consists of wax effigies of the five successive Generals of the Mackerel Brigade, with the peculiar personalities of each one, and the superiority of each over the other, unmistakably stamped on the forms and features of each ! " Being a moral man, my boy, and much addicted to entertainments which differ from the prevailing drama of the day in obviating the necessity for steadily blushing, I repaired to the Effigynia the other evening and was much edified by the spectacle presented. Five mirrors standing at different angles with a wax figure of the first General of the Mackerel Brigade, were made each to reflect said figure ; and I could not help feeling, my boy, that the likenesses were correct. I saw before me the counterfeit presentments of the five soldiers who had successively arisen to the highest Mackerel Command, and I found myself wondering how many more

166 ORPHEUS C. KERR PAPERS.

mirrors the exhibition would need before the war came to a head — containing brains.

It was on Tuesday morning that I ascended majestically to the slanting roof of my Gothic steed, the sagacious Pegasus, and moved perceptibly across Long Bridge once more, toward the camp of the Mackerel Brigade. It is worthy of note, my boy, that the architectural animal in question has greatly improved of late upon a diet of condemned straw hats, and now trots an hour in sixty minutes with the greatest ease of manner. An occasional cough but adds to the melancholy interest of his funereal cast of countenance; and as his head grows more and more vivid in its resemblance to an infant's coffin, his whole effect deepens in its churchliness and sepulchral solemnity.

As I neared the national head-quarters, the Mackerel Surgeon-General saluted me, and I observed that he kept his glance dreamily fixed upon the Gothic Pegasus.

" As I gaze upon that bony fabric," says he, biting a piece of calamus in soft professional abstraction, — " as I gaze upon that fleet skeleton you bestride, I cannot help thinking that Rule Britannia is frequently right in speaking of a horse as an 'oss; though she may use a superfluous ' s ' in the word. You see," says the surgeon, pausing to take a gray powder, and to try his lancet on his left thumb-nail, — " you see, the classical term ' os ' signifies bone; and as bone is the prevailing aspect of your present charger, he might be termed an ' 'os ' without violence to the lingual proprieties."

I have always suspected this surgeon, my boy, of being an accursed secessionist in disguise, and now I feel confi-

THIRD SERIES. **167**

dent that he would not hesitate, if opportunity offered, to carry his fiendish affection for the well-known Southern Confederacy to the extent of actually differing with me upon some point in conversation. In such times as these, my boy, there can be no middle ground for a man; he must either be heart and soul with his country's murderous foes, or ready to agree entirely with me in anything I may say or think. God save the Republic!

Upon arriving at a locality, which I refrain from naming, lest I should thereby betray my beloved country or make a mistake in spelling, I found the venerable and spectacled veterans of the thrice-valorous Mackerel Brigade just returned from a spirited pursuit of certain regiments of disreputable Confederacies who were stealing farms on the outskirts of Paris. These Confederacies had even penetrated into storied Accomac, and removed everything they found upon the farms there except the mortgages. Hence the demand upon the aged and unconquerable Mackerel Brigade for an immediate walk in that direction, and there they had gone by the most circuitous and profoundly strategical route afforded by the county maps. General John Smith, the latest edition of Mackerel Commander, gave leadership of his advance guard to Captain Villiam Brown, and immediately five-and-twenty inflamed reporters frantically telegraphed to as many excellent and reliable morning journals, that all the thieving Confederacies were about to be bagged, and that all the revolting details would be given in our next issue. It was toward evening, my boy, when Captain Villiam Brown, mounted upon his geometrical steed, Euclid, came riding up to the advanced head-quarters of the new general to report results.

8

168   ORPHEUS C. KERR PAPERS.

"Well, young man," says the General, with Spartan equanimity, "have we bagged the enemies of human freedom?"

Villiam looked up from the demijohn under the table, upon which he had been earnestly gazing, and says he, "No, sire; but the very next thing to bagging them has occurred."

"Relate the tale," says the General, with dignity.

"Why," says Villiam, "instead of our bagging them, they have been sacking us."

It is a remarkable and beautiful peculiarity of our flexible language, my boy, that its semi-syno-nymical effects permit the transmission of trying intelligence in terms of soothing similarity to those which might have been employed had the news been more felicitous. Thus are we let down easily from pride to humiliation, and spared much intervening agony of soul.

So the Mackerel Brigade turned their gleaming old spectacles once more in the direction of our National Capital, and are again a characteristic of the landscape enclosing Washington. Further consummate strategy is postponed for a time on account of the weather, which has become villanously hot through the fanatical machinations of the insidious Black Republicans. Thus are Greeley, Beecher, Wendell Phillips, and their deluded followers weakening the military arm of the government and endeavoring to obtain fat contracts for worthless fans!

Methinks I hear you ask, "Has the new general of the Mackerel Brigade made a failure, after all the credit the public have given him for superiority over his predecessors?"

THIRD SERIES. 169

Far be it from me to judge hastily, but I may be permitted to say, my boy, — I may be permitted to say, that men in the military line have this point in common with men in a mercantile business; by obtaining too much on credit at the start, they are very apt to make bad failures, leaving nothing but their lie-abilities for the consolation of those who trusted them.

Upon reaching the Mackerel camp, and exchanging festive salutations with Captain Bob Shorty, who was trying to purchase the dressed skin of a handsome copperhead snake from Corporal Veller, of the California Reserve, to use as a sword-belt, — after exchanging salutations, I repaired to the tent of the chaplain, to witness the marriage of one of the younger Mackerels to a pretty Shenandoah belle. As the happy pair stood before the drum to be made wife and man, I noticed that the bride's rosy cheeks paled like a sunset under the twilight, until the languishing stars of her eyes shone only upon snow.

And now, my boy, let me say a few words respecting the recent attempted draft of Abe L. bodied men in thrice-famous Accomac, and the freedom-loving spirit in which it was met by the Sovereign People. With a prescient view to being amply prepared for an overwhelming assault upon combined Europe, which is shortly to be made by Secretary Seward and the muscular United States of America, our Uncle Abe ordered a draft of Accomackians to be made at once. Hereupon the Accomac " Morning Dog," an excellent daily journal, indulged in a high-minded editorial on the fiendish proclivities of the Governor of Accomac, and the general wildness of all the Accomackians to be drafted if he would let them. With

170   ORPHEUS C. KERR PAPERS.

great promptness, that admirable palladium of human freedom, the " Evening Cat," avowed that it spit upon the gubernatorial scurrility of its growling contemporary ; that it deprecated mob violence and trusted that no mob would resist the draft ; but could not help believing that the Sovereign People might possibly arise in their majesty and occasion a speedy funeral in the family of the editor-in-chief of the venomous and intolerable " Morning Dog."

It was at 10 o'clock A. M., my boy, when the drafting commenced in Accomac, and in half an hour thereafter the Sovereign People, consisting of several gentlemen from Ireland, were asserting the dignity of a free community in a manner worthy of the sacred cause of Emigration. It is a touching fact, my boy, — a touching and æsthetical fact, that the American people are ever so able to find foreign champions to protect their freedom from governmental infringement that they seldom have occasion to do any fighting for it themselves.   .

The Sovereign People of Accomac, being fully aroused and slightly inebriated, proceeded to vindicate the majesty of our excellent national Democratic Organization by relieving a bloated aristocracy of their watches and loose change, ransacking sundry private residences on account of the great draft of their chimneys, and performing other awe-inspiring acts of rude majesty, equally well calculated to evince a freeborn people's distaste for despotism. Furthermore, the Sovereign People fearlessly attacked a large and aristocratic Hospital, beating many of the patients to death ; for, by some corrupt chicanery, these patients were barefacedly exempted from the Conscription which bore so heavily upon the down-trodden and

THIRD SERIES. 171

healthy poor man. The "Evening Cat," in a special edition, was genial enough to express a hope that "the outraged people now muttering ominously in the air," would not burst upon the office and editor of the "Morning Dog" with *too* much just fury; whereupon the incensed Sovereign People said that, bo ja'bers, they'd come mighty near forgetting that entirely; and forthwith proceeded to stone the office of the "Dog" until the hasty discharge of an ink-stand from one of the upper windows thereof induced them to make a hasty change of base.

Without indulging in farther details, suffice it to say that the Sovereign People finally desisted from their struggle for liberty upon being satisfied that no more watches, purses, nor sick despots were to be got at conveniently, and the "Evening Cat" came out in a spirited article in favor of an immediate war with France.

How grateful should it be to our national pride, my boy, that even the stranger that is within our gates feels inspired by the very atmosphere with a jealous, a fighting love for perfect freedom, — especially if said gates be those of a State prison.

Yours, exuberantly,

ORPHEUS C. KERR.

LETTER XCVIII.

RECOUNTING A CHASTE "RECONSTRUCTION" ANECDOTE OF THE SIXTH WARD, AND DIVULGING CAPTAIN VILLIAM BBOWN'S INGENIOUS ALPHABETICAL EXPERIMENT WITH COMPANY THREE.

WASHINGTON, D. C., Sept. 25th, 1863.

IT is a high-moral idea of poets, congressmen, and the writers for our improving weekly journals of exciting romance, my boy, that it is a noble and majestic thing to feel warmly for one's country; but when the thermometer stands at 90 in the shade, and we join with our fellow-beings in shedding tears from the tops of our foreheads, I find my disinterested patriotism fully equal to the self-abnegation of the remark, that I had rather be cool than be President. Our brethren are already in the field; why stand we here idle? Is ice so dear, or peace so sweet as to be purchased at the price of chains and slavery? Forbid it, Almighty Dollars! I know not what other gentlemen would have; but as for me, give me liberty, or give me a fan. Thus, my boy, after the manner of the departed Patrick Henry, did I expose myself to the conservative Kentucky chap, as we stood panting together in the vestibule of the Treasury Buildings the other day; and says he:

"The loyal State of Kentucky, of which I am a part, has no objections to warm weather in the summer-time; provided it is not indorsed by the fanatical Black Repub-

(172)

THIRD SERIES. 173

licans. Warm weather," says the conservative Kentucky chap, thoughtfully, " is of much service to the old rye crop of Kentucky ; but Kentucky would forego even her old rye, rather than see retarded the movements of that army whose constitutional duty it is to restore the Union — not reconstruct it."

The regular list of dead idiots for this year being not quite full yet, my boy, there are still persons living who can perceive no very immense difference between Restoring the Union and Reconstructing the Union ; which reminds me of a chaste little incident that once occurred in the Sixth Ward.

A highly-respectable liquor-selling chap, of enlarged stomach and overwhelming shirt-collar, having just been elected Alderman, through the influence of his excellent moral character, and about two thousand dollars judiciously invested in Irishmen, gave a fashionable party to celebrate this triumph of the purity of elections, and invited about two-thirds of the Fire Department to bring their wives and sweethearts. Promptly at nine o'clock, two Hose Companies, of unblemished reputations for noise, four Engine Associations noted for saving one pine table from the devouring element to every two Brussels carpets they ruined with water, three Hook-and-Ladder Societies greatly distinguished for climbing into the third-story windows of the building two doors from the burning domicil, and an equivalent number of the cotton-hearted women of America, were on hand in the aldermanic drawing-rooms. The new public dignitary received them all with that exquisite blandness of demeanor which is so becoming to

174 ORPHEUS C. KERR PAPERS.

great men who have just made a rush from obscurity:
and says he, —

"Make yourselves at home now, boys, only don't spit
on the carpet. If there's a fire while the swarry is goin'
on, I'll let the old woman listen for the district and announce it from the airy. We'll keep the winders up,
and when the hall-bell rings, you fellers as has to leave,
can just slip down onto the front stoop without breaking
up the entire swarry."

Here the large-hearted aldermanic chap was called
hastily downstairs to attend the bar, several army officers
having just arrived in the ward, and the "swarry" commenced as merrily as a fire in a carpenter's shop. It set
in for a heavy dance at about eleven o'clock, and then
were seen as many elaborate verses in the poetry of motion, as any pair of eyes could wish to enjoy. "Fifty's"
foreman, who danced with a very pretty dotted muslin,
produced a very striking and picturesque effect by rolling
his inexpressibles up over his boots, and giving a life-like
imitation of the working of an engine with his heels and
toes; whereupon the assistant foreman of "Thirty's
Truck" suddenly threw off his dress-coat and appeared in
full red shirt, simultaneously striking into a fine, artistic
shuffle, intended to imitate the hauling-in and reeling-up
of the wet hose after a conflagration. These and other
graceful novelties were greatly admired by the ladies,
each of whom said so many spicy and spiteful things
about the other's bare arms and forward manners, that
a stranger might have taken them all for the very cream
of Fifth Avenue or any other Best Society.

It was about midnight when "Fifty's" foreman, grow-

THIRD SERIES. 175

ing reckless with the passionate splendors of excitement, scuffled away with his flushed dotted muslin to a luxurious chintz sofa near one of the windows, and intemperately whispered in her ear, "Miss Perkins, it were madness for me longer to conceal my insanity, and to remain silent would but render me speechless. Here let me lay my heart and trumpet at your feet, and " —

She had fainted ! Ay, sir, swooned !

Instantly the whole brilliant saloon was in confusion ; the dancing ceased, the dust commenced to settle, and the assistant foreman of " Thirty's Truck " was seen to put on his coat.

" Bring your hose here, quick, and play on her face ! " shouted " Fifty's " foreman, half-crazed by what he had done. But the dotted muslin's mother now clutched her in her arms, and says she, " Let's get her into the dressing-chamber, and somebody bring a little sally wolatile."

Here another dowager seized an arm of the fainting girl, and the two bore her tenderly into the retiring-room, followed by some two or three sympathizing young ladies. And now, my boy, it becomes my delicate duty to hastily sketch a scene which the masculine pen cannot too carefully touch upon. It being one of the principles of woman's nature that some relaxations must be admitted in her toilet before she can revive from syncope, the second dowager commenced to relieve the fainting fair one of such articles of fashionable addenda as might retard her recovery. She took off her side-curls and back-hair and laid them upon a table ; with great care she removed her upper teeth and placed them upon a chair ; softly wetting a corner of her handkerchief in her mouth she effect-

8*

ually wiped away the eyebrows and a part of the cheek of the young sufferer; and she was proceeding to make other dissections which I shall dismiss with the remark that they are merely matters of form, when the patient gave a gentle sigh as she rested in her mother's arms, and says the mother to the dowager : —

"There, Mrs. Jobbins, I guess you needn't do any more." Mrs. Jobbins gave a sagacious look at the patient, and says she :

"Very true, mem; she is getting better. It wont take us many minutes to reconstruct her."

"I beg your parding, Mrs. Jobbins," says the maternal, shaking her cap, — "I beg your parding Mrs. Jobbins; but your language is ineddicated, highly; you should say ' restore' her."

Mrs. Jobbins straightened herself up, with a glare, and says she : "Perhaps, mem, you can teach *me* eddication, and my own daughter a teacher these two years in the public schools! The ideor! I repeat it — to reconstruct her — put her together again."

"Restore," says the maternal, savagely.

"Reconstruct!" screamed Mrs. Jobbins.

"You're a artful, ignorant old copperhead!" howled the maternal, dropping her daughter's head upon the floor.

"And you're a spiteful, stuck-up, toothless old — ab'litionist!!" yelled the dowager, stamping until her snuff-box hopped out of her pocket.

Drawn to the room by the noise, a hard old nut, a retired foreman of old "Sixty," stuck his head in at the

THIRD SERIES. 177

door, and says he : "What are you old fools scrimmaging about ? You're keeping the swarry back."

Both the old ladies made at him at once to know which, in his opinion, was the right word, — 'Reconstruct,' or ' Restore ? '

The old nut took a thoughtful bite of tobacco, and says he: Let the girl herself tell you when she *revives*."

Revive was the word, my boy ; and while the old women were quarrelling over the two terms aforesaid, poor nature got tired of waiting, and realized the right one in action for herself. The girl revived without being either restored, or reconstructed.

And thus, my boy, I sometimes think, that, whilst noisy old political grannies are quarrelling as to whether the Union shall be Restored, or Reconstructed, the fainting young Union will suddenly revive of itself. At any rate, it bids fair to have plenty of time to do so.

In a recent letter I noted the return of the main body of the invincible and time-honored Mackerel Brigade to what may be termed the place of its military birth ; but I did not, nor can I, describe justly the many touching incidents of the retrogression. Once more, my boy, does this standard national martial organization find itself on the right side of Awlkuyet River, and many a sensitive Mackerel, as he gazes through his tear-dimmed spectacles upon the surrounding scenery of his youth, fancies himself a boy again, and newly experiences in all his muscles that tingling sensation which, in the full-blooded lad, equally follows a public compliment and a private flogging. As the gory and venerable Brigade wound slowly back

178   ORPHEUS C. KERR PAPERS.

into the well-known fields rendered historically famous for making Washington safe, one very ancient Mackerel grounded his musket by the roadside, took off his spectacles, looked with deep emotion upon the scenes of his early years, and says he to another Mackerel: —

"Thank Heaven! we have at last reached the end of the war."

The other Mackerel paused in his work of cracking an army biscuit between two rocks, and says he: "Which end do you mean, Sammy?"

"Why," says Sammy, "the end we commenced at."

Could it be possible, my boy, that there was a serious and profound truth in that unconsidered Mackerel remark? If so, we are indeed approaching the beginning of the war, and there is rather less of Mars than of Grand-Ma's in the management of the Virginia campaign.

But why should my pen linger upon this monotonous theme, when the grim Fort Piano on Duck Lake, and the ancient city of Paris on the nether shore thereof, are being besieged on all sides by the Mackerel iron-plated patent squadron under the hoary Rear Admiral Head, and the Mackerel contingent and Orange County Howitzers under Captains Samyule Sa-mith and Villiam Brown. Several times, my boy, has Fort Piano been entirely destroyed and taken by all our excellent and reliable morning journals, the columns of American newspapers being led on to victory — or leaded on to victory — with rather more ease than a dozen times as many columns of any troops in the world; but, inasmuch as the unseemly but well-known Southern Confederacy still keeps store there, it has been deemed proper to make

THIRD SERIES. 179

another iron-clad experiment in that salubrious vicinity. This time, however, the army takes part in the effort, as well as the navy, and Captain Samyule Sa-mith, with the Orange County Howitzers, bombards the atmosphere from the banks of the Lake, whilst the aged Rear Admiral Head, with his iron-plated squadron, performs fiery antics upon the briny element.

The sailing of the squadron inside the bar was a beautiful sight, and was witnessed by a couple of English and French consuls who had come down to the banks of Duck Lake to see if they could recognize the Confederacy at that distance. First advanced Rear Admiral Head's flagship monitor, the "Shockingbadhat;" followed in close order by the "Aitch," the "Yew," the "Em," the "Bee," the "You" and the "Gee."

And now, my boy, you may probably imagine that I am about to relate, with Homeric fervor and the graphic eloquence of Tacitus, how the Mackerel Squadron poured whole foundries of shot and shell into Fort Piano; and how the Orange County Howitzers rained Greek Fire (Irish whiskey) into all the basement windows of Paris; but I have various reasons for doing nothing of the kind, inasmuch as the War Department does not desire that the enemy should be prematurely informed of the capture of the Fort and City. Suffice it to say, that everything is progressing favorably, though recent heavy rains have greatly incommoded such of the land forces as are not supplied with umbrellas.

I think, however, my boy, that I may venture to describe Captain Villiam Brown's alphabetical experiment with Company 3, Regiment 5, which constitutes the pres-

180

ORPHEUS C. KERR PAPERS.

ent Mackerel reserve on the edge of the Lake. Villiam having heard of Jeff. Davis's experiment with his regiment in Mexico, when he formed it into a V shape to receive a cavalry charge, resolved to give his regiment that shape for the purpose of a roundabout sally upon Fort Piano from the rear, or land side.

" Comrades," says Villiam, impressively, " V stands for Victory, Vengeance and Vashington, and I desire you to take its shape."

The Mackerels formed themselves into a V, my boy; but when Villiam gallantly retired behind a tree to be out of the way, and gave the order " Forward — double-quick, — march ! " Sergeant O'Pake modestly stood out of the ranks, and says he:

" Of course *you* will go ahead of us, Captain ? "

" Ha ! " says Villiam, haughtily, " why ? "

" Oh ! " says the sergeant, " V., you know, always follows U."

Villiam was lost in thought for a moment, my boy, and then says he : " That's true, Sergeant ; and as U never comes until after T, we'll defer that ere charge for the present."

Incidents of this kind are but common in this war between brethren, which is so abhorrent to Democrats and the high-moral members of the church.

Hoping, my boy, that, by relating the success of Rear Admiral Head and Captain Samyule Sa-mith in my next, I may add two more illustrious names to the list of candidates for the Presidency in 1865, I remain,

Yours, electorally,

ORPHEUS C. KERR.

LETTER XCIX.

IN WHICH OUR CORRESPONDENT IS BETRAYED INTO ARGUMENT; BUT
RECOVERS IN TIME TO GIVE US THE USUAL CHRISTMAS SONG AND
STORY OF THE RENOWNED BRIGADE.

WASHINGTON, D. C., Dec. 27th, 1863.

ANOTHER Christmas finds our great stragetic country in
the toils of war, my boy, and the chiming of the bells is lost
in the roar of ingenious artillery. Where blazes the yule
log that misses not at least one manly form from its genial
ring of quivering Christmas light; and where hangs the
mistletoe bough beneath which at least one gentle, womanly heart beats not the quicker with fond thoughts of
the lad whose first kiss upon her half-reluctant lips was destined to burn in future there as her keepsake from a hero?
Dear old Christmas! rich to memory in all the simple joys
and fond, familiar sanctities of home, thou comest sadly
upon me in my exile with the iron men of war, the waxen
men of politics; and though I hail thee merry for thy
cheery evergreens, God knows it is thy snow that presses
nearest to my heart. But a truce to sentiment, my boy,
when the most sentimental object I have seen for a week is
the Conservative Kentucky Chap, whose imbibing method
of celebrating the approach of Christmas invariably leads
him into disquisitions upon the wrongs of the heroic White
Man. On Tuesday, as we took Richmond together,

(181)

182 ORPHEUS C. KERR PAPERS.

with the least bit of sugar in the world, he leaned heavily upon me, and says he:

" The ancient State of Kentucky, of which I am a part, is growing sick at the stomach to see how the Black Man is continually being raised above the White Man ; and Kentucky demands to be immediately informed whether or no this war is to be prosecuted in future for the White Man ? "

" For the White Man," my boy, he said ; " for the White Man ! "

And was he not right ? The noble being to whom he alluded is certainly richly justified in a very high pitch of pride over the gratifying fact, that his natural complexion is considerably whiter than anything at all darker. In the abstract, my boy, it is not a positive white, and its general hue, if characteristic of a napkin would hardly enable that napkin to pass muster at the feast of an Apicius or a Lamia ; but, as compared with other complexions, it is properly colorless, and strikes the eye very pleasantly when regarded by a single person in a mirror. So highly, indeed, do many possessors of this complexion admire its prevailing whiteness, that they perform their ablutions with an artistic design to leave here and there certain picturesque streaks of delicate shading, thereby causing the whiteness of the intervening spots to appear all the more dazzling. Others, again, religiously refrain from water outwardly as well as inwardly, for the apparent purpose of incrusting the purity of their valuable complexion in a protecting coat ; thus preserving it from any possible bad effect of the sun. Still others, my boy, continue to practise the thorough ablution of the ancients, but signally

THIRD SERIES.

succeed in throwing out the whiteness of the level of their faces in excellent relief, by adopting measures to implant a contrasting red on the tips of their noses. And a fourth class, having an eye to beauties of a White background for the exhibition of chaste neutral tints, incur the frequent freckle and the graceful pimple with great judgment and taste.

Considering the character of the White face with due profundity of thought, my boy, I am led to regard it as a canvas, expressly intended by nature to receive quick and vivid paintings of all the virtues ; and so nicely adapted to the least of humanity's desires, that the woman who has no virtues to limn themselves thereon, may yet paint it to suit herself.

This cannot be said of the Black skin, my boy. Upon that the beautiful virtue of Modesty cannot paint itself in a blush when its owner is detected in the act of taking a bribe ; nor is it susceptible of that beautiful sunset-tint which the genial merit of being able to punish four bottles at a sitting delights to leave upon a face of Caucasian extraction. It is even incapable of receiving those exquisite sub-ocular shades which adorn a White face after an evening's innocent enjoyment at the Club, and it fails signally to absorb the delicate tint of yellow not unfrequently perceptible near the outer corners of the busy dental department of the tobacconizing White man's physiognomy.

Taking all these facts into calculation, my boy, it is plainly evident that the variously-ornamented White skin is an article much superior to the Black, and certainly designates its wearers as beings intended to move in nothing but the highest natural circles.

184   ORPHEUS C. KERR PAPERS.

Such being the case, we cannot blame the White Man
for entertaining a wholesome contempt and loathing for
the Black Man ; and the truly hearty manner in which
many of our more pallid fellow-countrymen breathe ingenious execrations whenever the latter is mentioned, may
be accepted as a beautiful and touching proof that they
appreciate God's benignity in giving them a superiority
of skin; even though He may have seen best, in His
infinite wisdom, to leave them occasionally without
brains.

Having been informed that the ancient and spectacled
Mackerel Brigade had returned from its monthly walk
toward the well-known and starving Southern Confederacy,
I ascended to the roof of my architectural steed, the Gothic
Pegasus, on Thursday morn, my boy, and galloped slowly
to the stamping ground of the unconquerable veterans.
Let me pass over the events of the day in camp, when the
sedentary warriors, whom it is my glory to celebrate,
were reviewed after the manner of Napoleon's Old Guard.
Let me pass over this, and come directly to Christmas Eve,
and the literary entertainment in the Mackerel Chaplain's
tent. Captains Villiam Brown, Bob Shorty, Samyule
Sa-mith, a young reporter from Olympus, the Chaplain,
and myself, were the members of the party, and we sat
round a camp-table with two lanterns swinging right over
the bottles.

Rear Admiral Head shortly came in ; and when the
Olympian reporter was requested to open the intellectual
festival with a song, he complimented the iron-plated
branch of the service with

THIRD SERIES. **185**

"THE BOATSWAIN'S CALL.

I.

"THE lights upon the river's brink
  In constellation bright,
- Are winking down upon the tide
  That twinkles through the night;
When in a gayly dancing skiff
  The boatswain leaves his ship,
And as his oars a moment cease
  Within the flood to dip,
          He winds his call,
          The boatswain's cheery call.

II.

"A maiden stands upon the shore,
  Where land and ocean meet,
And breakers cast their pearly gifts
  In homage at her feet;
While through the causeway of the night
  She gazes o'er the sea,
To where a stately frigate rides
  In lonely majesty,
          And waits the call,
          The gallant boatswain's call.

III.

"'Oh! tarry not, my boatswain bold,'
  Her parted lips would say;
But when the heart is vexed with doubt,
  The soul can only pray;
And sorely doubtful is the maid,
  Till on her ear there falls
The music of the merriest,
  The clearest, best of calls —
          A winding call,
          Her faithful boatswain's call.

IV.

" A shining keel is on the sand,
 The oars are laid aside,
And to the shore the sailor leaps
 To greet his chosen bride;
His arms about her waist are thrown,
 And through her rosy lips
He breathes a dainty boatswain's call,
 Though not the call of ships;
   But Cupid's call,
   The boatswain Cupid's call.

V.

" And when the moon has drawn a path
 Of light upon the sea,
A skiff is floating o'er the deep,
 To where a frigate free
Is nestled in the ocean's breast,
 With all her canvas furled;
Though ere the morn makes Hesper blush
 Upon a waking world,
   ' Make sail, men, all!'
   Will round the boatswain's call.

VI.

" A shadow follows in her wake,
 And, through its depths is seen
The figure of a widowed wife
 Upon the shore of green;
And ever as the tempest moans
 Above the mocking wave,
A sound is wafted to her ears
 From out a moving grave,—
   A boatswain's call,
   A ghostly boatswain's call."

THIRD SERIES. **187**

At the termination of the last stave, Captain Villiam Brown cleared his throat, and says he, —

" As our friend has commenced the services with melody, I will proceed to keep the feeble intellecks of this assemblage excited with a terrifying moral ghost tale which the Dickens himself might grow pale under. It was sent to me," says Villiain, majestically, " by a former writer for the Track Society, and reflects much credit upon the literary resources of the United States of America."

Whereupon, Villiam took some sheets of paper from his breast-pocket, my boy, and introduced

" MR. PEPPER'S GHOST.

" In the heart of a great city, whose corruption and wickedness in continually growing larger and richer, were evident to every smaller, and, consequently, more pious, town on the globe, dwelt a shamefully rich banker, named Pursimmons, who, notwithstanding his vile and enormous wealth, had refused to give it all to the virtuous poor. That it was utterly impossible for such a man to enter the Kingdom of Heaven need not be told ; since we all know that honest poverty, alone, can hope for such entrance ; and as poverty covers at least three-fourths of the human race, and is invariably honest, according to its own touching account, there is likely to be enough of it to fill up all the standing room in Paradise, leaving no space for even the repentant wretch of a millionaire. Hence, it naturally follows, that old Pursimmons was miserable, with all his wealth. In fact, a slim, black-dressed gentleman of

188   ORPHEUS C. KERR PAPERS.

much spectacles and severe countenance, who had vainly
solicited him to subscribe for ten thousand extra-gilt copies
of his new work on ' The Relation of Sunday Schools
with the Moral Organism of Normal Creation,' to be sent
to the starving heathen of the Choctaw Nation, was heard
to remark, emphatically, that he would rather be 'a
ignorant but religious slave in the desert of Sahara, my
brethren, than that godless man with all his filthy lucre.'
Therefore, old Pursimmons *must* have been a continual
prey to the most horrible twinges of guilty conscience that
any one man, in the abundant excess of his own spiritual
serenity, ever attributed to another of different views.
All the year did this unhappy but fleshy old man sin
against everything that is poor and pious by accepting
all — ay, all! — the profits his business was iniquitous
enough to produce ; and even rode in a carriage ; though
hundreds of noble-hearted Irishmen in the honest brick
and mortar business had to walk, — ay, walk ! — becoming so terribly exhausted thereby as to be invariably
compelled to pause for rest, on their way home, at some
humble liquor establishment.   When Christmas Eve came
round, it found this enemy of his race meanly retiring to
bed, instead of scouring the highways and byways in
search of reduced private families who might at that very
moment be despairingly praying to have his last cent at
their disposal.   A man so thoroughly bad could not fail
to be a pitiable coward, and it is not at all surprising that
he was somewhat startled to suddenly perceive, between
himself and his scandalously-comfortable bed, Mr. Pepper's
Ghost ! — the very same ghost once in full blow at all our
moral temples of the drama.   ' Unreal Novelty !' ex-

THIRD SERIES. 189

claimed old Pursimmons, chewing the strings of his night-cap, 'hie thee away to thy native footlights ; or, if thou must keep somebody awake all night, betake thee to some great tragedian when Shakspeare's murder lies heavy on his soul.' Mr. Pepper's Ghost winked with great archness as it replied : " Ghosts have no terrors for the sons of Thespis, who are even merry with a ghost — of a chance to get their salaries. My mission is to you, to whom I must a wholesome lesson teach. Behold ! '

" The spirit waved its hand, and lo ! one whole side of the vile banker's chamber fell magically away, disclosing to view a room entirely destitute of velvet carpet and pictures by the Old Masters. On a sofa reclined a middle-aged young girl, whose poor dress of braidless merino was so inclemently low in the neck as to suggest for its down-trodden wearer a purse too scanty to procure a sufficiency of material. The daughter of penury had just reached the hundred and fifty-second exciting page of the cheap but excellent work of fiction she was reading, when a door opened and her crushed husband entered, smoking his meerschaum.

" ' Old boy,' said the Ghost, ' do you remember that man ? '

" ' Yes,' responded the banker, sadly ; 'he came to me yesterday for some money to keep him from starvation ; and as he would not take ' greenbacks,' I did not help him.'

" ' Listen,' said the Ghost.

" The crushed husband threw himself into a chair which was not covered with Solferino satin, and ate a peanut.

" ' Well, what luck ? ' asked the daughter of penury.

190 ORPHEUS C. KERR PAPERS.

" ' Old Pursimmons has refused, and I ' —

" ' And you !! ' —

" ' Must ' —

" ' Must ? ' —

" ' *Support myself ! ! !* '

" It was too much. The daughter of penury fainted, the crushed husband sniffed aloud, and the landlady knocked at the door for the week's board.

" As this agonizing picture of human misery faded away, old Pursimmons turned with an inaudible groan to Mr. Pepper's Ghost:

" ' And I,' said he, — ' and I am the cause of this woe ? '

" The spectre silently and solemnly nodded an awful affirmative, and waved its hand for another scene.

" This time, the presentment was the interior of a shop, around which were shelves full of boxes containing all sorts of delicious little gaiters, ties, slippers, bootees and kid pumps, whilst the same kind of articles hung suspended from various hooks and pegs on the wall. On a bench in one corner of this shop, busily working upon a dainty pink satin gaiter-boot, was a narrow young man of pensive countenance, weak eyes, pink nose and an intellectual head of hair, in a workman's paper cap manufactured from an admirable weekly journal of romance.

" As the deeply-affected banker gazed upon this figure, he sorrowfully murmured : ' Ah! that is the deep-voiced youth who last week desired of me five hundred dollars to insure the publication of his new novel of Fashionable Life, which was destined to instantly sweep Dickens, Victor Hugo, Thackeray, and other demoralizing writers from the field of literature.'

THIRD SERIES. 191

" ' Yes!' said Mr. Pepper's Ghost, severely ; ' and your miserly refusal to aid struggling genius with your miserable wealth has driven a giant intellect into the ladies' shoemaking business. In which,' added the spectre, ' I am bound to say, that he is doing tolerably well.'

" The guilty old banker buried his face in his trembling hands ; and when he looked up again, the vision had changed, and he saw before him the inside of a soldier's tent on the banks of the Rapidan, with two gentle Zouaves arraying themselves in their new uniforms, which had just arrived. Owing to some trifling mental aberration, accompanied by hiccups, which often attacks the members of an army confined to damp localities, these two troops had somehow mistaken their jackets for their pants, and were struggling with Herculean strength to thrust their dainty nether limbs into the sleeves of the first-named garments. After an animated struggle of about a quarter of an hour, something was heard to tear ; whereupon, one of the Zouaves tore his fractured jacket from his limbs, and dashed it furiously to the ground, hurling imprecations upon all hard-hearted wretches who coined money by making clothing out of rotten rags for the glorious defenders of their homes and firesides.

" ' Old boy,' thundered Mr. Pepper's Ghost, reproachfully, ' did you not have an interest with your brother, the —— street tailor, in that Government contract for uniforms ? '

" ' I did,' replied the mournful banker.

" ' Then behold,' said the spirit, ' how you have earned the eternal hate of your country's gallant volunteers, and will be handed down to future scorn and infamy as a

9

member of the 'Shoddy Aristocracy.' 'And now,' continued Mr. Pepper's Ghost, 'that I have shown you these illustrations of your wickedness as a rich man, how do you feel ? '

" ' Well,' responded old Pursimmons, ' to tell the truth, I feel greatly bored and very sleepy.'

" ' And you wont bestow all your wealth upon the next poor widow with six small children ? '

" ' Not exactly.'

" ' Nor at least one half of it upon the Mission for the Regeneration of the starving Choctaw Nation ? '

" ' I'd rather be excused.'

" ' Well, then,' exclaimed Mr. Pepper's Ghost, plaintively, ' wont you — *wont* you, oblige *me* with — a loan of five dollars ? '

" ' Yes — if you will take greenbacks.'

" At the word, Mr. Pepper's Ghost uttered a scream of despair, smote its breast frantically, and gave the chair upon which old Pursimmons had just seated himself such a vicious kick that the flinty-hearted banker suddenly awoke, found it all a dream, and, — went outrageously to sleep again ; thereby giving convincing proof of that utter callousness of soul which all worthy poor men know to be the sure accompaniment of riches ! "

As Villiam ceased reading, we all retired silently from the tent, greatly improved by what we had heard. And now, my boy, let me conclude with a little story of my own :

Some months ago, a certain western General gave an order to an Eastern contractor for a couple of peculiarly

THIRD SERIES. 193

made gunboats for his service ; but, happening to pass the White House, shortly after, saw what he took to be the models of two just such gunboats protruding out of one of the windows. Thinking that the President had concluded to attend to the matter himself, he immediately telegraphed to the contractor not to go on with the job.

Quite recently, the contractor came here again, and says he to the General, —

" I'd like to see the model of those White-House gunboats."

The General conducted him toward the White House, my boy, and the two stood admiring the models, which protruded from the window as usual.

Pretty soon a Western Congressman came along, and says the contractor to him :

" Can you tell me, sir, whether those models of gunboats up there are on exhibition ? "

" Gunboats ! " says the Western chap, looking. " Do you take those things for gunboats ? "

" Of course," says the contractor.

" Why, you fool ! " says the Congressman, " those are the Secretary's boots. The Secretary always sits with his feet out of the window when he is at home, and those are the ends of his boots ! "

Without another word, my boy, the General and the contractor turned gloomily from the spot, convinced that they had witnessed the most terrific feet of the campaign.

Yours, merrily,

ORPHEUS C. KERR.

LETTER C.

GIVING DIVERS INSTANCES OF STRANGELY-MISTAKEN IDENTITY; AND REVEALING A WISE METHOD OF SAVING THE COUNTRY FROM BANKRUPTCY.

WASHINGTON, D. C., March 5th, 1864.

THIS gray-headed pen of mine, my boy, — which is mightier than the sword, inasmuch as it can, itself, " draw " the sword when it chooses, quite as accurately as any pencil-vanian, — has run the blockade recently imposed upon it, and once more gambols nervously down the lines of contemporaneous military history. When first I heard that aphorism of the elegant and ghostly Bulwer, by which the sober sceptre of the scribe is magnified above the fancy-dress weapon of the hero, I took it to be like any other high-sounding sentiment of the stage, whereby the poor but virtuous editor was nobly and improvingly encouraged to believe himself rather more powerful in this universe than all its great captains put together. Being a child of the pen myself, I felt benignantly inflated by the venerable " Richelieu's " excellent remark, and looked with much generous pity upon a crushed young army officer in the box next to mine ; but, at the same time, I remember that it reminded me of the exceedingly moral popular delusion making starving virtue a much pleasanter and more admirable thing to possess than a king's crown ; and I also remember how it thereupon dawned upon me, that

THIRD SERIES.

the pen was possibly mightier than the sword only in the far-removed sense of Might being Write. Since I have lived in Washington, however, I have learned, my boy, that the sentiment in question is capable of demonstration as a very plain fact; seeing, as I do, that off-hand strokes of the pen can in a very few minutes promote into Major Generals and Brigadiers certain pleasing brass-buttoned chaps whose actual swords could never have done as much for them in all their lives. And yet, my boy, if all those powerful, unsordid creatures, our country editors, had their youths to live over again, I verily believe that two-thirds of them would sooner be put to the sword than put to the pen. Such is man!

Nevertheless, mighty as the pen may be, it must fail equally with the well-known Southern Confederacy to do justice to this Capital of our distracted country in its present social peculiarities. The cackling of geese once saved the Capitol of the Roman Empire, my boy; but it will take more geese than those who have come hither with the expectation of being respected for their virtues, to save Washington from permanent investment by all the speculative chaps on earth who have no other capital to invest. The present social circle around the family hearth of this Capitalian and Congressional town, my boy, is somewhat more remarkable than it was, even in the palmiest and most mutually abusive days of our eloquent National Legislature, and fully equals the frequent domestic symposium of Albany when the State Legislature meet *there*. Look into a Washington home, and you shall find the venerable grandfather, who sits nearest the fire, talking and chuckling to himself over his success that day in depreciating the national currency by first frightening a country squire on the street almost into fits by prating learnedly about "repudiation," and then buying all his treasury notes from him at fifty per cent. discount! Next sits the younger husband and father, cataloguing to his devoted wife, with the forefinger of his right hand upon all the fingers of his left, the successive pecuniary advantages sure to accrue from a contract he has just obtained to supply our national troops with patent suspenders, and which will enable him to return to New York in the spring, purchase a palatial residence on Fifth Avenue, and sign urgent and influential calls for Peace Conventions. Thirdly, my boy, we have the interesting wife and mother who listens to her lord and master's revelation with beaming satisfaction, glancing occasionally at her youthful son and heir, who, with two thimbles, is practising upon the rug at her feet the curious and ingenious game of the "Little Joker," whereby he hopes to reap profit from his small associates on the morrow. The fourth figure of this prayerful group around the home altar is the highly elaborated daughter, reading over her lover's shoulder, from a newspaper held conveniently by him, a spicy, exciting, moral tale of a daring spirit who had sold a sloop-load of hay, just as it floated, to the Government, and then — when he had got his pay — set fire to it and burnt the whole concern so effectually, that very few could presume to think that at least two-thirds of it had been old straw.

It is a noble and beautiful thing to remember, or note, my boy, that the true and real Home, — the shrine of parental Love and Honor, and of childhood's Innocence and fearless trust, — is ever held sanctified by an unseen

THIRD SERIES. 197

angel-circle, into which a few men can bring even so much of the scheming outer world as its cares; that its name, long, perhaps, after it has ceased to be, lives for our voices only in that plaintive medium tone, which, like the master-string of an instrument responding to a passionate touch, sums up, by its very cadence, all the noblest music of a life.

It is this state of things in Washington that greatly confuses the stranger, and causes him to make strange and horrible mistakes as to personal identities. On Monday afternoon, as I stood musing in front of Willard's, after a dispassionate conversation with the Conservative Kentucky Chap as to the probability of Kentucky's consenting to the setting apart of the first of January as New-Year's day, I overheard a conversation between a middle-aged chap of much vest pattern from the rural districts, and one of the Provost Marshal's disguised detectives. The rural chap chewed a wisp of straw which he had been using as a toothpick, and says he:

"That gentleman in a broad-brim hat, going along on the other side of the street, is a prominent New York politician, — is he not?"

The detective involuntarily rattled a pair of miniature handcuffs which were hanging from his watch-chain, and says he:

"Ha! ha! truly! That's a queer mistake. Why, that's Nandy Brick, the incendiary and negro-killer."

Not at all discouraged by this failure at guessing, my boy, the rural chap glanced knowingly at another passer-by, and says he:

198 ORPHEUS C. KERR PAPERS.

"Well, this here other one who just went by is the French Minister, I believe?"

"Really!" says the detective, with a slight cough, "Really, you're wrong again, for that's 'Policy Loo,' the notorious Mexican murderer and thief."

The rural chap bit his right thumb-nail irritatedly, and says he:

"At any rate, I know who yonder tall, gentlemanly person in the black gloves is. It's a famous leader of fashions from Fifth Avenue."

The detective opened his eyes widely at this, and says he:

"Why, there you miss it again. I think I ought to know 'Slippery Jim,' who got that fat contract to supply the army with caps, and made half of them of shoddy."

The chap from the rural districts seemed very much ashamed of himself, my boy, for doing such a wrong to our admirable and refined Best Society; but he was bound to try it once more, and so says he, shortly:

"Perhaps you'll tell me that fleshy individual in a black silk vest, coming this way, an't the British Minister?"

"Wrong again, by thunder!" says the detective; "for all the world knows that respectable cove to be 'Neutral John,' the celebrated rebel-spy and blockade-runner."

Indeed, appearances go so entirely by contraries here, that I really fear, my boy,— I really fear, that many of our veritable great politicians, diplomatists, and Missouri Delegates, are frequently taken for unmitigated rogues by blundering amateurs in physiognomy.

It was on Wednesday that the Venerable Gammon

THIRD SERIES. 199

being seized with a fresh and powerful inspiration to confer a new benefaction on his favorite infant, his country, came post haste from his native Mugsville, and was quickly blessing the idolatrous populace in front of the Treasury Buildings with some knowledge of his benevolent scheme for paying the cost of the War.

"War?" says the Venerable Gammon, fatly, — pronouncing the word as though he had just invented it for the everlasting benefit of some poor but virtuous language, — "War costs money, and money costs gold. What we want is gold, to pay for the money that pays for the war. And where shall we get that gold?" says the Venerable Gammon, with a smile of knowing beneficence.

"By reference to a California journal, I find that California and Nevada contain about twenty columns of gold mines, and that each mine is worth so many millions that its directors are obliged to levy daily assessments of Five, Ten, and Twenty-five cents per share, or 'loot,' in order that the shareholders, in their immense wealth, may not forget that their distracted country has a decimal currency to be countenanced and supported. Now I propose," says the Venerable Gammon, magisterially pulling out his ruffles with his fat thumb and forefinger, "I propose that the War debt and the board of our Major Generals be paid by an especial tax on these mines, thus " —

"Killing the goose which lays the golden egg," broke in an aged Treasury Clerk standing near, whose countenance possessed all the oppressive respectability that large spectacles and a pimple on the nose can possibly bestow.

The Venerable Gammon was hereupon seized with such

9*

200 ORPHEUS C. KERR PAPERS.

a violent fit of coughing that farther argument was imprac-
ticable; and it is not decided to this day whether it would
be in keeping with the eternal fitness of things to tax the
miners to pay the majors.

ORPHEUS C. KERR.

LETTER CI.

EXPLAINING THE WELL-MEANT DUPLICITY OF THE JOURNALS OF THE OPPOSITION; AFFORDING ANOTHER GLIMPSE OF THE IRREPRESSIBLE CONSERVATIVE SENTIMENT; AND SHOWING HOW THANKSGIVING DAY WAS KEPT BY THE MACKERELS.

WASHINGTON, D. C., Dec. 10th, 1864.

THANKSGIVING Day, my boy, is an able-bodied national festival which has dwelt unctuously in all my less spiritual annual reminiscences, since that poetical and beautiful time of life when the touching innocence of childhood tempted me to surreptitiously pick a chicken-leg while my good grandfather was asking a blessing; and to receive therefor that wholesome box of the ears, which not unfrequently imparts a temporary and excessive warmth to the brain of virtuous boyhood. 'Tis sweet to remember that old-fashioned Thanksgiving Eve, my boy, when the venerable and widowed Mrs. McShane, our cook, would renew her annual custom of inveigling us children into the kitchen on pretence of admiring our new shoes; and then proceed, by divers artful and melancholy phrases, to darken our little souls with a heart-sickening conviction of her utter failure to procure, in her recent trip to market, that long-anticipated Turkey! 'Tis pleasant to recollect how entirely we were cast down thereat, and how rigidly we refrained from so much as a single glance toward the old " Dresser," whereon stood the well-known market-basket

(201)

202   ORPHEUS C. KERR PAPERS.

of Mrs. McShane, with the plump legs of the choicest of
gobblers protruding very obviously therefrom! 'Tis joyous to recall how we stared mercilessly at every possible
thing in the kitchen except that " Dresser ; " and how
desolately we received certain sadly-philosophical remarks
from Mrs. McShane, as to the unspeakable admiration
assuredly merited by those " rale good childers," who
could, for one Thanksgiving Day, endure starvation without tears.

The little deception was most tenderly and kindly
meant, my boy ; it was the artless roguery of a dear old
heart — the gentlest of cheats — the fondest of frauds ;
and the very remembrance of it, at this remote moment,
not only fills my manly bosom with the softest charity,
but endows me with a nicer mental perception of actual
good in seeming wickedness, than any yet disclosed by my
more obtuse fellow-countrymen.

Thus, my boy, when I note how some of our excellent
Democratic daily journals attempt to prove, with great
sadness of manner and profound sincerity of reluctant
reasoning, that all the celebrated advances, conquests, and
flankings of our remarkable national armies are really so
many heart-breaking defeats in deep disguise ; and that
the well-known Southern Confederacy is actually quite intoxicated with its continued remorseless successes over us ;
when I note this, my boy, I am moved to pleasant tears
over that inherent and ineradicable goodness of human
nature, which instinctively inspires the nobler of our species to first delude their fellow-beings to despondency with
the most innocent of falsehoods, only that their consummate
bliss may be the greater when the glorious truth can no

THIRD SERIES. 203

longer be thus fondly concealed. Join with me, my boy, in a noble tribute of affection to the humble but tender Editors of these excellent Democratic daily journals, who would lovingly make us, children of the nation, believe, that the Turkey of Victory is not to be had at any price, though none of us need look very far to see the plump legs of that very same turkey sticking out of the family-basket. Thanks to thee, thou dear old Mrs. McShane, with thy perpetual atmosphere of roast-beef gravy, and eternal rims of crusted flour about thy finger-nails — thanks be to thee for that humanizing remembrance of thy loving fraud, which thus enables me to rescue our excellent Democratic daily journals from the unseemly imputations of degenerate Black Republicans.

My long absence with our somewhat tedious national troops, my boy, — troops now constituting a flaming necktie about the throat of this exciting Rebellion ; — my long absence, I say, has given this Capital City of our distracted country an opportunity to thrive apace in the development of those public and private virtues, which so thoroughly unpopularize Vice in this chaste locality, that even the Vice President is never heard of. True it is, that one misses those pleasant and gorgeous chaps of much watch-chain and an observable extent of diamond breastpin, who were wont, in the days of genial Southern preponderance, to lend lustre to the hall-ways of the more majestic hotels, and occasionally induce the inebriated son of Chivalry to join them at Faro his table. We miss these light and airy chaps, each of whom is now an unblushing Confederacy without hope of Reconstruction ; we miss the high and lofty Carolina chap of much hat-

204 ORPHEUS C. KERR PAPERS.

brim, whose playful moments after the bottle were now and then illustrated with a lively shot from a revolver at a waiter, or cheerful pass with a bowie-knife at his opponent in conversation. And oh! we miss those languishing magnolia belles, whose eyes always reminded me of fresh drops of ink on tinted paper, and whose beautiful belief in the utter vulgarity of all Northern ladies it was really quite delightful to hear. Yes, my boy, all, all are gone; but we have in their places such representatives of genuine republican simplicity as you shall not see again in a circuit of the globe. Our hotel-halls are brightened by youthful forms in the self-sacrificing uniform of our national army; and these youthful forms, being mostly from the country, confine their innocent gaming, almost exclusively, to the athletic game of "checkers." The prominent walking-gentlemen of Willard's wear black velvet vests all the year round, and, so far from shooting waiters, are always on the most familiar terms with that oppressed race; joking freely with them and recognizing them as intimate equals, as all genuine citizens of a true Republic should do. And as for our present Washington ladies, — wearing Lisle-thread gloves at the dinner-table and putting almonds and raisins into their pockets before leaving it, God bless 'em! — why they know no more of anything vulgar, than a maniac does of insanity.

Reflecting upon these things, on Monday last, my boy, I strolled abstractedly into an establishment where they sell army stores, such as lemons by the slice, sugar by the half-ounce, etc. I strolled dreamily in, when who should I see at the crockery-counter but the Conservative Kentucky chap, whose hat was very far down over his eyes,

THIRD SERIES. 205

like one who has just come through a severe election. He appeared to be taking Richmond at the moment, my boy, with a spoon in it; and as quickly as I entered, he let the hand grasping it fall suddenly down on his obverse side, and gave his entire and most unremitting attention to the picture of a flesh-colored young lady on the farthest wall. I slapped him on the shoulder, and says I:

" Well, my ancient Talleyrand, how are we ? "

The Conservative Kentucky chap gloomily placed his tumbler upon the stomach of a gentleman in checked pants, who was calmly sleeping on three chairs near the stove, and says he : " Kentucky can no longer blind herself to the fact that we are on the brink of a monikky. Yes ! " exclaimed the Conservative chap, — wildly tearing off his hat, and then putting it on again so that it entirely covered his left eye, — " Yes, sir, a monikky with a Yankee for its Austrian tyrant ! "

Here the Conservative Kentucky chap deliberately buttoned his coat to the very neck, turned up his collar, and gazed sternly at a bowl of cloves near by. I called his attention to the Ten of Spades, which was edging itself down between his hat and his right ear, and says I, —

" Hast proof of this, Horatio ? "

" Proof? " says the Conservative Kentucky chap, with such a start that the gentleman in the checked pants vibrated as though sleeping on springs, — " Proof ? You know Smith, — John Smith, — that little apothecary from Connecticut ? Well, sir, he voted in this here last election for the Austrian usurper, and now he's knighted ! Yes, sir, by A. Lincoln's recommendation he's now SIR

JOHN SMITH!! I've heard him called so myself. And this — this — is Kentucky's reward!"

At this crisis the Conservative Kentucky chap shut the stove-door with great violence, and seemed for a moment to meditate personal outrage on the young assistant oysterer, who had just arrived with the coal-skuttle.

Before I could make rejoinder, my boy, there approached us a middle-aged gentleman in a shocking bad hat and an overcoat very shiny about the seams, who had cordially invited himself to take a little something that morning, and had accepted the invitation with pleasure. Straightening himself suddenly, with a violent start, to restrain an unruly hiccup, or make me believe that he made the noise with his feet, he eyed the Conservative chap with a benignant smile, and says he:

" You're mistaken there, sir, — muchly, sir, hem! Mr. Smith is my friend, sir; my bosom friend, till time shall end. — Beautiful idea, that. — My friend, I say; and he's only been appointed to the medical department by recommendation of the President. — Let nature do her best, and then your doctors are of use to men. — Byron. — Yes, sir, Mr. Smith is now a military doctor; and that's how you've made the mistake. You thought it was ' Sir John' Smith they said, when it was ' *Sur-geon* ' Smith!"

As he said this, the middle-aged gentleman became aware that one of his toes was sticking very much through his boot, and retired to confidentially ask the assistant-oysterer if any one had yet found that valuable diamond scarf-pin which he (the middle-aged gentleman) had recently lost.

THIRD SERIES. 207

I looked at the Conservative Kentucky chap, my boy, and his chin had sunk down upon his breast. He felt that his mistake was also the mistake of Kentucky, and his heart was too full for further conversation.

'Twas on Thursday morn, — Thanksgiving Day, — that I blithely scaled the heights of my faithful Gothic steed, the architectural Pegasus, and softly urged that ruined temple of a horse to trot me a lively reminiscence of his youth. Forward we went with a unique, chopping motion, with now and then a stumble to keep the blood in circulation, interpersed with occasional plunges at stumps and shyings at fluttering withered leaves. When you have mounted a beloved horse, on a fine, bracing autumnal morning, my boy, did you ever feel like a kind of new and superior being; as though you and your steed were one consummate individual, inspired by one bounding, uncontrollable impulse, and impatiently regarding the line of the horizon as a tyrannical limit to a ride that should else tear gallantly and recklessly forth into illimitable space? Did you ever feel thus, my boy? . . . .

Because, if you did, your feelings were not at all like mine.

. . . . . .

Onward we go, like a wrecked centaur before the wind, and soon these eager eyes behold once more the camp of the aged and thrice-valiant Mackerel Brigade. Far and near, the spectacles of the decrepit veterans are flashing in the sun; whilst before them is the much-besieged City of Paris, and behind them (in consequence of recent rains) the storied waters of Duck Lake. The veterans are clustered around Paris, my boy, like so many exceedingly thirsty chaps around the tall and well-spiked fence inclosing a cherished pump, and if ever they get at it, they will at least drink it dry. Scarcely had I reined-in, near the edge of Duck Lake, where certain members of Rear Admiral Head's iron-plated mackerel squadron were discharging cases and barrels by the score, — scarcely had I dismounted from the Gothic Pegasus and hitched him to the body of a slumbering Mackerel chap, who had already overdone his Thanksgiving, when I beheld Captain Villiam Brown approaching, on his geometrical steed, the angular Euclid. Following him, but on foot, was Captain Bob Shorty in command of the famous Conic Section of the Mackerel Brigade.

"Ha!" says Villiam, leaping down to meet me in dreadful entanglement with his sword, and hastily plunging into his bosom a small black bottle of regulation cough-drops, "have you flown hither like an narrer from a bow, to view the sublime spectacle of the troops at their feed? Ah!" says Villiam, quickly clasping his hands to save the bottle from slipping out of his breast-pocket, "the beautiful pageant of a nation feasting these martial beings on turkey, is something for besotted Europe to tremble at. Next to serving up ice-cream to the sailors in a gale of wind at sea, this" —

Here a venerable Mackerel tottered from the ranks, and says he: "Is them the birds in them ere cases and barrels, Capting?"

Villiam attempted to rattle his sword threateningly at this interruption; but observing that the hilt of his weapon had got around to his spine, he rattled the keys in his pockets instead, and says he:

THIRD SERIES. 209

" How now, Sarah ! "

(He meant to say " sirrah," my boy, — he meant to say " sirrah ; " having recently learned, from the perusal of a moral tale in one of our excellent weekly journals of exciting romance, that said aristocratic term is of frequent occurrence in all the conversations of the great.)

" Why," says the aged Mackerel, coughing into his hand, " if them's the turkeys the people have sent us for Thanksgiving, we're ready for 'em."

" You're right, Sarah," says Villiam, magnanimously, " and we'll open this first case at once. The trade-mark of this case," says Villiam, learnedly, " is ' 50 Turkeys with Care.' "

They were prying the lid off, my boy, with bayonets, and the eyes of the surrounding Mackerels had commenced to glisten fierily through their spectacles, when I saw Villiam and Captain Bob Shorty exchange looks of deep meaning, and shake their heads like a couple of melancholy mandarins.

" Robert S.," says Villiam, with a look of deep perplexity, " this is indeed a strange oversight."

Captain Bob Shorty shook his head sadly.

" And yet," says Villiam, sternly, " we must tell these beings about it."

" There's no avoiding it, by all that's Federal ! " murmured Captain Bob Shorty.

Captain Villiam Brown sighed deeply, and says he :

" Soldiers, the people of the United States of America meant well in sending such beautiful birds for our Thanksgiving bankwick ; but they've made a strange mistake. Really," says Villiam, toying with the cork of the bottle

210 ORPHEUS C. KERR PAPERS.

of cough-drops, as it protruded from his ruffles, — " really, I find, that *not one of these Turkeys is stamped !* "

At this juncture the same old Mackerel again stepped forward, and asked if the turkeys came by mail ?

" No," says Villiam, with much sympathy of manner. " I don't mean postage-stamps, but the Internal Revenue. Turkeys," says Villiam, reasoningly, " come under the head of ' Unnecessary Luxuries,' and are not legal unless stamped. But," says Villiam, with sudden benignity, " your officers possess the necessary stamps, and will sell them to you at twenty-five cents apiece."

It was a beautiful proof of the untiring vigilance and energy of our national regimental officers, my boy, that they happened to have the stamps on hand just as they did ; though, if there happened to be stamps required on geese, I am afraid that every Mackerel who paid his twenty-five cents would come in for one of those chaste little pictures on himself.

And now, the stamps being purchased and the New England eagles distributed, there commenced such a scene of martial revelry and good-nature as the world never saw before. In every direction — at the openings of tents — around open-air fires — everywhere, the jolly festival went on.

Strolling to the outer picket-line, I saw a Mackerel chap lay aside his gun, seat himself upon the ground, and commence handling a nice little turkey which had just been brought to him by a comrade. He smacked his lips audibly, my boy, and was just in the act of tearing off a " drumstick " when I saw him suddenly look up to a point ahead of him, and instantly cease all motion. Curious to know what had thus fascinated him, as it were, and so abruptly checked his feast, I also looked in that direction.

Right across the little field in front of us, seated on the last remaining post of a ruined fence, was a ragged Confederacy, in a perfect whirlpool of tatters, who had rested his musket upon the ground, and was alternately gnawing an army biscuit and casting longing looks toward his happier enemy. He was a dreadfully thin, hollow-eyed chap, my boy, and shivered in the cold. The Mackerel stared at him without motion for some minutes, and then commenced to handle his turkey again. Then he stared again, dropped his turkey, picked it up, and finally rose to his feet impatiently — looked toward his nearest comrade — and then seated himself with his back toward the Confederacy. Still the latter gnawed and looked longingly. The Mackerel said, " damme ! " quite distinctly and stoutly, and vigorously grasped at a " drumstick " again. He gave it a twist, paused, wavered, and *looked over his shoulder.*

In another instant, my boy, that Mackerel sprang to his feet, faced about, shouted :

" I'll do it, by G—d! if I swing for it " — dashed across the field like a stark madman, and, before the astonished Confederacy could budge an inch, had hurled the turkey into his arms and was tearing back to his own post.

There is a chivalry, my boy, that makes a man a hero with the sword of a patriot, or bears him triumphantly through perils and obstacles to the arms of the bride he has won. There is a chivalry that inspires a man to spurn with contempt the fortune not fraught with all honor, and gives him the graces of a gentleman through all the glooms and burdens of honest poverty. But in that grander Chivalry native to the soul, which raises the tenderness of our best humanity far above the highest point all enmity can reach, and lets it fall, like God's own dew, upon the other side, none, none more fairly ever won a knighthood, than that poor Mackerel picket-guard on last Thanksgiving Day.

Yours, gently,

ORPHEUS C. KERR.

LETTER CII.

SHOWING THE INGENIOUS FINANCIAL ENERGY OF A GREATLY-REDUCED POLITICIAN; AND DESCRIBING A COMBAT, ILLUSTRATIVE OF THE PHILOSOPHICAL CONTENTMENT OF THE WELL-KNOWN SOUTHERN CONFEDERACY UNDER ALL REVERSES.

WASHINGTON D. C., Dec. 17th, 1864.

IT is a sublime thing, my boy, — a high moral and exciting thing, — to note a wealthy nation's outburst of gratitude to Providence and our national military organization, for a succession of Mackerel triumphs without parallel either in history or her story. As I look abroad upon the exulting hosts of our distracted fellow-countrymen from an upper front window of Willard's, — having first wafted a fascinating salute to the pleasing young woman of much back hair at a window across the avenue, — as I look abroad, my boy, upon this whole remarkable people, I am deeply impressed with a sense of that beautiful, national characteristic which makes us all buoyant over Mackerel victories only as they bring us nearer to virtuous peace and universal brotherhood, and am convinced that our otherwise inexpressible thankfulness to Heaven may be divided into two equal parts :

I. An ardent desire to destroy combined Europe.

II. A disposition to set fire to combined Europe, bringing off the women and children in small boats.

Hah, hah! does combined Europe tremble? Does C. E. offer a certain sum to be let off?

(213)

214   ORPHEUS C. KERR PAPERS.

" Shall I ever forget, my boy, the recent terrible remark of that grim old sea-dog, Rear Admiral Head, just
after that late tremendous capture of Fort Piano, on
Duck Lake, by the Mackerel Chalybeate squadron, — shall
I ever forget it ?

" Chip my turret!" says that venerable salt, in his
iron-plated manner, —" Chip my turret if I couldn't take
my flag-ship, the ' *Aitch*,' and crush Europe like a perish-
ing insect, — unrivet my plates if I couldn't ! "

But why should I dwell upon the dreadful suggestions
of a theme like this? Europe — crowded Europe —
millions of people — bright summer morning — everybody
in the streets — Bang ! whiz! — Great combinations of
the Lieutenant General — Victoria and Louis N., do you
surrender ? — We DO !

Solemnly do I say to you, my boy, let us mix plenty
of this sort of thing in our devout gratitude to Providence
for His mercies to us as a people, and henceforth we may
confidently count upon the support of Providence — Rhode
Island.

Fairly and benignantly shone the blessed sun over val-
ley and hill on the morning of that recent memorable day
when I scaled the architectural heights of my Gothic
Pegasus, and turned his front-elevation toward the Mackerel camp before the much-banged City of Paris. Bright-
ly gleamed the fluted roof of my ancient pile of a steed as
he went blithely forward on three legs, keeping one in
reserve in case of accident : joyous was the alacrity with
which he waltzed an imitative earthquake and tossed his
child's-coffin of a head. The exhilaration of the motion,
the proud sense of being borne again, might ultimately

THIRD SERIES. 215

have plunged me into a delicious dream of being divided into two parts, my boy, had I not suddenly discovered, on the road-side, some twenty yards ahead of me, the figure of a being seated upon a camp-stool. Hastily dismounting from my architectural animal, and tying him to an oak in such a manner that he presented somewhat the perspective of a modest country church with a tree before the door, I stole carefully upon the being in my front, and found it to be the Conservative Kentucky chap, engaged in the muscular game of " Bluff" with himself.

His venerable hat, my boy, sat far down over his ears, like some shabby bird of night just stooping to carry off two oysters; a curious antiquity in the shape of a black stock loomed gloomily under his chin, as a memorial sepulchre in which some departed collar was supposed to be sacredly entombed ; his face was toward Kentucky, and in his hands he was vivaciously shuffling a number of cards.

" Hum, hem ! " soliloquized the Conservative Kentucky chap, complacently — " ten of spades — king of diamonds — king of hearts — ace of clubs — ace of hearts — ace of " —

Here the Conservative Kentucky chap uttered an absolutely startling cough and, at the same instant, passed three of the aces up his left sleeve !

" Yes," said the Conservative Kentucky chap, still to himself, " the pasteboards are all right — hem ! — it's your deal. Ah! ten is it? — I'll go twenty better — forty — sixty ! Hem! Ace and two Kings is it? Look here — three aces ! Good-night, gents." — and the Conservative Kentucky chap at once sang, with triumphant and great effect :

10

> " Four years the war have looked upon,
>   But haven't brought the end meant ;
> Nor anything except the Con-
>   stitutional Amendment ;
>   Oh, Kentucky! an't this a go, Kentucky?
>   Oh, Kentucky! an awful blow, Kentucky!"

As the last note of exquisite melody died away upon the air, I slapped him on the shoulder, and says I :

" Well done, my son of Hoyle ! "

The Conservative Kentucky chap sprang wildly to his feet, my boy, simultaneously " making a pass " of the cards into his pocket, and commenced dancing insanely before me with a view of hiding from my notice the four of clubs, which he had dropped to the ground and was anxious to conceal in the mud.

" Ha! ha! " observed the Conservative Kentucky chap, somewhat hysterically, in the midst of his dance ; " of course you didn't see what I was doing ? "

Then it was, my boy, that I folded my arms after the manner of Hamlet, threw forward my right knee, shook my head profoundly thrice, and murmured, with the poet :

> " Were his old mother near him now, how would that mother grieve,
>   To see two aces in his hand, — another up his sleeve."

" My mother ! " exclaimed the Conservative Kentucky chap, suddenly descending into Cimmerian gloom ; " Kentucky is my mother, and from her maternal fount I drew the old rye of my existence. But now, Kentucky becomes a indigent pauper under the Constitutional Amendment and the failure of the Bankrupt Bill, and I find myself compelled to take to bluff and poker in the prime

THIRD SERIES. 217

of life." Here the poor chap made a move toward tearing his hair, but thought better of it and only scratched a pimple on his chin.

Arm in arm we walked slowly forward together, each busied with his own thoughts, until, from a clump of trees by the road-side, there unexpectedly emerged before us that ornament of our national service known as Captain Bob Shorty, with his cap at a fierce cock, his hands in his pockets, and a supernaturally knowing air clothing him as with a garment.

" By all that's Federal!" said Captain Bob Shorty, starting at sight of me, " if I didn't take you at first for that ere Confederacy of the name of Munchausen, which has privately appointed to meet me here in single combat."

" Why then, really, you know," observed the Conservative Kentucky chap, suddenly coming forward and pleasantly rubbing his hands, " really it would be a good plan for me to go forward and meet him with a view to peace negotiations. Being a Confederacy, he is Kentucky's brother," warbled the Conservative chap, with soft enthusiasm, " and I might tell him that you would pay all his debts, black his boots, run errands for him, and send the President to tell him a little story, if he would give up this conflict. Should he refuse, and even proceed to the extremity of kicking me," said the Conservative Kentucky chap, with awful sternness, " why, then, I should be in favor of letting the matter proceed to the bitter end, — as it had already in my own case."

" I am not aweer," observed Captain Bob Shorty, " that you have any business in the matter at all, my old Trojan ; but there's the road open to you."

218   ORPHEUS C. KERR PAPERS.

It was beautiful, my boy, — touchingly beautiful, and withal unctuous, to observe with what a benignant smile the peaceful Conservative Kentucky Chap departed up the road. We saw him reach a turn in the path, around which the sound of stately approaching footsteps was already becoming audible. We saw him turn it; heard all the footsteps cease; heard a confused murmur, — a sharp scratching as of heels upon gravel; and Kentucky's favorite son was observed to be coming again to his place, with a slight limp in his walk.

Right behind him came a remarkable being attired in fragments of gray cloth and a prodigious thicket of whiskers, through the latter of which his eyes glared yellowly, like the bottles in an apothecary's shop down the street. As he approached nearer, he hastily put on a pair of partially-dissected white cotton gloves, and casually re-arranged the strip of carpet-binding which served him as a full-dress cravat.

" Yours, truly," said Captain Bob Shorty.

" Vandal!" hissed Captain Munchausen, removing from his brow an unexampled conglomeration of rags in the last stages of cap, and handing it to a faithful contraband who attended him.

" Why, then," said Captain Bob Shorty, doffing his own cap, and tucking up his sleeves, " in the name of the United States of America, I propose to move upon your works immediately."

And now, my boy, do I particularly lament my lack of those unspeakable intellectual gifts, which enable the more refined reporters of all our excellent moral daily journals to describe the fistic achievements of the noted Arkansas

THIRD SERIES. 219

Mule and celebrated Jersey Bantum in a manner that delights every well-conducted breakfast-table in the land, and furnishes exquisite reading for private families.

Forward hopped Captain Bob Shorty, as though on springs, — his elbows neatly squared, his fists held up like a couple of apples on sticks, and his head poised as though it had just started to look round a corner. With fists to match, and eyes shining like the bottoms of glass bottles, the wary Munchausen scuffles cautiously back from him in a half circle. Now they make skips toward each other; and now they skip back. Anon an arm is raised, and is parried; and then they balance to partners; and then they hop back.

I was gazing at all this, my boy, in speechless admiration, when suddenly I saw the dexter hand of Captain Bob Shorty pierce the enemy's lines, and explode with tremendous force on Munchausen's nose. For a moment there was a sound as of Confederate blasphemy, but in a moment the chivalric Munchausen was himself again.

" Ah ! " said Captain Bob Shorty, agreeably, " did you see the star-spangled banner that time ? "

" Sir," said Munchausen, with tears in his eyes, " I am thankful that my nose *is* broken. It is a blessing; for I had nothing to smell with it, and only wasted my strength in its special defence."

Here Captain Bob Shorty looked jovially at me, my boy, and says he, " By all that's Federal! an't he jolly ? "

" Come on to thy ruin," roared Munchausen from behind his rapidly increasing nose; and again the battle raged.

220 ORPHEUS C. KERR PAPERS.

Now did Captain Bob Shorty sidle to the left, with a view to flanking; but two columns of the enemy met him there. Next the agile Munchausen attempts, by a quick turn, to take him in the rear of his position, but finds a strong body of five divisions hurled upon his headquarters with an impetuosity that knocks out half his teeth.

" Art satisfied, Horatio?" said Captain Bob Shorty, with more or less Bowery Theatre in his manner.

An awful smile appeared upon what were left of the features of Captain Munchausen. It was so full of scorn, you know.

" Sir," said he, with much chivalry of bearing, and some difficulty of utterance, " my jaw may be broken, but I thank fate for it. It's a long time since I had anything to eat with my mouth, and to defend it at all was useless."

" Ha! ha! ha!" roared Captain Bob Shorty; " I really never did see anything so jolly."

" Madman!" yelled Munchausen, " your destruction is decided!"

Then were all the skips and hops repeated, my boy; with such ornamental bits of occasional fine art as the refined reporters of our excellent moral daily journals love to dwell fondly upon. Were I but such a reporter, I would describe the scene in a way to make you take it home to your children. But let me not waste time in lamentation; for, just then, a something heavy fell upon the right eye of Captain Munchausen, and effectually closed it for a week.

" Ah!" said Captain Bob Shorty, pleasantly, " did you count the stars upon our Flag that time, my grayback?"

THIRD SERIES. 221

"Sir," retorted Munchausen, staggering about, and wildly pulling handfuls of imperceptible hair out of invisible heads in the air, — "I consider the loss of that eye a blessing in disguise; for I can now concentrate my WHOLE strength on the other."

"Well, now, really," said Captain Bob Shorty, — "really, you know, I never see anything half so jolly."

"Extermination is now your doom," howled the Confederacy, reeling deliberately forward upon the first fist he met, and falling heavily to the ground with his other eye emphatically darkened.

Instantly was Captain Bob Shorty at his side, exclaiming, "I'm sorry for this, old chap. I wish you'd only consented to stop before — EH?" ejaculated Captain Bob Shorty, — "what's that you say?"

As true as I live and breathe, my boy, — as true as I live and breathe, — when Captain Bob Shorty put his ear to the mouth of the fallen Confederacy, he heard, slowly spoken, these remarkable words:

"I'm — glad — this — has — happened — because —I — can — now — develop — my — REAL — resources — of ——strength!!!"

Yours, speechlessly,

ORPHEUS C. KERR.

LETTER CIII.

BEING ANOTHER AND FINAL CHRISTMAS REPORT; INCLUDING A SMALL STORY FROM OUR UNCLE ABE; A CIRCULAR FROM THE SECRETARY OF STATE; A SUPERNATURAL CAROL FROM SERGEANT O'PAKE; AND A TREMENDOUS GHOST STORY FROM AN UNAPPRECIATED GENIUS.

WASHINGTON, D. C., Dec. 27th, 1864.

UPON these holy anniversary-days of "Peace on Earth, good-will toward men," the American human mind is naturally prone to regret that the well-known Southern Confederacy still survives, in a degree, all its inexpressible spankings, and still compels the noblest of us to pour out our substitutes like water. You, my boy, have poured out your substitute; other great and good men have poured out *their* substitutes, and your devoted pockets bleed at every pour.

O war! thirsty and strategical war! how dost thou pierce the souls of all our excellent Democratic journals, against whom the increased war-tax on whiskey is an outrage not to be mentioned without swearing.

On Christmas-day, my boy, there came to this city a profound Democratic chap of much stomach, who wore a seal-ring about as large as a breakfast-plate, and existed in a chronic condition of having the bosom of his shirt unbuttoned to such a degree as to display picturesquely the red flannel underneath. He ran for Sheriff of Squankum last month, my boy; and having been defeated with great slaughter, concluded that all was gall and bitterness,

(222)

THIRD SERIES. 223

and that he couldn't do better than come to Washington and improve the President's mind.

At the time of the interview, our Honest Abe was sitting before the fire, peeling an apple with a jack-knife; and the fact that part of his coat-collar was turned inside, did not lessen in him that certain generous dignity which hale good-nature ever wears, as morning wears the sun.

"Mr. President," says the profound Democratic chap, spitting with dazzling accuracy into a coal-hod on the opposite side of the room; "I call upon you to-day, sir, not as a politician, but as a friend. And as a friend, sir" — here the Democratic chap wore a high-moral look, and his shirt-bosom yawned as though eager to take all the world into the red-hot depths of his affectionate flannel heart, — "as a friend, sir, I feel bound to tell you, that your whole administrative policy is wrong; and as for your Emancipation Proclamation, it has had no effect at all, as I can see."

Here the profound Democratic chap stuck a cheap bone eyeglass into his right eye, and seemed to think that he rather had him there.

The Honest Abe peeled his apple, and says he:

"Neighbor, the sane men of all parties think differently from you in that matter."

"That proves, I suppose," says the Democratic chap, wrathfully, "that I'm a lunatic."

The Honest Abe ate a piece of apple, and says he:

"Not at all, neighbor; not all; nothing so serious as that. But talking about what a difference of opinion 'proves,'" says the Honest Abe, balancing one boot upon the toe of the other, and smiling peacefully at his jack-

10*

224   ORPHEUS C. KERR PAPERS.

knife ; "talking about what it ' proves,' reminds me of a small tale :

"When I was a law-student out in Illinois, and wore spectacles to appear middle-aged and respectable, we had in our district-court the case of a venerable Sucker, who was. prosecuting another man for spreading a report that he was insane, and greatly damaging his business thereby. The defendant made reply, that he had honestly supposed the plaintiff to be insane on one point, at least, and that was the motion of the world around the sun. This motion was denied *in toto* by the plaintiff, who had frequently, of late, greatly astonished everybody and shocked the schoolmaster, by persisting in the assertion that the world did not spin round at all, inasmuch as *he* had never seen it spin round.

"Various witnesses were called for both sides," says the Honest Abe, pleasantly scratching his chin ; "various ones were called, to testify as to whether such difference of opinion from all the rest of mankind would seem to prove the insanity of the venerable Sucker ; but nothing decisive was arrived at until old Doctor Dobbles was examined. Old Dobbles," says the Honest Abe, winking softly to himself, "was not quite such a teetotaler as may be told about in the ' Lives of the Saints,' and when he took the stand we expected something.

"Says the Court to old Dobbles :

" ' In your opinion, doctor, does a man's denial that the world turns round, inasmuch as he has never seen it go round, prove his insanity ? '

" ' No,' says Dobbles.

" ' Ah ! ' says the Court, ' what then ? '

THIRD SERIES. 225

"'Why,' says old Dobbles, deliberately, 'if a man denies that the world goes round, and has never *seen* it go round, it simply proves that he — *never was drunk.*'

"As it happened," says the Honest Abe, balancing his jackknife on the tips of all his fingers; "as it happened that the Court himself had frequently seen the world go round, the justice of the idea flashed upon him at once, and the defendant was found guilty of six dollars' damages, and ordered to treat the Court.

"Now," says the Honest Abe, with a winning smile, "I am far from inferring, neighbor, that you have never been intoxicated; but it seems to me, that when you say the Proclamation has had no effect at all, it proves you can't be speaking soberly."

The profound Democratic chap came away, my boy, with a singing in his head, and has been so tremendously confused ever since, that he asked me this morning at Willard's, if I thought, that what we of war see is anything like what Thaddeus of Warsaw.

On Monday, while I was on my way to the Mackerel camp, before Paris, to be present at the usual Christmas song-singing and story-telling in the tent of Captain William Brown, I met an affable young chap, driving a wagon, in which were some thousands of what appeared to be newly-printed circulars. I knew that the young chap came from a large printing-office in the lower part of the city, and says I:

"Tell me, my young Phæton, what have we here?"

The affable young chap closed one eye waggishly at a handy young woman who was cleaning the upper windows of a house near by, and says he:

226   ORPHEUS C. KERR PAPERS.

" These here, are five thousand copies of a blank form, just printed down at our place for the State Department. And I should think," says the affable young chap, taking a dash at a small boy who had just " cut behind" his cart — " I should think that pile ought to last a month, at least, though the last one didn't."

I made bold to examine a copy of the blank form in question, my boy, and found it to read as follows :

" CITY OF WASHINGTON, U. S. A.,
     DEPARTMENT OF STATE.

" *Dear Sir :*

" *Permit me to beg you will inform the Government of* ——, *so admirably represented by you, that the Government of the United States entirely disapproves the action of the Commander of the* ——, *in the matter of* —— ——, *and will make whatever reparation may be deemed adequate therefor by the Government of* ——.

" *With the profoundest respect, I am your Excellency's most obedient humble servant,*   —— ——.

" HIS EXCELLENCY —— ——.
    MINISTER FROM ——."

As I read this document, I thought to myself: Verily my distracted country's Secretary of State wishes to save as much writing as possible ; and who knows but that he is like one of own frontier riflemen, who kneels only that he may take the more deliberate aim at the heart of the wolf?

And now, as I push on again for my destination, let

THIRD SERIES. 227

me say to you, my boy, that few who read my wonderfully lifelike picture of Mackerel strategy and carnage, have any idea of the awful perils constantly assailing a reliable war-correspondent of the present day.

Thus : during a great battle which I attended in Accomac, a piece of shell tore off my head, — that is to say, the head of my cane.

At the second battle of Paris, while I was in the act of taking notes of the prevailing strategy, a cannon-ball took my legs off, — that is to say, the legs of my camp-stool.

In the summer of '62, as I was sitting in the doorway of my tent, on the shores of Duck Lake, a case-shot, of immense size, entered my chest, — that is to say, the chest in which I carry my linen.

Cherish me, my boy, make much of me ; for there is no telling how soon some gory discharge of artillery may send me to join the angel-choir.

But here we are in the tent of Captain Villiam Brown ; and the manner in which the Mackerel officers are clustered about the round table in the centre, reminds me of flies around a lump of sugar — supposing a lump of sugar to be shaped exactly like a portly black bottle.

Sergeant O'Pake rises with a manuscript in his hand, and says he :

" Comrades, — let me read to you a weird legend, of which I am the sole author and proprietor, and to which I would draw your most political attention."

228   ORPHEUS C. KERR PAPERS.

And the sergeant forthwith delivered this remarkable poetical report of

"THE IRISHMAN'S CHRISTMAS.

"Hic!"—TERENCE.

" Ould Mother Earth makes Irishmen her universal pride,
   You'll find them all about the world, and ev'rywhere beside;
   And good Saint Peter up above is often feeling tired,
   Because of sainted Irishmen applying to be hired.

" Thus, being good and plentiful, 'tis proper we should find
   A spacious house stuck full of them where'er we have a mind,
   And unto such an edifice our present tale will reach,
   With sixty nice, convaynient rooms — a family in each.

" No matter where it stands at all; but this we'll let you know,
   It constitutes itself alone a fashionable row;
   And when a bill of " Rooms to let" salutes you passing by,
   You see recorded under it, " No Naygurs need apply."

" Now, Mr. Mike O'Mulligan and servant boarded here, —
   At least, his wife at service spent a portion of the year, —
   And when, attired in pipe and hod, he left his parlor-door,
   You felt the country had a vote it didn't have before.

" Not much was M. O'Mulligan to festive ways inclined;
   For chiefly on affairs of State he bent his giant mind;
   But just for relaxation's sake he'd venture now and then,
   To lead a jig, or break a head, like other Irishmen.

" Says Mrs. Mike O'Mulligan, when Christmas came, said she :
' Suppose we give a little ball this evening after tea;
   The entry-way is broad enough to dance a dozen pairs,
   And thim that doesn't wish to dance can sit upon the stairs.'

THIRD SERIES. 229

" ' And sure," said M. O'Mulligan, " I don't object to that ;
But mind ye ask the girls entire, and ev'ry mother's Pat ;
I'd wish them all, both girls and boys, to look at me and see,
That, though I'm School Commissioner, I'm noways proud,"
    says he.

" The matter being settled thus, the guests were notified,
And none to the O'Mulligans their presences denied ;
But all throughout the spacious house the colleens went to fix,
And left the men to clane themselves and twirl their bits of sticks.

" 'Twas great to see O'Mulligan, when came the proper hour,
Stand smiling in the entry-way, as blooming as a flower,
And hear him to each lady say, " Well now, upon me sowl !
Ye look more like an angel than like any other fowl."

" And first came Teddy Finnigan, in collar tall and wide,
With Norah B. O'Flannigan demurely by his side ;
And Alderman O'Grocery, and Councilman Maginn,
And both the Miss Mulrooneys, and the widowed Mrs. Flynn.

" The Rileys, and the Shaunesseys, and Murphys all were there,
Both male and female creatures of the manly and the fair ;
And crowded was the entry-way to such a great degree
They had to take their collars off to get their breathing free.

" O'Grady with his fiddle was the orchestra engaged,
He tuned it on the banisters, and then the music raged ;
' Now face your partners ev'ry man, and keep your eyes on me,
And don't be turning in your toes indacently,' says he.

" And when the dance began to warm, the house began to shake,
The windows, too, like loosen'd teeth, began to snap and break ;
The stove-pipes took the ague fit, and clattered to the floors,
And all the knobs and keys and locks were shaken from the doors.

ORPHEUS C. KERR PAPERS.

" The very shingles on the roof commenced to rattle out :
The chimney-stacks, like drunken men, insanely reeled about;
A Thomas cat upon the eaves was shaken from his feet,
And right and left the shutters fell into the startled street.

" It chanced as M. O'Mulligan was fixing something hot,
The spoon was shaken from his hand, as likewise was the pot;
The plaster from the ceiling, too, came raining on his head,
And like a railway-carriage danced the table, chairs, and bed.

" He tore into the entry-way, and ' Stop the jig!' says he :
' Its shakin' down the house ye are, as any one can see;'
But not a soul in all the swarm to dance at all forbore,
And thumping down their brogans came, like hammers on the
floor.

" And then the house commenced to sway and strain and groan and
crack,
And all the stairs about the place fell crashing, front and back;
The very air was full of dust, and in the walls the rats
Forgot, in newer perils found, all terror of the cats.

" Then swifter flew O'Grady's bow, and ' Mike, me lad,' he roared,
' They'll dance until they haven't left your floor a single board;
It's sperits that they are,' says he, ' and I'm a sperit, too;
And sperit, Mike O'Mulligan, is what we'll make of you!'

" ' And sure,' said M. O'Mulligan, though turning rather pale,
' Its quite a handsome ghost ye are, and fit for any jail :
But tell me what I've done to you offinsive in the laste ;
And if I don't atone for it, I'm nothing but a baste.'

" ' It's faithless to Saint Tammany ye are,' O'Grady cried, —
And wilder, madder, grew the jig as he the fiddle plied, —
' It's faithless to Saint Tammany, who bids the Irishman
Attain the highest office in this country that he can.'

THIRD SERIES. **231**

" ' Och hone !' says poor O'Mulligan, ' it's pretty well I've done,
To be a School-Commissioner before I'm thirty-one ;
'Tis barely just a year to-day since I set out from Cork,
And now, be jabers ! don't I hold an office in New York ? '

" ' Why, true for you, O'Mulligan,' O'Grady roared again ;
' But what's a School-Commissioner to what ye should have been ?
It's County Clerk, the very laste, an Irishman should be,
And, since you're not, receive the curse of Good Saint Tam-
many !'

" Then wilder danced the spirit crew, the fiddler gave a scowl;
And scarce could fated Michael raise a good old Irish howl,
When all the timbers in the house went tumbling with a crash,
Reducing M. O'Mulligan to bits as small as hash!

" Take warning now, all Irishmen, of what may be your fate,
If you come home on Christmas-night an hour or so too late ;
For sleeping on the garret stairs, and rolling down, may be
To you, as unto Mike, a dream of good Saint Tammany ! "

The deep, terror-stricken silence following this ghastly
legend was suddenly broken, my boy, by a frenzied shriek
from my frescoed dog, Bologna, who had followed me
down from Washington, and whose stirring tail had been
accidentally trodden upon by the absorbed Mackerel
Chaplain. The picturesque animal, with a faint whine
not unlike the squeaking of a distant saw, walked toward
Captain Bob Shorty and gazed inquisitively for an instant
into his face ; then took earnest nasal cognizance of the
boots of Captain Samyule Sa-mith ; then sat for an instant
on his haunches, with his tongue on special exhibition ;
and, finally, went out of the tent.

" Ah ! " exclaimed Captain Villiam Brown, who sat

232

ORPHEUS C. KERR PAPERS.

nearest the bottle, and had, for the past hour, been unaccountably shedding tears, — "how much is that dorg like human life, feller-siz'ns! Like him, we make a yell at our firz"'pearance. Like him, we make our firz advances to some brother-puppy. Like him, we smell the boots of our su-su-superiors. Like him, we put out our tongues to see warz marrer with us; and, at last, like him, we — (hic) — we go out."

At the culmination of this sublime burst, Villiam again melted into tears, smiled around at us like a summer-sunset through a shower, and gracefully sank below the horizon of the table, like an over-ripe planet.

"By all that's Federal!" said Captain Bob Shorty, "that was dying young, for Villiam; but who can tell whose turn it may be next? To guard against possibilities, my blue-and-gold Napoleons, I will at once proceed to read you a Christmas-story, written expressly for the Mackerel Brigade by my gifted friend, Chickens, who should be in every American library, and would like to be there himself. The genius of my friend, Chickens," says Captain Bob Shorty, enthusiastically, "cannot be bought for gold; but, in a spirit of patriotic self-sacrifice, he would take ' greenbacks,' if the sordid persons having control of the press should conclude to give him that encouragement which, I am indignant to say, they have hitherto, with singular unanimity of sentiment, entirely denied him. Indeed, my friend Chickens has, at times, been placed in charge of the police by certain editors with whom he has warmly argued the value of his talents, and I trust that the four shillings we have appropriated for our Christmas-

THIRD SERIES. 233

story may be given him for the following tale." And
Captain Bob Shorty proceeded to read : —

"THE GHOST'S ULTIMATUM.

" England, merry England! Land of our forefathers!
Having seen several attractive stereoscopic pictures of thee,
— not to mention various engravings, — I love thee! Yes,
I am of passionate temperament; I am thy fond American
child; and I love thee. Ay, me lud, we all love thee;
and the best of us cannot pay the shortest visit to thy
shores without bringing back such a wholesome contempt
for everything at home, as none but affectionate American
hearts can feel. Having inherited the money realized by
our deceased paternal from his celebrated patent Fish-
scales we put our aged mother comfortably into the Old
Ladies' Home, and fly to thee, dear, dear motherland, by
the most expensive steamer to be had. Then we associate
with the footmen of thy nobility, and go to see thy dukes'
houses while the dukes are absent, and ask the dukes'
housekeeper how much such a house costs, and come
away stupefied with the atmosphere of greatness. We
return to America with mutton-chop whiskers and our
hands in our pockets, while our wife wears a charity-boys'
cap on her head, and carries a saddle-whip forever in her
left hand. We haven't seen the fashion-plates in the
London shop-windows for nothing. We find New York
rather small. There's no Tower, ye know, nor Abbey,
nor Pell Mell, my dear boy. What's Pell Mell? Oh, I
suppose *you'd* call it Pall Mall; ha, ha, ha! quite provin-
cial, to be sure. Really, this new Fifth-avenue house of

ours is not quite equal to the Earl of P.'s town-house ; but we can add a private theatre and a chapel, and make it do for a while, eh ? Day-day, Tomkins, my good fellow, how-de-do ? How are your poor feet ? Ha, ha, ha, quite the joke in London society, Tomkins. What's new ? Yanks had another Bull Run ? Every nobleman I met in England is with the South, my dear boy, and so am I.

" O England ! If I could but visit thee just once, —just a little tiny bit of a once; but no matter, I haven't the money ; never mind. Honest poverty in this country will yet — but it's of no consequence.

" Persons with money may have noticed, that as you turn from Cheapside into Whitefriars, and go on past St. Paul's and the Horse Guards into Pell Mell, keeping straight to the right to avoid Waterloo Bridge and the Nelson Monument, you come to an English house.

" At the particular period of which I write, the night of the 24th of December was Christmas-eve in this house, and Mr. R. Fennarf had just devoured a devilled kidney, some whitebait, a plate of Newcastle pickled-salmon, and some warm wine and toast, as it is believed customary for all English gentlemen of the better class to do before going to bed. Having thus prepared commodious stabling for a thoroughbred nightmare, he looked at his hands, looked at his watch, looked at the fire-irons, looked at his slippers in perspective, and at once fell into an English revery, — which differs materially from an American one, as everybody knows, being much superior.

" ' Can it be,' said Mr. R. Fennarf to himself, ' that my pride was really sinful, when I drove my daughter Alexandra from my house, because she would have wed a

THIRD SERIES. 235

potboy? It must be so; for I have not seen a happy hour since then. Here is Christmas-eve, and here am I a lone, lone man. Oh that by the endurance of some penalty, however great, I might bring back my girl, and ask her forgiveness, and be my old self again.'

"'Thy wish shall be granted!!!'

" This last terrible remark came from a being in white, with a red silk handkerchief tied about the place where he was murdered.

"'Ah!' exclaimed Mr. R. Fennarf, 'have I the pleasure of seeing a Ghost?'

"'You have,' said the being.

"'Wont you take a seat, Mr. G.?'

"'No,' sighed the spectre, 'I haven't time. I just dropped in to let you know through what penance you might be enabled to atone for your unjustifiable arrogance with your daughter, and recall her to your side. Your sin was pride; your atonement must be humiliation. You must get yourself Kicked!'

"'Kicked!' ejaculated R. Fennarf, in a great state of excitement; 'why, really, Mr. G., I would bear anything to gain my desire; but that's rather a severe thing; and, beside, I don't know that I have an enemy in the world to do the kicking for me — except it is the potboy, and his legs are too short.'

"'Nothing but a kick will do,' said the Ghost, decidedly; 'and I will help you to the extent of handing you this rod, by aid of which you can transport yourself in any, or every, direction, until the kick is obtained.'

" As the Ghost spoke, he laid a small black rod upon the table, and — was gone.

236   ORPHEUS C. KERR PAPERS.

"Mr. R. Fennarf fell into a revery: where could he go to make sure of a kick? He might go out into the street and tweak the nose of the first brother-Englishman he saw; but would that Englishman kick him for it? No! He would only sue him next day for damages. No Frenchman would kick a Britisher; because it is the policy of France just now to appear immensely fond of all that's British. Nor German. Nor Spaniard. 'Ah!' exclaimed Mr. R. Fennarf, joyously, 'I have it! The very place for me is "the formerly-united Republic of North America." They hate the very name of Englishman there. Read the articles in their papers; hear the speeches at their meetings: Oh, how they hate us! So here's a wave of the magic rod, and wishing I may be transported to the presence of some good England-hating Yankees. Hey, presto!'

"In an instant he found himself being announced, by a servant in livery, to the company in the drawing-room of Mr. Putnon Ayres, of Beacon Street, Boston, who is quite celebrated for having said some thousands of times that England is the natural enemy of this country, sir; the natural enemy, sir; and if war were declared against England to-morrow, I, for one, sir, would close my store and shoulder a gun myself, sir.

"'Now,' thought Mr. R. Fennarf, 'I shall be kicked, sure enough, and have it over.'

"He couldn't help shrinking when he saw Mr. Putnon Ayres approaching him; but the Bostonian foe of Britain whispered hurriedly to Mrs. Putnon Ayres: 'It's the English gentleman, my dear; a *real* one, and cousin to a Lord! Tell everybody to drop their aitches, and not to

THIRD SERIES. 237

say anything in favor of the war. Oh, ah! delighted to see you, my dear sir, in my 'umble 'ouse.'

" Mr. R. Fennarf was astonished. He must actually say something insulting, or that kick wouldn't come even here.

" ' Thankee, my old muff,' said he, in a voice like a cabman's ; ' but it's a dewcied bore, you know, to answer all the compliments paid one in this blawsted country. I'm fond of wimmin, though, by George ! ' —

" Before he could finish his sentence, twenty managerial mothers, each dragging a marriageable daughter by the hand, made a desperate rush for him ; but Mrs. Putnon Ayres reached him first, and placed the right hand of a pretty young lady in his own.

" ' Take my 'arriet, sir,' she exclaimed, enthusiastically, ' and be assured that she will make you a good wife. It 'as always been my 'ope to 'ave such a son-in-law.'

" Mr. R. Fennarf felt that his case was becoming desperate ; his chance of regaining his daughter further off than ever. Fairly crazy to be kicked, he familiarly chucked Miss Harriet under the chin, and, assuming a perfectly diabolical expression of countenance, deliberately tickled her !

" ' Haw ! haw ! haw ! ' roared Mr. Putnon Ayres, holding his sides with delight, ' that's the real English frankness, my dear son, — for such I must already call you, — and no American girl could be less than 'appy to perceive it.'

" In utter despair, Mr. R. Fennarf involuntarily placed a hand upon the magic rod in his bosom, and wished himself elsewhere. Quick as thought he was elsewhere, and entering the sumptuous private office of the gifted St. Al-

238   ORPHEUS C. KERR PAPERS.

bans, editor of the New York 'Daily Fife,' whose 'leaders' on the propriety of an immediate slaughter of all
Britons within reach, have excited much terror in the
bosom of Victoria.

"'My dear sir,' screamed the sturdy St. Albans, spring-
ing to meet his visitor, 'I am delighted to welcome you
to the United States!'

"Mr. R. Fennarf's heart sank down to his very boots.

"'You mean what there is left of your United States,'
he yelled, like a very ruffian. 'You Yankees never did
know how to speak the English language.' And he actually spat upon a file of the 'Daily Fife' hanging near
him, and sneered pointedly at a lithograph of the editor
over the fireplace.

"St. Albans grasped his hand convulsively.

"'Spoken like Carlyle, sir; spoken like Carlyle. Your
English honesty is worthy your English heart of oak, my
dear friend.'

"'Sir!' roared R. Fennarf, frantic to be kicked, and
backing temptingly toward the gifted St. Albans all the
time he talked; 'you and your paper be demn'd! What
do *you* know about Carlyle, bless my soul! *Who* are you
smiling at? WHAT d'ye mean?'

"Here he knocked St. Albans down.

"'You shall hear from me — step into that next room
— will write to you instantly,' panted the editor.

Half-crazed with his continued failures, the unhappy
R. Fennarf walked abstractedly into the next room, half
hoping his antagonist wanted an opportunity to put on a
pair of extra-heavy boots.

In two minutes a boy put a note into his hand.

THIRD SERIES. 239

"'My dear Sir: Name your own terms for contributing a daily article to the Fife. Select your own subjects.   St. Albans.'

"The miserable Briton involuntarily groaned, shook his head hopelessly, and once more touched the Ghost's rod. He heard the roll of drums, the scattering cracks of muskets, and found himself seated in the tent of that same Major General Steward who has so nobly said, on innumerable appropriate occasions, that he was ready to fulfil his whole duty in defeating the Southern rebels; but could not help wishing, as a man, that the enemy were Englishmen rather than our own brothers. *Then* he would show you!

"'I want to take a look at your military shopkeepers,' observed Mr. R. Fennarf, with great brutality, 'and see how you Bull Runners make your sandbanks — fortifications, as you absurdly call them. You're "Brute Steward," I suppose.'

"'Ha! ha!' laughed the able General, cheerily, 'that's what you English gents call me, I believe. We're going to have a battle, to-day, and you must stop and see it.'

"'A battle!' growled R. Fennarf. 'What do you mean by that? I've got a permit from your vulgar blunderers at Washington to go through your so-called lines to Richmond, as that's the only place where one can find anything like gentlemen in this blawsted country. I intend to go to-day, too; so you must put off your so-called battle.'

11

240 ORPHEUS C. KERR PAPERS.

"He'll certainly kick me after that, thought R. Fennarf, beginning to feel quite hopeful.

"'Put off the battle?' said the great commander, cordially. 'I'll do it with pleasure, sir.'

"The Englishman stared at him in utter despair, and, for the last time, clasped his mystical rod, murmuring: 'Back to England, back to my own street. I give up all hope!' .

"No sooner said than done. In a second he was at the corner of his own street, and, with the rod in his hand, started upon a distracted run for his own lonely house. Not looking where he ran, he went helter-skelter against a fine, fleshy old English gentleman with a plum nose and a gouty great-toe, who had hobbled out for a mouthful of night-air. Bang against this fine, fleshy old English gentleman went he, and down came one of his heels on the gouty great-toe.

"There was a tremendous roar, as from the great Bull of Bashan; the countenance of the fine, fleshy old English gentleman became livid, and, in the deep anguish of his soul, he saluted the disturber of his peace with a tremendous — KICK!

"The black rod vanished in a moment from the hand of Mr. R. Fennarf, and his very soul jumped for joy.

"'Merry Christmas!' he shouted, violently shaking the hand of the now bewildered old gentleman with the plum nose.

"Then, on he darted toward his house. It was lighted up in every window. There was music in the house, too, and dancing. In he flew, with a delightful presentiment

THIRD SERIES.   241

of what was going on. Sure enough, his daughter Alexandra had come home, with her husband the potboy, and a score of friends, and all hands were hard at a cotillon.

" ' Father, forgive us ! ' screamed Alexandra.

" ' Your pariental blessing,' suggested the potboy with much feeling.

" ' Support them for life,' murmured the friends.

" ' My children,' said Mr. R. Fennarf, rubbing his back, ' you must forgive *me*. Henceforth we live together, and celebrate every coming Christmas-eve by meeting all our friends again, as now. I am a new man from this time forth ; for on this very night I have learned a great and useful lesson.'

" Then all was jollity again, and the potboy, notwithstanding the shortness of his legs, danced like a veritable Christy minstrel.

" Meantime, a certain retired hackney-coachman in the company, who had attentively noted the reconciliation of father and daughter, called the former into a corner of the room, and said very gravely to him :

" ' You said you had learned a lesson to-night ? '

" ' Yes.'

" ' What is it ? ' asked the hackney-coachman.

" ' It is,' said Mr. R. Fennarf, with solemnity, ' that no man need go out of his own country to be kicked ! '

As Captain Bob Shorty finished reading, he looked about him for the first time, and lo ! all the Mackerel chieftains were slumbering, with their chins upon their breasts.

242   ORPHEUS C. KERR PAPERS.

And now, my boy, as the New Year rolls in, let
me tender you the compliments of the season, and sign
myself;

Yours for festivity

ORPHEUS C. KERR.

LETTER CIV.

EXPLAINING, IN A LUCID AND PERFECTLY SATISFACTORY MANNER, THE POWERFUL INACTIVITY OF THAT PORTION OF THE VENERATED MACKEREL BRIGADE RESIDING BEFORE THE ANCIENT CITY OF PARIS, AND PRESENTING CERTAIN GENIAL DETAILS OF A RECENT FESTIVE CONGLOMERATION.

WASHINGTON, D. C., March 6th, 1865.

METHINKS, my boy, that I see you sagely assuming a pair of massive ears, a pair of silver spectacles, and a blue cotton umbrella, for the purpose of accurately personating the celebrated Public Sentiment, and, in that gifted character, peremptorily requiring me to explain the present use of the venerable Mackerel Brigade!

Mastering for a moment the noble rage of the unimperilled patriot at a request so vulgarly practical, I sternly refer you to the latest able articles in all our exciting and learned morning journals; wherein you will be taught that such portion of the aged Mackerel organization as has of late years invested Paris is in reality the gorgeous Pivot around which revolve all the other brass buttons of ultimate national triumph. And is not each editor of these excellent and sanguine morning journals well qualified by his military genius to represent a General Ism, oh?

But perhaps, my boy, you fail to find ocular demonstration in that illumination. It is barely possible that you refuse to acknowledge optical conviction in a lucidity of

244   ORPHEUS C. KERR PAPERS.

that description.   It may be that your cornea lacks ability to transmit a specific image in that polarization of pris-
matics.   It strikes me as not improbable that you — can't
see it in that light.

Then come with me to the Mackerel camp before Paris,
and mark where the antique Brigade is sitting-up with the
expiring Confederacy.   Observe how each morning's sun
is reflected from the gleaming spectacles of the venerable
military organization ; while occasional rains make those
same innumerable glasses resemble fairy lakes with dead
fish in them.   Note with what a respectable air of a reliable family physician each patriarchal warrior exhumes,
from somewhere down his leg, the massive gold watch
which he has been induced to buy for $10 of one of those
national benefactors in jewelry who advertise affection-
ately in our more parental weekly journals of romance —
and remarks, oracularly :

" It being exactly three o'clock by this here nineteen-
carat repeater, that air Confederacy has got just one hour
less to live."

The fact, my boy, that this timely observation would
apply with about equal accuracy to the whole human family, need not deter your insidious self from answering in
the affirmative, when I ask you, calmly, if it does not
seem that a military organization of such intellect, *must* be
engaged in some unspeakably profound scheme of victory,
even though to the uneducated eye it may present somewhat the aspect of a muddy old gentleman with his head
against a stone-wall ?

And this business of showing the possible identity of
apparent dead-pause with actual velocity, reminds me of

THIRD SERIES. 245

a chap I once knew in the Sixth Ward. He was a cast-iron chap, my boy, whose most powerful conception of enterprise in trade was vividly associated with the duty of being forever in his shirt-sleeves; and he kept a hard-ware shop at which the economical women of America could get such bargains in flat-irons and door-plates, as were a temptation to marry none but the most impover-ished young men.

Many customers had this very practical hardware chap, and one of them was an aged file in a broad-brimmed hat, blue spectacles, and a silk umbrella, who had about him that air of Philadelphia which at once suggests an equal admixture of chronic slumber and profundity. Being a widower and a happy man, it was the daily custom of this aged file to spend several hours of intellectual refreshment in the hardware shop, smiling benignantly upon the ancient maidens who came thither to buy curling-tongs, and enlivening the soul of the cast-iron chap with fine, la-borious treatises on the general idiocy of popular percep-tion.

"I tell you, my child," this aged file would remark, polishing his spectacles with a red silk handkerchief, — "I tell you, the popular perception wants nicety; wants del-icacy; wants capacity to distinguish between the noisy, bustling style of operation by which it loves to be deceived, — *Populus vult decipi*, — and the silent, almost impercep-tible agencies through which all really great results are ac-complished."

Having heard this chaste sentiment repeated daily for about three years, my boy, the very practical hardware chap began to find his nature growing embittered, and re-

246 ORPHEUS C. KERR PAPERS.

solved to do something desperate. So, one morning, after listening quietly to the essay of the aged file, and refusing to tell a small boot-blacking child of six years old the lowest price for one of Jones's Patent steam-ploughs, this cast-iron chap suddenly removed his hands from around an object on the counter, which he had, apparently, been attempting to conceal, and revealed to view a boy's lignum-vitæ peg-top, which stood seemingly exactly balanced on its steel tip.

" Who would think now," said he, reflectively, " that it could be turning all the time ? "

The aged file advanced his blue spectacles to the very verge of the top, and says he :

" Well, now, it's wonderful, an't it? Any one would think, to look at that simple toy, that it stood perfectly still ; and yet its velocity of movement must be prodigious. Go into yonder street," exclaimed the aged file, dropping his umbrella in the excitement of the moment, — " go into yonder street and bring in any man you please, and that man could swear that this top is not spinning at all. And why ? Simply because the velocity of this top, being several millions of revolutions per minute, is greater than his ignorant eye can comprehend. Upon my soul!" ejaculated the aged file, bending once more to the top, with great enthusiasm, " upon my soul ! it's wonderful."

Over the counter came the hardware chap, with one bound, and says he :

" Why, you durned old fool, *the top an't moving at all !* "

And sure enough, the very practical cast-iron chap had just stuck the top up with his hand, in order to bring the popular perception theory of the aged file to grief.

THIRD SERIES. 247

Ordinary persons, my boy, observing the Mackerel Brigade any time these three years, might think it was not moving at all; but we know its General to be the Top of the heap, and we know that he is making revolutions — in the whole art of war.

Let, then, the venerable and strategical Mackerel Brigade strike off impressions of itself in the mud before Paris; while the conic section, under Colonel Wobert Wobinson, walks calmly through the depths of storied Accomac; while Captain Samyule Sa-mith and the Anatomical Cavalry prosecute Confederate railroad researches, and Rear Admiral Head's iron-plated squadron keeps watch and fishes for bass near the captured Fort Piano, on Duck Lake. For the present, be mine the pleasanter duty of imperfectly reporting that stately Ball at the Patent Office, which clinched the re-inauguration of our Honest Abe, and was attended by none of the old aristocracy of the capital, save those who had received invitations.

The old aristocracy of the capital, my boy, having been accustomed only to association with the ministers from combined Europe, and the chivalry who had, now and then, a nice wife or daughter to sell, could not be expected to countenance a plebeian carnival for which they had not received invitations. They could not be expected so soon to forget those elegant family entertainments of the olden time, when the hospitable board, with its green covering, groaned under the weight of gold and silver; when, instead of salads and pates in crockery platters, the plates were of delicately enamelled pasteboard, containing from one to ten diamonds each, or, perhaps, a king or queen served up cold with mint sauce.

11*

248   ORPHEUS C. KERR PAPERS.

The Old Aristocracy! lineal descendants of the British cavaliers! I should weep, my boy, over their possible extinction forever, were it not that the assiduity of the London Prisoners' Aid Society, in sending ticket-of-leave men to New York, promises to keep the species going.

Behold me, at the proper hour, suspended between the shoulders of three or four fat citizens of America in the entrance-hall, and being thus borne into the festive scene like a being too delicate to walk. This, too, at the expense of only the linen "duster" which I had donned to preserve my broadcloth from the dust in the dancing room, and which I had the satisfaction of seeing distributed in ribbons around the necks and bodies of a score of my neighbors, like so many charms to keep off enchantments. The crowd, the management, and the number of guests with umbrellas and top-boots, were all the subjects of ill-disguised sneers among the old aristocracy of the capital who had not received invitations.

And now I emerge into fountains of satin and mechlin cascades, with numerous citizens of America up to their waists in the surf, and looking about as comfortable as though bathing at Newport in full dress. Yonder stands our Honest Abe, in sombre costume, like a funeral procession standing on end to let something pass under it.

Leaning thoughtfully against the wall, my boy, I was gazing meditatively upon this scene, and thinking how many of these fair beings would be destroyed by railroad accidents on the way to their homes in other cities — I was thinking of this, my boy, when I heard a voice saying :

"How powerful is human instink! let a fire-bell ring,

THIRD SERIES. **249**

and at least half of these manly beings would make a bust for the street to join their native fire departmink. Let the hall-bell ring, and nearly all these fair petticoats would involuntarily rush to 'tend the door. Such is human instink."

Like one in a dream, I turned me where I stood and beheld the form of Captain Villiam Brown, his left hand upon his hip and his right caressing the neck of a small case-bottle in his bosom. I eyed him pleasantly a moment, and, said I:

" Well met, my Union Blucher ! "

" Ah ! " says Villiam, pensively, " how powerful is Human Instink ! "

" Explain, my Blue and Gold."

" Human Instink," says Villiam, softly, " is an involuntary tendency to our normal condition."

" Ahem," said I, sagely, " that sounds like Seward."

" Come with me," says Villiam, gravely, " and I will show you the power of Human Instink."

He led me quietly, my boy, to a corner of the great room, where the guests were nearly all males, and suddenly roared out this extraordinary question :

" Say, Johnny-y-y, how's yer do-o-org ? "

The magical sound caught them unprepared, my boy, and before there was time to remember where they were, they unanimously responded with :

" Bully ! "

" Ah ! " says Villiam, " that's Instink. They all were fellow-firemen last year, and remember the language of the Departmink."

Deeply impressed with a sense of that subtle sympathy

250 ORPHEUS C. KERR PAPERS.

with early usages which never leaves a man in life, I again let the hero of a hundred battles lead the way to another corner, where fifty fair ones stood apart in a cluster, waiting for their escorts. Then it was that Captain Villiam Brown suddenly assumed an air of unspeakable abstraction, and commenced humming the tune of the song :

> " Bridget, tend the airy bell,
> Don't you hear it tinkle ?
> Butcher's brought the bacon home, —
> Cook it in a twinkle."

Without at all thinking or knowing why they were doing so, my boy, two-thirds of those fair ones took up the tune at the first note and hummed it through !

" The fair sect," says Villiam, cautiously, " once heard its mother sing that song, as she had learned it in her native palace ; and has the Instink to remember it."

Thus, taking new and beautiful lessons in the ever-fresh volume of animate nature, we sauntered into the ballroom, where our Honest Abe and his lady were viewing the performances from a pair of handsome elevated chairs. Ay, sir : handsome (!) chairs ; and that, too, when many an honest poor man in the land has not a single chair with a gilt back to rest upon. Thus are we drifting toward (start not!) — yes sir and madam, toward — Royalty ! ! Thus, too, are we incurring the highest scorn of the old aristocracy of the capital who had not received invitations.

There was dancing of the ordinary sort in plenty ; many solid men of Boston of the oldest age going to the verge of apoplexy in their efforts at double-shuffle ; but how can description do justice to the Honorable Gentleman from

THIRD SERIES. 251

the Sixth Ward, who performed the celebrated Conflagration Hornpipe!

First, the Honorable Gentleman threw his whole weight upon his left leg, elevated one ear as though intently listening, and tapped distinctly upon the floor with his right heel the number of the district. Then came a confused scuffling, first upon one foot and then upon the other, to represent the hurry and excitement of getting the machine out of the house and whirling her to the scene of the conflagration. The next figure, performed alternately upon the toe, heel, and side of the shoe, was an imitation of the noble machine in motion; the whole winding up with the Honorable Gentleman's seizing his partner around the waist and plunging into a polka, symbolizing the gallant fireman's rescue of a consuming female from a sixth-story window.

This beautiful dance, my boy, was considered an unanswerable argument in favor of a Volunteer Fire Department; but its finishing effect was somewhat marred by a piercing note from the famous night-key bugle of the Mackerel Brass Band: who, in an enfeebled state of mind, was found wandering about the palace a trifle intoxicated, and received prompt direction to the apartments of Detective Baker.

After witnessing, also, the noted walk-around known as the Revenue Stamp, we joined the march for supper, and I sweetly expressed to Captain Villiam Brown my fear of being crowded from the eatables.

"Oh!" says Villiam, catching his case-bottle just in time to save it from sliding through his ruffles to the floor; "I shall work upon human Instink."

252   ORPHEUS C. KERR PAPERS.

Here, this ornament of our National Mackerel organization inserted an elbow under the right ear of a fair being in blue just before us, and says she :

" I don't admire to see you men treating ladies in that manner. The ideor ! "

" Ah, Mrs. Nubbins," says Villiam, pleasantly, " when your father, the milkman, used to serve our house, I " —

" Here — you can pass, sir," said the fair being in blue ; and Captain Villiam Brown walked forward deliberately upon the trailing skirts of a beauteous object in pink."

" You're tearing my things — creature ! "

" Ah ! " says Villiam, abstractedly, to me, " you don't remember stand Number Twelve, Fulton Market, where Miss Poodlem's grandmother used to " —

" There's plenty of room here, sir," observed the beauteous object in pink, and Captain Villiam Brown accidentally brushed against a beatitude in white.

" Plebeian ! "

" My fren," says Villiam, as though he and I were entirely alone together on a desert island, " when old Binks gave up the soap-boiling business last fall, and came to " —

" Did you wish to pass, sir ? " said the beatitude in white ; and we soon found ourselves beside the banquet board, where all went merry as a fire-bell.

Then did we gorge ourselves, my boy, like the very First Families under similar circumstances ; revelling in such salads as were known to the ancients just before the breaking out of the Asiatic cholera, and paying general attention to a bill of fare which was heartily despised by the old aristocracy of the capital who had received no invitations.

THIRD SERIES.   253

It was past midnight when we retreated to a double-bedded room at Willard's, and as Captain Villiam Brown took his goblet of final soda, he gracefully tipped my glass, and says he:

"I propose a sentimink."

Villiam raised the Falernian nectar aloft, gazed solemnly at me, and says he:

"Human Instink!"

Let us believe, my boy, that the instincts of those who come to the higher social surface in this, our trying time of war, are, by their own purity from anything actually malignant, sure indications that the nation's heart is good to the very bottom. Let us believe that the pride of Ascent, vain-glorious as it may seem, is nobler in raising the public laugh than is the tyrannical pride of Descent, which too often forces the public tear. Let us believe that, in the course of time, when the soft white hand of Peace shall have thrown a wreath of flowers across the muzzles of our guns, these unaccustomed tradesmen-courtiers who now throng the halls of our upright First Citizen and Friend will prove the sound ancestral stock of a race of brave gentlemen and women fair, to defend and adorn our Republican Court.

Yours, blithely,

Orpheus C. Kerr.

LETTER CV.

BEING OUR CORRESPONDENT'S LAST EFFORT PRIOR TO THE COMMENCE-
MENT OF A NEW MACKEREL CAMPAIGN; INTRODUCING A METRICAL
PICTURE OF THE MOST REMARKABLE SINGLE COMBAT ON RECORD; AND
SHOWING HOW THE ROMANCE OF WOMAN'S SENSITIVE SOUL CAN BE
CRUSHED BY THE THING CALLED MAN.

WASHINGTON, D C., March 12th, 1865.

THIS sagacious business of writing national military
history once a week, my boy, has at times presented
itself to my mind as a public obligation nearly equal in
steady mutual delight to the wholesome occupation of
organ-grinding. Mark the Italian nobleman who dis-
courses mercenary twangs beneath your window, and
you shall find him a person of severe and gloomy vis-
age, — a figure with an expression of being weighed
down to the very earth by a something heavier than
the mere mahogany box of shrieks out of which he
grinds popular misery by the block. Not that he has
a distaste for music, my boy; not that he was the less
enthusiastic at that past period "when music, heavenly
maid, was young" to him; but because the daily recur-
rence to his ears of precisely the same sounds for ten
years, has a horribly depressing effect of unmitigated
sameness; and music has become to him an ancient
maiden of exasperating pertinacity. It quite affects me,
my boy, when I see one of those melancholy sons of

THIRD SERIES.   255

song carrying a regularly organized monkey around with him ; for it is evident he finds in such companionship a certain relief from the anguish of monotony. Guided by the example, I sometimes get a Brigadier to keep me company also, and you can hardly imagine how often I am saved from gloom by the amusement I experience in seeing his shrewd imitation of a real soldier.

But even this resource may fail ; for there are periods when such imitations are very bad indeed ; and then the mind of the wearied scribe, like that of my departed friend, the Arkansaw Nightingale, may at any moment expire for want of food. Shall I ever forget the time, my boy, when the Nightingale came to Washington, as President of the Arkansaw Tract Society, for the express purpose of protesting against the war, and procuring a fresh glass of the same he had last time ?

" This war," says he, waiting for it to grow cooler, and thoughtfully contemplating the reflection of himself in the bowl of a spoon, — " this war, if it goes on, wont never shet pan till the hair's rubbed off the hull country, and the 'Merican Eagle wont hev enough feathers in his tail to oil a watch-spring. Tell you! stranger, it'll be wuss than Tuscaloosa Sam's last tackle ; and that wasn't slow."

" What was that ? " says I.

" What ! " says the Nightingale, stirring in a little sugar, " did you never hearn tell of Tuscaloosa's last? Then here's the screed done into music under my pen and seal ; and as it an't quite as long's the hundred nineteenth psalm, you don't want a chair to hear it."

Whereupon the Arkansaw Nightingale whipt from

256 ORPHEUS C. KERR PAPERS.

some obscure rear pocket a remarkable handful of written
paper, and proceeded to excite me with

"A GREAT FIT.

> " There was a man in Arkansaw
> As let his passions rise,
> And not unfrequently picked out
> Some other varmint's eyes.

> " His name was Tuscaloosa Sam.
> And often he would say,
> ' There's not a cuss in Arkansaw
> I can't whip any day.'

> " One morn, a stranger passin' by,
> Heard Sammy talkin' so,
> When down he scrambled from his hoss,
> And off his coat did go.

> " He sorter kinder shut one eye,
> And spit into his hand,
> And put his ugly head one side,
> And twitched his trowsers' band.

> " ' My boy,' says he, ' it's my belief,
> Whomever you may be,
> That I kin make you screech, and smell
> Pertikler agony.'

> " ' I'm thar,' says Tuscaloosa Sam,
> And chucked his hat away ;
> ' I'm thar,' says he, and buttoned up
> As far as buttons may.

THIRD SERIES.

257

" He thundered on the stranger's mug,
　The stranger pounded he ;
And oh ! the way them critters fit
　Was beautiful to see.

" They clinched like two rampageous bears,
　And then went down a bit;
They swore a stream of six-inch oaths
　. And fit, and fit, and fit.

" When Sam would try to work away,
　And on his pegs to git,
The stranger'd pull him back; and so,
　They fit, and fit, and fit!

" Then like a pair of lobsters, both
　Upon the ground were knit,
And yet the varmints used their teeth,
　And fit, and fit, and fit ! !

" The sun of noon was high above,
　And hot enough to split,
But only riled the fellers more,
　That fit, and fit, and fit ! ! !

" The stranger snapped at Sammy's nose,
　And shortened it a bit;
And then they both swore awful hard,
　And fit, and fit, and fit ! ! ! !

" The mud it flew, the sky grew dark,
　And all the litenins lit ;
But still them critters rolled about,
　And fit, and fit, and fit ! ! ! ! !

258   ORPHEUS C. KERR PAPERS.

" First Sam on top, then t'other chap ;
    When one would make a hit,
  The other'd smell the grass ; and so,
    They fit, and fit, and fit ! ! ! ! ! !

" The night came on, the stars shone out
    As bright as wimmen's wit ;
  And still them fellers swore and gouged,
    And fit, and fit, and fit ! ! ! ! ! ! !

" The neighbors heard the noise they made,
    And thought an earthquake lit ;
  Yet all the while 'twas him and Sam
    As fit, and fit, and fit ! ! ! ! ! ! ! !

" For miles around the noise was heard ;
    Folks couldn't sleep a bit,
  Because them two rantankerous chaps
    Still fit, and fit, and fit ! ! ! ! ! ! ! ! !

" But jist at cock-crow, suddently,
    There came an awful pause,
  And I and my old man run out
    To ascertain the cause.

" The sun was rising in the yeast,
    And lit the hull concern ;
  But not a sign of either chap
    Was found at any turn.

" Yet, in the region where they fit,
    We found, to our surprise,
  One pint of buttons, two big knives,
    Some whiskers, and four eyes ! "

There's dramatic genius for you, my boy, and you will join me in raining a pint or so of tears in memory of one who perished because his mind had nothing to feed upon, and who left his bottle very empty.

Deferring for the present all account of the Mackerel strategy now coming slowly to a head and on foot, let me relate a little incident illustrative of the delicious loyalty of the taper women of America, and the intolerable baseness of the repulsive object called man:

There is in this city an intensely common-place masculine from Pequog, who has, for a wife, a small, plump member of that imperishable sex whose eyes remind me of wild cherries and milk. There never was a nicer little woman, my boy, and she can knit scarlet dogs, play "Norma," make charlotte russe, and do other things equally well calculated to confer immeasurable happiness upon a husband of limited means. Ever since the well-known Southern Confederacy first respectfully requested to be let alone with Sumter, she has been eager to fulfil woman's part in the war, and does not wake up the Pequogian more than twice of a night to talk about it.

'Twas at one o'clock on the morning of Tuesday last that she roused up the partner of her joys and sorrows, and says she:

" Peter, I do wish you'd tell me what I can do, as a woman, for my country."

" Go to sleep," says Peter, fiendishly.

" No, but what *can* I do? Why wont you tell me what is really woman's part in the war?"

" Now, see here," says Peter, sternly. " I'm having so many nights, with the nap all worn off, over this business, that I can't stand it any longer. Just wait till tomorrow evening, and I'll think over the matter and tell you what really *is* woman's part in the war."

So they both went to sleep, my boy, and all next day that little woman wondered, as she hummed pleasantly over her work, whether her lord would advise her to go out as a Florence Nightingale, or turn teacher of intelligent contrabands.

Night came, and the Pequogian returned from his grocery store, and silently took a seat before the fire in the dining-room. The little woman looked up at him from the ottoman on which she was cosily sitting, and says she :

" Well, dear ? "

Slowly and solemnly did that Pequog husband draw off one boot. Deliberately did he take off a stocking and hold it aloft.

" Martha Jane ! " says he, gravely, " 'tis a sock your eyes behold, and there is a hole in the heel thereof. You are a wife ; duty calls you to mend your husband's stockings ; and *this* — THIS — is Woman's Part in the Wore ! "

Let us draw a veil, my boy, over the heart-rending scene that followed ; only hinting that hartshorn and burnt feathers are believed to be useful on such occasions, and produce an odor at once wholesome and exasperating.

Yours, sympathetically,

ORPHEUS C. KERR.

LETTER CVI.

WHEREIN WILL BE FOUND CERTAIN PROFOUND REMARKS UPON THE VARIATIONS OF GOLD, ETC., AND A WHOLESOME LITTLE TALE ILLUSTRATIVE OF THAT FAMOUS POPULAR ABSTRACTION, THE SOUTHERN TREASURY NOTE.

WASHINGTON, D. C., March 22, 1865.

THE venerable Aaron, my boy, was the first gold speculator mentioned in history, and it exhausted all the statesmanship of Moses to break up the unseemly speculation, and bring Hebrew dry goods and provisions down to decent prices. Were Aaron alive now, how he would mourn to find his auriferous calf going down at the rate of ten per cent. a day, while the Moses of the White House reduced that animal more and more to the standard of very common mutton!

Alas, my boy, what madness is this which causes men to forget honor, country, ay, even dinner itself, for ungrateful gold! Like all writers whose object is the moral improvement of their kind, I have a wholesome contempt of gold. What is it? A vulgar-looking yellow metal, with a disagreeable smell. It is filthy lucre. It is dross. It is also 156.

Not many months ago I knew a high-toned chap of, much neck and chin, who made five hundred thousand dollars by supplying our national troops with canned peaches,

(261)

262   ORPHEUS C. KERR PAPERS.

and was so inflated with his good luck in the cholera-
morbus line, that he actually began to think that his canned
peaches had something to do with the successes in the field
of our excellent military organization. Being thus elevated, this finely-imaginative chap believed that his services
deserved the mission to France ; and, as that was refused
him, it was but natural for him to become at once a Southern Confederacy in sentiment, and pronounce our Honest
Abe a tyrant of defective education.

Just before the last election, I met him at the Baltimore
railroad depot, and says he : " I have just invested a cool
five hundred thousand in gold.   It is positively sure," says
he, glibly, " it is positively sure that the reëlection of our
present despot will send gold straight up to five hundred.
I tell you," says he, in a wild ecstasy, " it'll ruin the country, and I shall clear a half million."

He was a Jerseyman of fine feelings, and took a little
hard cider for his often infirmity.

Yesterday I saw that man again, my boy, and I gave
him a five-cent note in consideration of his great ability in
sweeping a street-crossing.   He deserted his canned peaches, and was cr-r-rushed.

But what is this manuscript upon my table, as I write ?
It is a veracious and wholesome little tale of

" THE SOUTH. — BY A NORTHER.

" 'Twas night, deep night, in the beautiful city of Richmond ; and the chivalrous Mr. Faro was slowly wending
his way through Broad street to the bosom of his Confederate family, when, suddenly, he was confronted by a venerable figure in rags, soliciting alms.

THIRD SERIES. 263

" ' Out of my path, wretch !' ejaculated the haughty Virginian, impatiently ; and, tossing two thousand dollars ($2000) to the unfortunate mendicant, he attempted to pass on.

" The starving beggar was about to give way, and had drawn near the barrel which he carried on a wheelbarrow, for the purpose of adding to its contents the pittance just received, when the small amount of the latter seemed to attract his attention for the first time, and again he threw himself in the way of the miserly aristocrat.

" ' Moses Faro,' he muttered, in tones of profound agitation, 'you have your sheds full ($000000000) of Southern Bonds, while one poor barrel full ($000) must supply me for a whole day; yet would I not exchange places with a man capable of insulting honest poverty as you have done this night.'

" The proud Virginian felt the rebuke keenly ; and as he stood, momentarily silent, in the presence of the hapless victim of penury, he could not help remembering that he had, on that very morning, willingly given his youngest son five thousand dollars ($5000) to purchase a kite and some marbles. Greatly stricken in conscience, and heartily ashamed of his recent meanness, he turned to the suppliant, and said, kindly :

" ' Give me your address, and to-morrow morning I will send you a cart full ($000) of means. I would give you more now, but I have only sixty thousand dollars ($60,000) about me, with which to pay for the pair of boots I now have on.'

" ' Moses Faro,' responded the deeply-affected pauper, ' your noble charity will enable me to pay the nine thou-

12

264 ORPHEUS C. KERR PAPERS.

sand dollars ($9000) I owe for a week's board ; and now let me ask, how goes our sacred cause ? '

" ' Never brighter,' answered the wealthy Confederate, with enthusiasm. '. We have succeeded to-day in forcing five more cities through the Yankee lines, and are draging three whole Hessian armies to this city.'

" ' Then welcome poverty for a while longer,' cried the beggar, pathetically ; and so great was his exuberance of spirit at the news, that he resolved to spend five hundred dollars ($500) for a cigar in honor thereof.

" Mr. Faro walked thoughtfully on toward his residence, pondering earnestly the words he had listened to, and astonished to find how easily a rich man could give happiness to a poor one. After all, thought he, there is more contentment in poverty than in riches. Show me the rich man who can boast the sturdy lightness of heart inspiring that hackneyed rhyme, the

" ' CAROL OF THE CONFEDERATE BEGGAR.

" ' Though but fifty thousand dollars
Be the sum of all I own,
Yet I'm merry with my begging,
And I'm happy with my bone ;
Nor with any brother beggar
Does my heart refuse to share,
Though a thousand dollars only
Be the most I have to spare.

" ' I am shabby in my seven
Hundred dollar hat of straw,
And my dinner's but eleven
Hundred dollars in the raw

THIRD SERIES. 265

> Yet I hold my head the higher,
> That it owes the hatter least,
> And my scanty crumbs are sweeter
> Than the viands of a feast.'

" Humming to himself this simple lay of contented want, Mr. Faro reached his own residence, gave eighty dollars ($80) to a little boy on the sidewalk for blacking his boots, and entered the portals of the hospitable mansion. His wife met him in the hall, and, as they walked together into the parlor, he noticed that her expression was serious.

" ' Have you heard the latest news, Moses ? ' she asked.

" ' No,' returned the haughty Southerner.

" ' Well,' said the lady, 'just before you came in, I gave Sambo a hundred and twelve dollars ($112) to get an evening paper, which says that the Confederate Government is about to seize all the money in the country, to pay the soldiers.'

" A gorgeous smile lit up the features of the chivalric Virginian, and he said :

" ' Let them take both my shedsfull ($00000000) ; let them take it all ! Sooner than submit, or consent to be Reconstructed, I would give my very life even, for the sake of the Confederacy ! '

Mrs. Faro still looked serious.

" ' Moses,' she said, with quivering lips, ' have you not got, hidden away somewhere, *a twenty-shilling gold-piece* ($2,500,000) ? '

" Ghastly pale turned the proud Confederate, and he could barely stammer, —

" ' Ye-ye-yes.'

266 ORPHEUS C. KERR PAPERS.

" ' Well,' murmured the matron, ' it's the gold they intend to take, I reckon.'

" That was enough. Frantically tore Mr. Faro into the street; desperately raced he to the city limits; madly flew he past the pickets and sentinels ; swiftly scoured he down the Boynton Plank Road. A Yankee bayonet was at his bosom.

" ' Reconstruction ! ' shouted he.

" They took him before the nearest post-commandant, and he only said, —

" ' Let me be Reconstructed.' "

Need the reader be informed that he is now in New York, looking for a house, and in great need of some financial aid to help him pay the rent of such a residence as he has always been accustomed to and cannot live without? Yes, far from home, family, and friends, he is now one of those long-suffering, self-sacrificing Union refugees from the South, whom it is a pleasure to assist, and whose manly opposition to the military despotism of the Confederacy commends them to our utmost liberality. He will accept donations in money, and this fact should be sufficient to make all loyal men eager to extend such pecuniary encouragement as may suffice to keep him above any necessity for exertion until the presidency of some Bank can be procured for him by the Christian Commission.

I may add, my boy, that any monetary contribution intended for this excellent man, may be directed to

Yours, patronizingly,

ORPHEUS C. KERR.

LETTER CVII.

RECORDING THE LATEST DELPHIC UTTERANCES OF ONE WHOM WE ALL HONOR WITHOUT KNOWING WHY; AND RECOUNTING THE TRULY MARVELLOUS AFFAIR OF THE FORT BUILT ACCORDING TO TACITUS.

WASHINGTON, D C., March 29th, 1865.

IT is a beautiful trait of our common American nature, my boy, that we should be stood-upon by fleshy Old Age, and find ourselves reduced to the mental condition of mangled infants thereby. It is an airy characteristic of our gentle national temperament, to let shirt-collared Old Age, of much alpaca pants, sit down on us and cough into our ears. It is a part of our social organization as a reverential people to be forever weighed-down in our spirits by the awful respectability of double-chinned Old Age, and the solemn satisfaction it displays at its elephantine meals.

Hence, my boy, when I tell you that the Venerable Gammon beamed hither from his residential Mugville last Saturday, with a view to benefiting that wayward infant, his country, you will be prepared to learn that the populace fell upon their unworthy stomachs before him, and respectfully begged him to walk over their necks.

" My children," said the Venerable Gammon, with a fleshy smile, signifying that he had made them all, and yet didn't wish to seem proud, — " My children, this war

(267)

268 ORPHEUS C. KERR PAPERS.

is progressing just as I originally planned it, and will end successfully as soon as it terminates triumphantly. Behold my old friend, Phœbus," says the Venerable Gammon, pointing an adipose forefinger at the sun, with a patriarchal air of having benignantly invented that luminary, though benevolently permitting Providence to have all the credit, " it is not more certain that my warm-hearted friend Phœbus will rise in the yeast to-morrow morning than that the Southern Confederacy will not be capable of fighting a single additional battle after it shall have lost the ability to take part in another engagement."

Then the entire populace requested immediate leave to black the boots of their aged benefactor and idol, and seven-and-thirty indefatigable reporters, with pencils behind their ears, telegraphed to seven-and-thirty powerful morning journals, that the end of the rebellion might be looked for in about a couple of hours.

I don't mind revealing to you, as a curious fact, my boy, that no mortal man is able to understand how the Venerable Gammon has done anything at all in this war. In fact, I can't exactly perceive what earthly deed he has actually performed to make him preferable to George Washington ; but it is generally inferred, from the size of his watch-seals and the lambency of his spectacles, that he has in some way been more than a parent to the country ; and the thousands now buying some beneficent Petroleum stock, which he has to sell, are firmly convinced that its sale is positively calculated to forever benefit the human race.

Oh ! that I were Ovid, or Anacreon, to describe fittingly the recent little wedding entertainment, at which

THIRD SERIES. 269

this excellently-aged teacher and preserver of his species was fatly present, diffusing permission for all mankind to be happy and not mind him. After beaming parentally upon the officiating Mackerel chaplain, with a benignity inseparable from the idea that all clergymen were the work of his hands, he took the dimpled chin of the bride between his thumb and forefinger, and says he:

"My children, I am an old, old man; but may ye be happy." Here he kissed the bride. "Yes, my children," says the venerable Gammon, with a blessing on the world in every tone of his buttery voice, "I am far down in the vale of years; but may ye be very happy." And he kissed the bride. "Still, my children," says the Venerable Gammon, with steaming spectacles, "I would be willing to be even older, if my country desired it; but may ye be forever happy." So he kissed the bride. "Oh!" says the Venerable Gammon, abstractedly placing a benefactor's arm around her waist, and looking benevolently about the room as though consenting to its possession of four walls, — "Oh!" says he, "it is a privilege to be old for such a cause as this; but may ye be supremely happy." At this juncture he kissed the bride. "I am old enough," says the venerable Gammon, "to be your brother." And he kissed every young woman there.

Whereupon it was the general impression that an apostle was present; and when the bridegroom subsequently hinted, in a disagreeable whisper, that two bottles of port were enough to confuse the mind of a Methuselah himself, there was a wonderful unanimity among the ladies as to the probable misery of the bride's future life.

But wherefore, O, Eros, dost thou detain me in such

270   ORPHEUS C. KERR PAPERS.

scenes as these, while the hoarse trumpet of bully Mars
calls me to the field of strategic glory ?   Hire an imaginary
horse, my boy, at a fabulous livery-stable, and, in fancy,
trot beside me as I urge my architectural steed, the
Gothic Pegasus, toward the Mackerel lines in front of
Paris.

Believing that you are entirely familiar with the very
fat works of C. Tacitus, and minutely remember Book
II. of his Annals, let me draw your attention to that fort
Aliso which he describes as being built upon the River
Luppia by Drusus, father of Germanicus, and constituting
the commencement of a chain of posts to the Rhine.   Just
such a work has been erected on the shores of Duck Lake
by Mackerel genius, as the key to a long line of remarkable mud-works.   It is modelled after Aliso, chiefly because
that work was notorious for being near the Canal of Drusus; and the whole world knows that canal-digging is inseparable from all our national strategy.

Fort Bledandide is the name of the Mackerel institution
destined to receive immortality in Mr. Tacitus Greeley's
exciting History of this distracting war ; but to me belongs
the earlier privilege of enabling a moral weekly journal to
confuse its readers with the first reliable report of the marvellous battle of Fort Bledandide.

It was at quite an early hour, my boy, on the morning
of my arrival before Paris, that a faint sound, as of gentlemen firing guns, was heard to proceed from a point
some six feet outside Fort Bledandide.   Nobody was up
at the time, save a few venerable Mackerels, who, in
daily expectation of some carnage, had selected that hour
at which to write their wills ; and it was left for these

antique beings to be the first of our troops disturbed by a shameless Confederacy who lifted his head slowly above our works, and deliberately aimed a deadly horse-pistol at Jacob Barker, the regimental dog. Hideous was the explosion ensuing, as the night-key with which the dread weapon was loaded went hurtling through the air some ten yards above its mark; and an aged Mackerel looked up from his penmanship.

"What!" says he, with some animation, "are, my spectacles guilty of a falsehood, or have I indeed the pleasure of seeing Mr. Davis?"

The Confederacy reloaded his horse-pistol with a handful of carpet-tacks, and says he:

"I am that individdle."

Raising a bell that stood by his side, the venerable Mackerel rang a hasty peal, which had the effect to arouse two or three of the other scribes from their writing, and cause them to apply ear-trumpets to their ears. Simultaneously the first warrior roared, through a fire-trumpet:

"Comrades! We are surprised."

At the same instant the Confederacy burst into a tempest of unseemly chuckles, and fired his carpet-tacks into the soft hat of the nearest Mackerel, causing that hoary veteran to drop his will and scratch his head with an air of hopeless bewilderment.

"Have you any tea that you could give me?" says the Confederacy, scrambling into the Fort, — "any Hyson senior or junior? Have you any coffee? Oh, *do* give me some coffee." Here the Confederacy winked profoundly, to indicate that his request was intended merely as a bit of surprising humor. Meantime, six other Con-

272   ORPHEUS C. KERR PAPERS.

federacies with horse-pistols had walked in to look for breakfast, and the facetious business of relieving the slowly-awakened garrison of their loud-ticking and rather cheap gold watches was performed with neatness and dispatch. After which the aged Mackerels were dismissed to join the main body of the ancient Brigade some ten yards to the rear of the work, with the remark, that their vandal rulers would find it somewhat difficult to reconstruct the sunny South.

Thus, my boy, was accomplished another of those surprises which not unfrequently give the most villanous cause an appearance of temporary success; though at times they prove real blessings to the good cause by including the capture of three or four brass-buttoned brigadiers.

But, pause, my feeble pen, ere thou venturest upon the hopeless task of putting into language the holy rage of the General of the Mackerel Brigade, when he learned the capture of Fort Bledandide. Pause, miserable quill, ere thou plungest into an insane effort to picture the awful state of vengeance exciting Captain Villiam Brown on the same occasion. As is his invariable custom at such junctures, the General at once retired to his tent to practise on the accordion, leaving Villiam to form a few regiments of the Mackerel reserve in line of battle for the recapture of the position.

" Ah!" says Villiam, spiritedly, " here's a chance for a baynit charge after the manner of Napoleon's Old Guard; and I hereby notify Regiment 5, that the eyes of the whole world are upon them."

Captain Bob Shorty and I had got ready our bits of

smoked glass, to preserve our eyes from the too-great glitter of the dazzling achievement about to come off, when we noticed that Villiam motioned with his famous sword, Escalibar, for the spectacled warriors to pause a moment.

"If any of you martial beings happen to have any small change about you at this exciting moment," says Villiam, paternally, "I will take charge of it, for safety."

This noble proposition, my boy, might have been accepted unanimously, had not the discharge, at that instant, of a horse-pistol from the ramparts of Fort Bledandide caused the entire regiment to partially disappear! That is to say, every man went down upon his stomach, according to the latest principles of regimental strategy.

"Ah!" says Villiam, "how are the mighty fallen!"

Loudly rang a tremendous horse-laugh from the Confederacies in the Fort, several of whom were seen making off toward Paris with Orange County howitzers under each arm. I could see, by the aid of my smoked glass, that the Chivalry on the ramparts was sitting on a chest, with his discharged horse-pistol across his knee, and a series of feeble winks chasing each other around his Confederate eyelids.

"By all that's Federal!" says Captain Bob Shorty, "the scorpion surrenders!"

At the word, up sprang Regiment 5, like the men of Roderick Dhu, and straightforward they swept into Fort Bledandide, as a wave of the angry sea will sometimes sweep into a doomed barrel on the beach. Such was the shock of this dare-devil charge, that the winking Confederacy on the ramparts incontinently rolled off his chest and was captured without much carnage.

274 ORPHEUS C. KERR PAPERS.

"Do you surrender to the United States of America?" says Villiam, with much star-spangled banner in his manner.

The Confederacy raised himself up on an elbow and hiccup'd gloomily.

"By all that's Federal!" says Captain Bob Shorty, "he's been drinking some of that air Commissary whiskey of ours."

Then, my boy, did Captain Villiam Brown evidence that exquisite quality of our humanity, which bids us forget all wrongs and enmities at the eloquent appeal of death. No sooner had Captain Bob Shorty made the above remark, than his whole aspect changed to pity, and he feelingly knelt beside the miserable captive.

"Have you any last request to make, poor inseck?" asked Villiam, much affected.

The misguided Confederacy was speechless; but made an attempt to scratch his breast.

"Ah!" says Villiam, with deep emotion, "you mean that your conscience is a still small woice."

Here the Confederacy scratched his left leg feebly; and says Captain Bob Shorty:

"According to your rule, Villiam, his conscience must be quite large, extending to his legs."

Nervously arose Captain Villiam Brown to his feet, with such a shudder running through his manly frame as caused every brass button to jingle.

"I think," says Villiam, with a ghastly smile, "that some of his conscience is a-walking softly down my backbone, with a hop now and then."

Alas! my boy, we all have consciences, save green

grocers and fashionable bootmakers; and who among us but has felt his conscience to be at times almost totally disregarded, until it has finally brought him to the scratch by turning to flee?

Scarcely was Fort Bledandide recovered by the valor of our arms when the General of the Mackerel Brigade let fly the following

" GENERAL ORDER.

" The General Commanding announces to the Mackerels that the Southern Confederacy has taken place. Also, that the unconquerable Mackerel Brigade has taken place back again.

" Yesterday morning the Confederacy massed himself and succeeded, through the unabated slumbers of the persons hired to sit up with him, in obtaining Fort Bledandide.

"Prompt measures were taken by Captain Villiam Brown, Eskevire; and, although an entire regiment fell in the assault, the work was retaken.

" Two lessons can be learned from these operations: First, that the notorious Southern Confederacy is now reduced to a mere shell; and, secondly, that said shell has a very short fuse.

" THE GENERAL OF THE MACKEREL BRIGADE.

(" GREEN SEAL.")

I was still reading this pointed document, when there arrived, from Paris, a Confederate being, in carpet slippers and white cotton gloves, whose name was Lamb, and who bore peace-propositions.

276 ORPHEUS C. KERR PAPERS.

" I have come," says he, affably, " to say, that the army of the North can now be admitted into the army of the Confederacy for a conjoint attack on combined Europe, after which the sunny South will forgive all her creditors, and see what can be done for the Northern masses."

Let this frank speech prove, my boy, what all our excellent democratic * morning journals of limited circulation have so long maintained, — that it rests entirely with the President to secure an immediate cessation of hostilities with the Southerners, by forgetting all the wrongs of the past, while they are for getting all the rights of the future.

Yours, pacifically,

ORPHEUS C. KERR.

* This letter was originally addressed to the editor of an excellent little democratic weekly journal, who went carefully over it and substituted the word " patriotic " for " democratic," whenever the latter occurred: — thereby achieving the most perfect and astounding perversion of meaning on record!

CVIII.

NARRATING THE UTTERLY UNPARALLELED CONQUEST OF PARIS BY THE VENERABLE MACKEREL BRIGADE, AFTER THREE DAYS' INCONCEIVABLE STRATEGY; IN FACT, A BATTLE-REPORT AFTER THE MANNER OF ALL OUR EXCITED MORNING JOURNALS; UPON PERUSING WHICH, EACH READER IS EXPECTED TO WRAP HIMSELF UP IN THE AMERICAN FLAG AND SHAKE HIS FIST AT COMBINED EUROPE.

WASHINGTON D. C., April 4th, 1865.

To loud huzzas our flag ascends, as climbs a flame the dizzy mast, while all its burning glory bends from where the planets seal it fast; and, pliant to the chainless winds, a blazing sheet, a lurid scroll, the Compact of the Stars it binds in fire that warms a nation's soul!

All of which, my boy, is the poetry of that banner whose union of a starry section of evening with the hues of dawn and sunset makes it a very good marriage-certificate of the wedding of old Mr. Day and the Widow Night. (Let us hope that Mr. Day will never be without a sun.)

And do you ask me wherefore I thus burst into red-hot song? — wherefore I inflict further verses upon a flag already washed almost to pieces in a freshet of poet's tears? — wherefore I jingle rhymes of Bostonian severity at the commencement of an epistle whose readers may not all be Emersons?

278   ORPHEUS C. KERR PAPERS.

Know, then, my boy, that the chant is to celebrate the conquest of the ancient City of Paris, which, for many years past, has actually waxed prosperous against Mackerel strategy, but now rests a prize beneath that glorious bunting which we all like to see our poor relations die for: beneath that ensign of freedom for which every man of us would willingly sacrifice his life, did he not feel that his first great duty was to his helpless family, who like to have him stay at home and take them to the opera.

O my country ! — sublime in thy wounds, chivalrous in thy triumph, more than royal in the kingless magnificence of thine undaunted power ; — forget not the patriots who have stayed at home on account of their families ; for surely such a disinterested and general demonstration of domestic virtue seems to indicate that our police force is uselessly large.

Let me not, however, waste time in national boasting, while the crowning result of consummate Mackerel strategy demands of me that narrating exercise of the pen without which even brigadiers might fail to receive public credit for deeds after the manner of Napoleon.

Retrace, my boy, to the happy days of your youth, and you may remember that I once described the ancient city of Paris as a house founded upon a bar-room and surrounded by warlike settlements of Confederacies. Here were collected all the lemons, glassware, sugar, spoons, and cloves of the sunny South ; and — though all else were lost — while these remained to them, the Confederacies were still unbroken in spirits and only spoke of Columbia to observe : " She may attack our chivalrous banner of Stars and Bars, and capture all the stars if she pleases ;

but while our Bars remain, we shall still be able to liquor." Therefore it is, that the aged and aristocratic city of Paris has stubbornly brought to grief so many of our admirable brass-buttoned generals, several of whom are now enjoying that unblemished obscurity which ungrateful republics are apt to bestow upon unappreciated greatness.

On the day succeeding the sanguinary affair of Fort Bledandide, my boy, while notes of busy preparation were rising from all parts of the Mackerel camp, one of our pickets was awakened by the sound of many equestrians riding over his body, and immediately put on his spectacles to discern whether they were friends or foes. The inspection lasted until one skeleton charger had stepped upon his canteen; whereupon the Mackerel picket discovered that the new-comers were the Anatomical cavalry, under Captain Samyule Sa-mith, just returned from operations in Confederate railway stock, which they had raised so far above par as to give it a very decided mar.

Proudly rode Samyule at the head of his triumphant bone-works, and the jingle of their spurs and sabres was like unto the collision of many tin pans. Gayly rode they to headquarters, and, says Samyule, " Sire, we have interrupted the railway travel of the Southern Confederacy for the season ; and obliterated the tracks of treason, that it may no longer rail against us. Further depot-nent saith not."

The General of the Mackerel Brigade laid aside his accordion, and says he :

" My sons, I would that every earthly foe to our distracted banner could at this moment be placed on board a

280 ORPHEUS C. KERR PAPERS.

railway train in any part of this country. Because, says the General, thoughtfully, "a ride on an American railway train of cars is foreordained car-nage."t

After this speech, my boy, it was generally allowed that the Mackerel commander was even with Samyule; and as the Anatomical Cavalry swept off to the left to flank the unseemly Confederacies defending Paris, the main body of the venerable brigade, under Captain Villiam Brown and Captain Bob Shorty, commenced strategical designs on that city.

Thus early in the engagement a bloodthirsty Confederacy had succeeded in training a fowling-piece from behind a chimney on the roof of Paris, greatly worrying our troops with dried beans, and the Orange County Howitzers were already concentrated upon him with a view to cutting off his legs; when there suddenly appeared within our lines a maiden, stricken in years, with a white plush bonnet, a green silk umbrella, and the ninety-ninth number of the History of this War under one arm. She waved a hand toward the Mackerels nearest her, and says she:

"On, to Paris! On, to Paris! or a decimated and indignant country, acting on the predictions in the ninety-ninth number of the most accurate History of the War now sold to subscribers only, will indignantly demand that EVERYBODY be at once removed!"

Here the General of the Mackerel Brigade made his appearance from the rear, and says he:

"What do you desire, Miss P. Hen?"

"On, to Paris!" shrieked the maiden. "On, to the capital of the brutalized dealers in human flesh and blood,

THIRD SERIES. 281

and drag them to the scaffold!" Here Miss P. Hen drew a long breath, and says she, "Let's have no vacillating."

"All right, Mamsell," says the General.

"And the country'd have more confidence in *you*," says Miss P. Hen, vigorously, "if you'd stop chewing that nasty tobacco, which is only fit for brutes and dealers in human flesh and blood. On, to Paris! or" —

At this juncture, my boy, the aged Miriam caught sight of the Conservative Kentucky Chap, haranguing against her down the Accomac road, and toddled furiously away to chastise him with her umbrella.

Meanwhile, the Orange County Howitzers had sent some pounds of shrapnel in the direction of the hostile Confederacy on the roof; and as the bricks began to fly from the chimney, and the dried beans came at longer intervals, Regiment 5 of the Mackerel Brigade moved nearer to the beleaguered capital, and opened an effective fire of musketry upon the azure zenith. Captain William Brown was about to order an assault, when certain windows in the upper stories of Paris were thrown up, and there rained therefrom such a hurtling tempest of stew-pans, hearth-brushes, shaving-cups, and boxes of blacking, that hundreds of Mackerel spectacles were broken. Simultaneously the sanguinary Confederacy on the roof put a double charge of dried beans through the coat-tails of Captain Bob Shorty, and our troops — " the object of the reconnoissance being fully accomplished " — withdrew in good order to their former position.

Quickly, thereupon, appeared a canvas banner from the

282   ORPHEUS C. KERR PAPERS.

garret windows of Paris, inscribed : "Chalk up the First
Round for the Southern Confederacy!" and the first
day's fight was over.

All that night, my boy, did the venerable Mackerel
Brigade lay upon their arms, finding all their hands
asleep, in consequence, when morning broke ; and as often
as a venturesome Confederacy skulked near Fort Bledandide to steal a cannon, just so often did one Mackerel
picket nudge another Mackerel picket and ask him if he
didn't think he heard something.

At last there came a gradual hush over everything, as
though the whole world were an antechamber to a room
in which rested some dear sick child.   Then the sharp
edges of this terrestrial bowl in which we hang over the
sun at night began to define themselves all around, as
though an early candle had just been brought underneath
to light the fire.   And at last a slowly-deepening lurid
glow appeared around the sides of the bowl, as though the
fire was just getting a start.   It was morning.

Fearful that if I go on in that strain any longer, some
sentimental Philadelphian may carry me off by main force
to write for the " Lady's Book," let me call your notice to
the extreme left of the Mackerel line, where Captain
Samyule Sa-mith and the Anatomical Cavalry, supported
by Sergeant O'Pake and Regiment 3, were formed in line
of battle, facing certain rickety Confederacies under Captain Munchausen.

" Comrades," says Samyule, vainly attempting to keep
the hind-legs of his anatomical steed from trying to sur-
round the two fore-legs — " comrades, one blow, and Syra-
cuse is free !   For-r-ward ! "

THIRD SERIES. 283

But what is this, starting up, as from the ground, right in the path of what else had been the most exorbitant cavalry charge on record ? It is the aged Miss P. Hen, with her white plush bonnet much mashed from a recent severe single combat with the Conservative Kentucky Chap, and the ninety-ninth number of the History of the War still unsold. She ate a Graham biscuit, and says she :

" Just once — I only want to say just once, that everybody is a-howling at me like wolves, and abusing me, because I said ' On to Paris.' So I want to say, just once, that I never, never will say one word about the war again, no matter how much you want me to. Now there's no use of your asking me, because I never, never will ! "

And she hoisted her green silk umbrella and stalked grimly from the field, like the horrid apparition of a nervous widower's dream.

" Really," says Samyule, irritably, " I don't think there's any other country where old women would be allowed on the field of battle without epaulets on their shoulders. But let us proceed with the war," says Samyule, earnestly, " or we shall not get through in time for our coming. conflict with combined Europe."

Loud ring the bugles, my boy, on either side, as when two chivalrous cocks crow defiance to each other from neighboring roosts ; and presently two rival circus-companies met in tremendous collision with two-up and two-down, two over and two under : guard — parry — feint — thrust ! Twick, thwack, slam, bang ; click-click, click-

click, click-click; chip, chop, higgledy-piggledy, crush, crowd, and helter-skelter.

"Let me get at you, foul Hessian!" roared the hairy Munchausen, with his horse hopping sideways in every direction.

"Die in thy sins!" shouted the excited Samyule, taking a slide toward his charger's ears, as that spirited animal ecstatically waved his hinder feet in the air.

"Coward, thou would'st fly me!" ejaculated Munchausen, just as his Arabian got a-straddle of a caisson.

"You are my prisoner!" thundered Samyule, endeavoring to restrain his blooded courser from climbing a tree near by.

"Beg for your life!" howled Munchausen, frantically clasping his arms about the neck of his Hambletonian colt as they went skipping against an ambulance together.

"Say thy last prayer!" yelled Samyule, backing frenziedly into the middle of the Christian Commission.

"This to thy heart!" screamed Munchausen, disappearing in a ditch.

"Victory!" ejaculated Samyule, rolling down a hill.

And the second day's fighting was ended.

Night again upon the battle-field. The wearied soldier, as he seeks a few hours of repose upon the damp and dreary ground, wonders what the people of the great patriotic cities will think of the battle of the day; whether they are indeed unspeakably proud and fond of the men perilling and losing their lives that the nation may live? Oh, believe it, thou most innocent of heroes; for is it not so written in all our excellent morning journals? Put no trust in the Satyrs who tell thee that thy countrymen at home, in the exultation of victory, hold thee only as an unconsidered part of the dumb and blind machine which hoists thy captain to eminence. Yet would I have thee turn thy fairest hope, thy perfect faith, to that one spot of all the world where kneels to-night some fond, familiar form ; where loving hands are humbly uplifted for an absent one, and quivering lips implore, Almighty Father, guard him still!

Now tremble, earth, and shake, ye friendly spheres, for the Mackerel Brigade, glittering with spectacles and gorgeous with red neck-ties and gold watches, advances for a third round with the unblushing Confederacies of Paris, several of whom are on the roof with duck-guns in their hands and slaughter in their hearts. As I gaze upon the wonderful scene through my bit of smoked glass, the Orange County Howitzers burst into a roar, not unlike a Dutch chorus, and the sun is in momentary danger of being hit.

To speak once more in a past tense : — Forward rolled the Mackerel tide of battle the whole length of the line, with skirmishers thrown out to catch Confederate chickens, and the deadly peal of treason's duck-gun mingled hoarsely with the angry bang of loyalty's random musket. Heading Regiment 5, and mounted on his geometrical steed, Euclid, Captain Villiam Brown essayed a daring charge at the front door of Paris; while Captain Bob Shorty, with a portion of the Conic Section just arrived from Accomac, thundered toward the window of the first floor ; but here a female Confederacy opened a heavy fire of pokers and gridirons

286 ORPHEUS C. KERR PAPERS.

from the basement, and there was too much danger to the spectacles of the ancient Brigade to warrant persistence in the bold attempt.

Far to the left, with his eyes blazing like the ends of two cigars, and his nose glowing like a transparent strawberry, Captain Samyule Sa-mith got himself and his celebrated horse-marines so ingeniously entangled and mixed up with Captain Munchausen's and everybody else's command, that the Schleswig-Holstein question was a very ordinary conundrum in comparison, and the fight in that part of the field bade fair to last for a few years without much definite carnage.

Then, again, on the calm waters of Duck Lake (now too deep for wading in consequence of recent rains), that hoary old salt, Rear Admiral Head, unhooked his famous flagship, the "Shockingbadhat," and set out with his improved swivel-gun and agile Mackerel crew to take a hand in the carnival of conquest.

"Loosen my plates!" swore the aged son of Neptune in his iron-clad manner, as he adjusted his spectacles and extracted a slow-match from one corner of his snuff-box, — "Loosen my plates! but the navy must kill a few Confederate insects, — bark my turret, if it mustn't."

It was really beautiful, my boy, to see an iron-clad tar of such great age light the slow-match with his own meerschaum, and aim the improved artillery directly at the rear-elevation of a Confederacy tying his shoe in one of the side windows of Paris.

Ker-bang! went the triumph of naval ingenuity, causing the flag-ship to hop only a few inches into the air; and a Confederacy with amputated coat-tails was instantly

THIRD SERIES. 287

seen to spin wildly around and rub himself like one in a bath.

Not to sicken you, my boy, with too much of such heart-rending slaughter, let me say that a dense cloud of sulphurous smoke soon entirely veiled the doomed City of Paris, into which the strategical Mackerels continued for hours to pour such torrents of lead as no number of windows could stand. Finally, as night approached, a person of black extraction, with wool on the brain, emerged from the cloud quite close to Villiam, and says he:

" De place hab surrender, sah."

" Ah! " says Villiam, pulling out his ruffles, " is the conflick too much for the scorpions ? "

The faithful black arranged a silver cake-basket more firmly under his coat, and says he:

" Dey's all gone over Jordan."

Wild were the cheers that rent the air at this intelligence, and right quickly were our national troops marching into the bar-room of captured Paris, to the inspiring strains of " Drops of Brandy," from the night-key bugle of the Mackerel band. Our distracted banner, too, was just being raised triumphantly upon the roof, when there suddenly emerged, from the shadow of the rear-guard, Miss P. Hen, leaning trustfully upon the arm of the Conservative Kentucky Chap !

" Now," says she, vivaciously, " is the very moment for the President to save our bleeding and bankrupt people, by paying four hundred millions of dollars to the sunny South for her losses in this war, and offering her such terms as may induce her to make that peace which is ab-

13

288 ORPHEUS C. KERR PAPERS.

solutely necessary to close the most accurate History of the War now sold to subscribers only."

Pause, my boy, ere you execrate the venerable Miss P. Hen ; for there is more than one fidgety old lady tendering advice to the Government at this crisis ; and the sisterhood is not without members who wear your own style of costume.

Yours, carefully,

ORPHEUS C. KERR.

LETTER CIX.

WHICH ENDETH THE THIRD VOLUME OF THIS INEXPRESSIBLY VERA-
CIOUS HISTORY OF THE WAR; AND SHOWETH HOW A GREAT RE-
PUBLIC FINALLY OVERCAME ITS SURPASSINGLY MENDACIOUS FOES,
AND HOW IT EVINCES ITS UNSPEAKABLE GRATITUDE TO PROVI-
DENCE FOR SUCH A VICTORY.

WASHINGTON, D. C., April 11th, 1865.

LOOK, my boy, upon the east wall of my luxurious presence-chamber, and mark how I have maliciously pasted thereon a map of besotted Europe; with all its capitals, rivers, mountains, and inland puddles laid down with an accuracy and multitudinosity to forever enlighten and utterly confound every sniffing little schoolboy-geographer in the land. What a shapeless chunk of inferior dirt is Europe! How like a minute and feeble skiptail does it appear, when compared with our own gigantic straddlebug of a country! Yet has the skiptail ventured to interfere offensively in the private affairs of the straddlebug; and the interference, and the private affairs, and the possible upshot of the whole matter, remind me forcibly of a spirited little event which once occurred in the Sixth Ward.

The male and female Michael O'Korrigan, my boy, occupied a spacious apartment on the fine, airy, eighth floor of the sumptuous Maison Mulligan in that celebrated Ward, and for several years the course of their true love ran so smoothly that it became hopelessly insipid and exasperating to all the old maids for blocks around. Nothing was ever equal to the peaceful unity of the male and female O'Korrigan ; and did Michael find it necessary, in the course of some friendly discussion with a neighbor on the stairs, to call for a hatchet till he broke the ugly nose of the spalpeen, it was the wife of his bosom that handed him his own bit of a stick, and joined in the argument herself with a poker for a referee. But nothing's perfect in this world except the wisdom of owls and Congressmen, and Mrs. O'Korrigan's military virtues and wholesome command of her husband had the slight drawback of a constitutional taste for poteen. Michael expostulated with her by the hair, and remonstrated with her by the shoulders, and plead with her over the head ; but all to no purpose ; and he was greatly assisted and comforted by a bit of a preacher named Father O'Tod, who took care of everybody's virtue except his own. It was Father O'Tod that sat down beside her quite pious and comfortable, and

" Ailey," says he, " it's clane disgusted I am at heart," says he, " to see a wake crature of the hen sex," says he, " a-cackling over a baste of a black bottle as if it was a fresh egg," says he. " And Ailey," says he, " if your husband was anything but a wake-minded bouchal of a man," says he, " it's with a bit of crab-thorn that he'd be persuadin' ye to give it up for good," says he.

" Oh, sorra the day," says she, " that I'm not behoolden to yer riverence," says she, " for such illigant advice," says she ; " but it's meself that's accountable to somebody else than yerself and Michael O'Korrigan," says she, " for what I do," says she. "Do ye mind that, Father O'Tod?" says she. "And when I'm afther takin' a drop for the good of me health," says she, "I don't bother any one," says she; "but stay shut up in my own room," says she, "and only ask to be let alone," says she.

Now it chanced that Mr. O'Korrigan, being invited by Father O'Tod, and especially aggrieved by having one of his best Sunday shoes coolly appropriated as a sort of fanciful leathern case for the aforesaid black bottle, finally resolved to at least recapture his property, and, mayhap, spill the poteen. So he placed the hair of his head in Mrs. O'Korrigan's left hand, and scraped his nose against the nails of her right, and was enjoying himself very much, when Father O'Tod came in, and

"Michael agrah," says he, "it's spaichless with horrors I am," says he, "to see ye brawling with yer own wife," says he, "and she a woman," says he.

"The marcy of Heaven on me!" says Mike, says he; "but isn't it yer own self," says he, "that's been advisin' me by the year," says he, "to stop her poteen?" says he.

"It's not the desthruction of the poteen yer after at all," says Father O'Tod, says he; "but only to wrinch from her," says he, "an owld brogan," says he, "that ye'd be as well without," says he.

Just at this moment Mr. O'Korrigan managed to get possession of the brogan referred to, and was commencing to use it most potently as an instrument of wholesome matrimonial correction, when the scuffle displaced the unfortunate black bottle from the pocket of Mrs. O'Korrigan, and it fell to the floor and — broke into fifty pieces.

"It's accident that did that," says Father O'Tod, says

292 ORPHEUS C. KERR PAPERS.

he, " and not yerself at all, Michael O'Korrigan," says he; "and it's not myself," says he, "that'll give aither of ye pardon," says he. " But I'm l'anin' to Ailey," says he, " and it's masses I'll say for her," says he, " if she's bate to death," says he.

" Ailey, avourneen," says Mike, says he, " the bottle's broke," says he, " and I've got me brogan," says he, " and ye may keep the rest," says he, " if ye'll make up," says he.

" Michael, darlint," says she, " ye can place yer big mout' in the middle of me faychures," says she; " but as for Father O'Tod," says she, " it's achin' I am to comb his hypocritical hair," says she, " with a poker," says she.

" Ailey, me angel," says Mike, says he, " it'll be showin' our gratitude to Saint Payter," says he, " that we an't both kilt intirely," says he, " lavin' aich other orphans," says he, " if we just slather the owld humbug together," says he.

So they both fell upon Father O'Tod with a heartiness not to be described, and that excellent and neutral old gentleman was much mussed in his linen.

Far be it from me, my boy, to say that combined Europe, and especially the step-mother country, is at all like Father O'Tod, or that Slavery in the remotest degree resembles a small black bottle; but interference in the quarrels of married folks is apt to excite the liveliest enmity of both parties, and two-against-one has been known to result quite spiritedly therefrom.

Therefore, let the skiptail of Europe beware! for even I, an humble historian and no warrior, am filled with that spirit of defiance to everything across the Atlantic which might serve to inspire a brigadier, the editor of an able morning journal, a fierce turkey-cock, or any other type of matchless valor. One week ago, this American breast of mine was wild for the immediate redemption of lovely Ireland, by reason of the marvellous and triumphant capture of Paris by the thrice-valiant Mackerel Brigade; and to-day such an accession of national triumph stares all through the columns of our more stentorian morning journals, that I demand the immediate disenthrallment from foreign tyrants of Hungary, Poland, Venetia, Mexico, Canada, Jersey City, and the Guano Islands.

Munchausen, my boy, has surrendered! That mirror of chivalry and hollow-eyed wanderer in a forest of whiskers has yielded to his noble desire for a piece — of something to eat, and gracefully permitted himself and his command to be wooed from their guiding star, — starvation.

Immediately after the unprecedented battle for Paris, and while yet the agitated Miss P. Hen and divers enterprising political chaps who had followed our troops were organizing a Republican caucus in the bar-room of the captured capital, the unconquerable Mackerel Brigade pushed on after the unseemly Confederacies, with a view to further carnage. Not a stump of a tree was seen but it was at once taken for Mr. Davis himself, and had the direful Orange County Howitzers concentrated upon it; yet such dangers did not deter our venerable Mackerel boys from their assigned pursuit, and ere long their glittering spectacles surrounded a goodly swamp, wherein were perceptible the caitiff Confederacies up to their chins in the sacred soil. With only their heads above the mud,

294   ORPHEUS C. KERR PAPERS.

these sons of chivalry looked not unlike a vast cabbage-patch romantically viewed by twilight; while far up the vegetable vista glowed the eyes of Captain Munchausen, like those of an irascible Thomas cat who sees a dog down the lane.

Pitching his tent in a spot where no vagrant stone could reach it, the General of the Mackerel Brigade took off his coat and vest, rolled up the legs of his inexpressibles, and commenced the following

CORRESPONDENCE.

MUNCHAUSEN, *Southern Confederacy :*

" SIR, —The result of the last strategical combat between us must convince you of the hopelessness of further military confusion in this country. I feel that it is so, and consider it my duty to shift from myself the responsibility of further carnage by asking of you the surrender of that portion of the sunny South known as the Southern Confederacy.

    " THE GENERAL OF THE MACKEREL BRIGADE.
(" Green Seal.")

You may observe, my boy, that the remark : " I feel that it is so," does not make the strongest kind of connection with the preceding sentence; but great warriors are apt to be shaky in their rhetoric; and the Confederacy responded thus :

" GEN. MACK. BRIG. :

" SIRRAH, — Though repelling with scorn the vandal insinuation that further military confusion on my part is

THIRD SERIES.   295

hopeless, I agree with you as to the stoppage of further carnage, and desire to know upon what terms you will haul the celebrated Southern Confederacy out of this swamp.

"MUNCHAUSEN X his mark."

(This chivalrous manner of signing a name with a Cross is a knightly expression of profound piety, descended from the ancient crusaders to the Southern chivalry of the present day.)

To the above epistle the General thus replied :

"MUNCHAUSEN, *Southern Confederacy :*

" SIR, — I propose to receive the surrender of the well-known Southern Confederacy on the following terms :

" Fresh rolls for all the officers and men to be made at once, and the boots of the Southern Confederacy to be blacked by officers duly appointed by the United States of America. All the officers to give their individual pay rolls, that they may be cashed by the United States. Such public and private property as has been stolen by the well-known Southern Confederacy to be turned over to the police-officers appointed to take charge of it.

" Each officer will be permitted to retain both of his arms, and, together with the men, is expected to return calmly to his family, and not commit assault upon the United States of America without due provocation.

" THE GENERAL OF THE MACKEREL BRIGADE.

(" Green Seal.")

It is related in tradition, that when the knightly Mun-

13*

296 ORPHEUS C. KERR PAPERS.

chausen received this epistle, he laughed horribly for the space of at least half an hour, as though greatly rejoiced at a bit of unparalleled waggishness. After which he delivered himself of four sinister winks at nothing, simultaneously exclaiming :

"By Chivalry ! here's magnanimity."

After which he wrote thus :

"GEN. MACK. BRIG. :

"SIRRAH, — I have received your scrawl of this date, containing what may be denominated terms of first-class board for the celebrated Southern Confederacy. Inasmuch as said terms give me rather more advantage than half a dozen strategical victories over your vandals could possibly have procured for us, I hereby permit you to capture us at once, in order to avoid further carnage in your ranks.

"MUNCHAUSEN X his mark."

Other letters incidental to this business passed between the two paladins, my boy ; but as the letters of all great men are proverbial for their great dignity and heaviness, and are immensely calculated to incline readers to untimely repose, I have spared you the infliction. Suffice it to say, that when Captain Villiam Brown read the Mackerel terms of surrender, he spasmodically applied his lips to a canteen, with the air of one who takes poison because the butcher's daughter has refused to be won by his manly shape.

"Ah ! " says Villiam, " such magnanimity ! "

Captain Bob Shorty was playing Old Sledge with three members of the Sanitary Commission when the document arrived.

"By all that's Federal!" says Captain Bob Shorty, "it appears to me — it really appears to me, Villiam, that I never see so much magnanimity!"

They took it to Captain Samyule Sa-mith as he sat by the roadside, straightening his highly-tempered sabre with a stone.

"I cannot always agree entirely with my brother officers on all points," says Samyule, reflectively, "for some of them are ineddicated: but I find in this document great magnanimity!"

Magnanimity, my boy, is the revenge of generous minds; as the venerable male parent feelingly observed when he made over his whole property to the interesting son who had just tried to poison him by putting arsenic into his coffee, and expressed an intention to burn him to death in his bed that night.

The glorious news of the surrender had no sooner reached the city of Paris than the aged and gifted Miss P. Hen organized an enthusiastic mass meeting of the decrepit Union element, and a speaker's stand was quickly erected, over which floated a banner inscribed

REGULAR MAGNANIMOUS NOMINATION
FOR
PRESIDENT OF THE UNITED STATES
IN 1869,
COLORADO JEWETT.

The meeting being called to order, Miss P. Hen came to the front with her umbrella, and addressed the populace.

She stated that this meeting was designed for no political purpose, but only to show Providence that a great nation knows how to be grateful for victory. Now was the time to heed the heart-sobs and gushing soul-pangs of the misguided Confederacies, and receive back all the Rebel leaders with kisses on their penitent noses. As for our present President, he meant well; but " —

The speaker was suddenly interrupted by a burst of fifes and drums coming up the Accomac road, and right quickly there appeared a procession of political chaps with immense stomachs, from Chicago, who carried a fine banner inscribed:

REPUBLICAN NOMINATION
FOR
PRESIDENT IN 1869,
THE
GENERAL OF THE MACKEREL BRIGADE.

At this apparition Miss P. Hen ate a Graham biscuit with great accerbity of bearing, and was about to go on with her *Te Deum*, when a fleshy Chicago chap lightly jumped upon the platform and pushed the venerable maiden aside. He said that no scheme of politics brought them together this time: but a humble, heartfelt wish to thank a benignant Heaven for the downfall of a mighty people's enemies. As for the chief of those enemies, the Rebel leaders, they must every one of them be hanged without mercy, or justice might as well be ignored forever. The present President was too " —

At this moment the hum of an approaching multitude drowned all other sounds, and there advanced from the

THIRD SERIES. 299

rear of Paris a great band of high-moral citizens, with a banner announcing

> UNION NOMINATION
> FOR
> PRESIDENT OF THE UNITED STATES
> IN 1869.
> *OUR UNCLE ABE.* *

Forward surged this new audience toward the platform, and both Miss P. Hen and the Chicago chap had recommenced their hymns of gratitude, when an athletic citizen from Baltimore made a dash for the front railing and eloquently addressed the meeting. He was proud to see such a glorious concourse assembled, for no wrangling party object, but solely to unite in thankfulness to a greater than all earthly powers for the blessing of returning peace. To make that peace permanent and solid," —

Here Miss P. Hen got to the front and brought down her umbrella with awful violence upon the bare head of the speaker, and says she : " I'm the Republican party myself ! "

" I beg your pardon, miss," says the Baltimore citizen, hotly, " but *I'm* the Republican party ! "

" You're both impostors ! " roared the Chicago chap, scientifically squaring-off ; " for I'M the Republican party ! "

Crash goes the platform ; down tumble the banners.

---

* Four days after the date of this letter, ABRAHAM LINCOLN — the wise, the just, the merciful — fell beneath the dastard blow of an ignoble assassin ! All that is beautiful and good in the world must mourn his irreparable loss ; and I need not say how consoling it is to me in this dark hour to feel, that, in all my extravagances of nonsense, I have never penned one word concerning the Martyr-President that was not inspired by a sentiment of actual affection for his genial and guileless character. Thank God ! his eternally-infamous murderer came of a line not native to my country ! O. C. K.

300 ORPHEUS C. KERR PAPERS.

Fists are plunging wildly in all directions, while such howls and screams arise from the tempest as though pandemonium were let loose to run a gamut of diabolical sounds.

Seated upon a barrel a short distance off, I was taking a deep interest, through my bit of smoked glass, in this scene of exciting National Thanksgiving, when a strange ringing noise, or lively bellow, and a sharp crash very unexpectedly sounded above the din, and, on looking up, I beheld the Conservative Kentucky chap joyously dancing upon the roof of Paris, with a huge dinner-bell in his right hand, and a smoking three-pounder beside him.

" Hooray ! " shouted the Conservative Kentucky chap, blissfully standing on one leg. " Go in ! That's the style ! Sic 'em ! Sic 'em ! Hit 'em again, boys. Hem ! " says the Conservative chap, with delirious enthusiasm ; " this here sort of thing in the enemy's camp is just the ticket for our National Democratic Organization, of which I am the large Kentucky branch ! "

Turn away your eyes, my boy, from such scenes as these, and look with me along that hill-side yonder, where the gentle sun casts his tenderest beams upon the new spring grass. You see there are irregular mounds scattered all the way up the slope, — hundreds, — hundreds ! Beneath them sleep the brave, the beautiful, the wept of the patriot home. Their loyal blood, poured in a fervid river to the twilight ocean of Eternity, has washed a pollution from our Flag, a blot from our escutcheon ; and, oh ! that it had also borne hence upon its purifying current that unholy, shifting beacon of political discord, which ever lures our Ship of State toward the breakers.

Yours, reverently,
Orpheus C. Kerr.

JUST PUBLISHED,

A VOLUME OF POEMS BY ORPHEUS C. KERR,

ENTITLED,

THE PALACE BEAUTIFUL,

AND OTHER POEMS.

———

12MO, CLOTH BOUND, WITH PORTRAIT   PRICE $1 50.

———

** The *Boston Transcript*, in speaking of this book, says : " Energy of feeling, sweet-
ness of sentiment, and grace and delicacy of fancy, are common characteristics
of the volume.   A number of the poems relate to the incidents, ideas,
and passions of the war, and rank among the most striking
lyrics called forth by the events of the time."
** Copies will be sent by mail, *free,*
on receipt of price, $1 50,

by

CARLETON, Publisher,

New York.

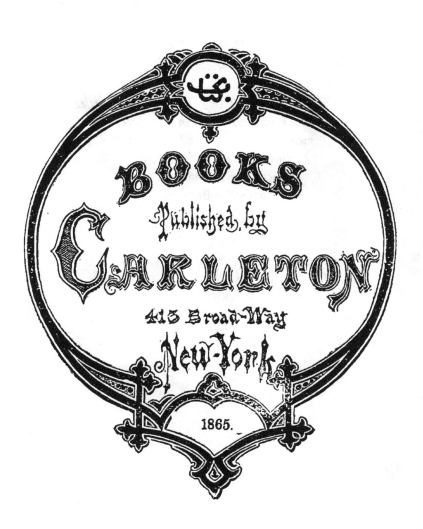

"There is a kind of physiognomy in the titles of books no less than in the faces of men, by which a skilful observer will know as well what to expect from the one as the other."—BUTLER.

NEW BOOKS
And New Editions Recently Issued by
CARLETON, PUBLISHER,
NEW YORK.
418 BROADWAY, CORNER OF LISPENARD STREET.

N.B.—The Publisher, upon receipt of the price in advance, will send any of the following Books, by mail, POSTAGE FREE, to any part of the United States. This convenient and very safe mode may be adopted when the neighboring Booksellers are not supplied with the desired work. State name and address in full.

Victor Hugo.
LES MISERABLES.—*The best edition*, two elegant 8vo. vols., beautifully bound in cloth, $5.50; half calf, . . $10.00
LES MISERABLES.—*The popular edition*, one large octavo volume, paper covers, $2.00; cloth bound, . . $2.50
LES MISERABLES.—Original edition in five vols.—Fantine—Cosette—Marius—Denis—Valjean. 8vo. cloth, . $1.25
LES MISERABLES—In the Spanish language. Fine 8vo. edition, two vols., paper covers, $4.00; or cloth, bound, . $5.00
THE LIFE OF VICTOR HUGO.—By himself. 8vo. cloth, $1.75

By the Author of "Rutledge."
RUTLEDGE.—A deeply interesting novel. 12mo. cloth, $1.75
THE SUTHERLANDS.— do. . . do. $1.75
FRANK WARRINGTON.— do. . . do. $1.75
LOUIE'S LAST TERM AT ST. MARY'S.— . . do. $1.75
ST. PHILIP'S.—*Just published.* . . do. $1.75

Hand-Books of Good Society.
THE HABITS OF GOOD SOCIETY; with Thoughts, Hints, and Anecdotes, concerning nice points of taste, good manners and the art of making oneself agreeable. Reprinted from the London Edition. The best and most entertaining work of the kind ever published. . . 12mo. cloth, $1.75
THE ART OF CONVERSATION.—With directions for self-culture A sensible and instructive work, that ought to be in the hands of every one who wishes to be either an agreeable talker or listener. . . . 12mo. cloth, $1.50

Miss Augusta J. Evans.
BEULAH.—A novel of great power. . 12mo. cloth, $1.75

4   *LIST OF BOOKS PUBLISHED*

Mrs. Mary J. Holmes' Works.

DARKNESS AND DAYLIGHT.—*Just published.*   12mo. cl. $1.50
LENA RIVERS.—   . . A Novel.   do. $1.50
TEMPEST AND SUNSHINE.— . do.   do. $1.50
MARIAN GREY. — .   do   do. $1.50
MEADOW BROOK.— . . . do.   do. $1.50
ENGLISH ORPHANS.— . . do.   do. $1.50
DORA DEANE.—   . . . do.   do. $1.50
COUSIN MAUDE.— . . . do.   do. $1.50
HOMESTEAD ON THE HILLSIDE.— do.   do. $1.50
HUGH WORTHINGTON.— *Just published.*   do. $1.50

Artemus Ward.

HIS BOOK.—An irresistibly funny volume of writings by the immortal American humorist. . . 12mo. cloth, $1.50
A NEW BOOK.—*In press.* . . .   do. $1.50

Miss Muloch.

JOHN HALIFAX.—A novel. With illust. 12mo., cloth, $1.75
A LIFE FOR A LIFE.— .   do. .   do. $1.75

Charlotte Bronte (Currer Bell).

JANE EYRE.—A novel. With illustration. 12mo. cloth, $1.75
THE PROFESSOR.—do.   do. .   do. $1.75
SHIRLEY.— . do. .   do. .   do. $1.75
VILLETTE.— . do. .   do. .   do. $1.75

Edmund Kirke.

AMONG THE PINES.—A Southern sketch. 12mo. cloth, $1.50
MY SOUTHERN FRIENDS.—   do.   do.   . $1.50
DOWN IN TENNESSEE.—Just published. .   do. $1.50

Cuthbert Bede.

VERDANT GREEN.—A rollicking, humorous novel of English student life; with 200 comic illustrations. 12mo. cloth, $1.50
NEARER AND DEARER.—A novel, illustrated. 12mo. clo. $1.50

Richard B. Kimball.

WAS HE SUCCESSFUL?—   A novel.   12mo. cloth, $1.75
UNDERCURRENTS.—   do.   do. $1.75
SAINT LEGER.—   do.   do. $1.75
ROMANCE OF STUDENT LIFE.— do.   do. $1.75
IN THE TROPICS.—Edited by R. B. Kimball.   do. $1.75

Epes Sargent.

PECULIAR.—One of the most remarkable and successful novels published in this country. . . 12mo. cloth, $1.75

BY GEO. W. CARLETON, NEW YORK.

A. S. Roe's Works.

A LONG LOOK AHEAD.— A novel.	12mo. cloth,	$1.50
TO LOVE AND TO BE LOVED.— do. . . do.		$1.50
TIME AND TIDE.— do. . . do.		$1.50
I'VE BEEN THINKING.— do. . . do.		$1.50
THE STAR AND THE CLOUD.— do. . . do.		$1.50
TRUE TO THE LAST.— do. . . do.		$1.50
HOW COULD HE HELP IT.— do. . . do.		$1.50
LIKE AND UNLIKE.— do. . . do.		$1.50
LOOKING AROUND.— *Just published.* do.		$1.50

Walter Barrett, Clerk.

OLD MERCHANTS OF NEW YORK.—Being personal incidents, interesting sketches, bits of biography, and gossipy events in the life of nearly every leading merchant in New York City. Three series. . . 12mo. cloth, each, $1.75

T. S. Arthur's New Works.

LIGHT ON SHADOWED PATHS.—A novel.	12mo. cloth,	$1.50
OUT IN THE WORLD.— do. . do.		$1.50
NOTHING BUT MONEY.— do. . do.		$1.50
WHAT CAME AFTERWARDS.—*In press.* . do.		$1.50

Orpheus C. Kerr.

ORPHEUS C. KERR PAPERS.—Three series. 12mo. cloth, $1.50
THE PALACE BEAUTIFUL.—And other poems. do. $1.50

M. Michelet's Works.

LOVE (L'AMOUR).—From the French. 12mo. cloth, $1.50
WOMAN (LA FEMME.)— do. . . do. $1.50

Novels by Ruffini.

DR. ANTONIO.—A love story of Italy. 12mo. cloth, $1.75
LAVINIA; OR, THE ITALIAN ARTIST.— do. $1.75
VINCENZO; OR, SUNKEN ROCKS.— 8vo. cloth, $1.75

Rev John Cumming, D.D., of London.

THE GREAT TRIBULATION.—Two series. 12mo. cloth, $1.50
THE GREAT PREPARATION.— do. . do. $1.50
THE GREAT CONSUMMATION.— do. . do. $1.50

Ernest Renan.

THE LIFE OF JESUS.—Translated by C. E. Wilbour from the celebrated French work. . . 12mo. cloth, $1.75
RELIGIOUS HISTORY AND CRITICISM.— 8vo. cloth, $2.50

Cuyler Pine.

MARY BRANDEGEE.—An American novel. . . $1.75
A NEW NOVEL.—*In press.* $1.75

LIST OF BOOKS PUBLISHED

Charles Reade.

THE CLOISTER AND THE HEARTH.—A magnificent new novel, by the author of "Hard Cash," etc. . 8vo. cloth, $2.00

The Opera.

TALES FROM THE OPERAS.—A collection of clever stories, based upon the plots of all the famous operas. 12mo. cl., $1.50

J. C. Jeaffreson.

A BOOK ABOUT DOCTORS.—An exceedingly humorous and entertaining volume of sketches, stories, and facts, about famous physicians and surgeons. 12mo. cloth, $1.75

Fred. S. Cozzens.

THE SPARROWGRASS PAPERS —A capital humorous work, with illustrations by Darley. . . 12mo. cloth, $1.50

F. D. Guerrazzi.

BEATRICE CENCI.—A great historical novel. Translated from the Italian ; with a portrait of the Cenci, from Guido's famous picture in Rome. . . 12mo. cloth, $1.75

Private Miles O'Reilly.

HIS BOOK.—Comic songs, speeches, &c. 12mo. cloth, $1.50
A NEW NOVEL.—*In press.* . . . do. $1.50

The New York Central Park.

A SUPERB GIFT BOOK.—The Central Park pleasantly described, and magnificently embellished with more than 50 exquisite photographs of the principal views and objects of interest. A large quarto volume, sumptuously bound in Turkey morocco, ... $30.00

Joseph Rodman Drake.

THE CULPRIT FAY.—The most charming faery poem in the English language. Beautifully printed. 12mo. cloth, 75 cts.

Mother Goose for Grown Folks.

HUMOROUS RHYMES for grown people ; based upon the famous "Mother Goose Melodies." . . 12mo. cloth, $1.00

Mrs. —— ——

FAIRY FINGERS.—A new novel. . 12mo. cloth, $1.75
THE MUTE SINGER.— do. *In press.* do. $1.75

Robert B. Roosevelt.

THE GAME FISH OF THE NORTH.—Illustrated 12mo. cl. $2.00
SUPERIOR FISHING.—*Just published.* do. do. $2.00
THE GAME BIRDS OF THE NORTH.—*In press* . . $2.00

John Phoenix.

THE SQUIBOB PAPERS.—With comic illustr. 12mo. cl., $1.50

BY GEO. W. CARLETON, NEW YORK. 1

N. H. Chamberlain.
THE AUTOBIOGRAPHY OF A NEW ENGLAND FARM-HOUSE.—$1.75

Amelia B. Edwards.
BALLADS.—By author of "Barbara's History." $1.50

S. M. Johnson.
FREE GOVERNMENT IN ENGLAND AND AMERICA.—8vo. cl. $3.00

Captain Semmes.
THE ALABAMA AND SUMTER.— . . 12mo. cl. $2.00

Hewes Gordon.
LOVERS AND THINKERS.—A new novel. . . . $1.50

Caroline May.
POEMS.—*Just published.* . . . 12mo. cloth, $1.50

Slavery.
THE SUPPRESSED BOOK ABOUT SLAVERY.—12mo. cloth, $2.00

Railroad and Insurance
ALMANAC FOR 1865.—Full of Statistics. . 8vo. cloth, $2.00

Stephen Massett.
DRIFTING ABOUT.—Comic book, illustrated. 12mo. cloth, $1.50

Thomas Bailey Aldrich.
BABIE BELL, AND OTHER POEMS.—Blue and gold binding, $1.50
OUT OF HIS HEAD.—A new romance. 12mo. cloth, $1.50

Richard H. Stoddard.
THE KING'S BELL.—A new poem. . 12mo. cloth, 75 cts.
THE MORGESONS.—A novel. By Mrs. R. H. Stoddard. $1.50

Edmund C. Stedman.
ALICE OF MONMOUTH.—A new poem. 12mo. cloth, $1.25
LYRICS AND IDYLS.— . . . . do. $1.25

M. T. Walworth.
LULU.—A new novel. . . . 12mo. cloth, $1.50
HOTSPUR.— do. . . . . do. $1.50

Author of "Olie."
NEPENTHE.—A new novel. . . 12mo. cloth, $1.50
TOGETHER.— do. . do. $1.50

Quest.
A NEW ROMANCE.— . . . 12mo. cloth, $1.50

Victoire.
A NEW NOVEL.— . . . . 12mo. cloth, $1.75

James H. Hackett.
NOTES AND COMMENTS ON SHAKSPEARE.— 12mo. cloth, $1.50

LIST OF BOOKS PUBLISHED BY CARLETON, NEW YORK.

Miscellaneous Works.

JOHN GUILDERSTRING'S SIN.—A novel. . 12mo. cloth,	$1.50
CENTEOLA.—By author " Green Mountain Boys." do. .	$1.50
RED TAPE AND PIGEON-HOLE GENERALS.— . do.	$1.50
THE PARTISAN LEADER.—By Beverly Tucker. do.	$1.50
ADAM GUROWSKI.—Washington diary for 1863. do.	$1.50
TREATISE ON DEAFNESS.—By Dr. E. B. Lighthill. do.	$1.50
THE PRISONER OF STATE.—By D. A. Mahoney. do.	$1.50
AROUND THE PYRAMIDS.—By Gen. Aaron Ward. do.	$1.50
CHINA AND THE CHINESE.—By W. L. G. Smith. do.	$1.50
THE WINTHROPS.—A novel by J. R. Beckwith. do.	$1.75
SPREES AND SPLASHES.—By Henry Morford. do.	$1.50
GARRET VAN HORN.—A novel by J. S. Sauzade. do.	$1.50
SCHOOL FOR THE SOLDIER.—By Capt. Van Ness. do.	50 cts.
THE YACHTMAN'S PRIMER.—By T. R. Warren. do.	50 cts.
EDGAR POE AND HIS CRITICS.—By Mrs. Whitman. do.	$1.00
ERIC; OR, LITTLE BY LITTLE.—By F. W. Farrar. do.	$1.50
SAINT WINIFRED'S.—By the author of " Eric." do.	$1.50
A WOMAN'S THOUGHTS ABOUT WOMEN — . do.	$1.50
THE SEA.—By Michelet, author of "Love." do.	$1.50
MARRIED OFF.—Illustrated satirical poem. . do.	50 cts.
SCHOOL-DAYS OF EMINENT MEN.—By Timbs. do.	$1.50
ROMANCE OF A POOR YOUNG MAN.—'. . do.	$1.50
THE FLYING DUTCHMAN.—J. G. Saxe, illustrated. do.	75 cts.
ALEXANDER VON HUMBOLDT.—Life and travels. do.	$1.50
LIFE OF HUGH MILLER—The celebrated geologist. do.	$1.50
LYRICS OF A DAY—or, newspaper poetry. . do.	$1.00
THE U. S. TAX LAW.—" Government Edition." do.	$1.00
TACTICS; or, Cupid in Shoulder-Straps. . do.	$1.50
DEBT AND GRACE.—By Rev. C. F. Hudson. do.	$1.75
THE RUSSIAN BALL.—Illustrated satirical poem. do.	50 cts.
THE SNOBLACE BALL.— do. do. do. do.	50 cts.
THE CHURCH IN THE ARMY.—By Dr. Scott. do.	$1.75
TEACH US TO PRAY.—By Dr. Cumming. . do.	$1.50
AN ANSWER TO HUGH MILLER.—By T. A. Davies. do.	$1.50
COSMOGONY.—By Thomas A. Davies. . 8vo. cloth,	$2.00
TWENTY YEARS around the World. J. Guy Vassar. do.	$3.75
THE SLAVE POWER.—By J. E. Cairnes. . . do.	$2.00
RURAL ARCHITECTURE.—By M. Field, illustrated. do.	$2.00